"I'll give you twe
bring the skull to

"If you do not comply, at precisely five minutes beyond the twenty-four-hour mark, I will kill you. Got it?"

Annja nodded. "How am I supposed to find you?"

Serge leaned close and hissed in her ear. "The Linden Hill cemetery off Starr Street. Tomorrow morning, this time."

"A graveyard? Swell," she mumbled.

Something sharp pricked her wrist. Annja let out a yelp as what felt like a knife entered her flesh and, with a forceful shove, traveled through to bone.

Serge gave the instrument a twist. Annja screamed. Agony felled her to her knees. Serge tugged it out and stepped back.

Struggling to maintain consciousness, and looking up to see the weird tubelike blade he tucked inside his coat, Annja reached out—for what, she didn't know. It seemed as though *something* should come to her hand. Something that could protect her.

Instead, she fell forward and blacked out....

Titles in this series:

ROGUE Angel™
Alex Archer

THE BONE CONJURER

A GOLD EAGLE BOOK FROM
W💧RLDWIDE®

TORONTO • NEW YORK • LONDON
AMSTERDAM • PARIS • SYDNEY • HAMBURG
STOCKHOLM • ATHENS • TOKYO • MILAN
MADRID • WARSAW • BUDAPEST • AUCKLAND

Recycling programs
for this product may
not exist in your area.

First edition May 2010

ISBN-13: 978-0-373-62143-9

THE BONE CONJURER

Special thanks and acknowledgment to
Michele Hauf for her contribution to this work.

Printed in U.S.A.

The
LEGEND

...THE ENGLISH COMMANDER TOOK
JOAN'S SWORD AND RAISED IT HIGH.

The broadsword, plain and unadorned,
gleamed in the firelight. He put the tip against
the ground and his foot at the center of the blade.
The broadsword shattered, fragments falling
into the mud. The crowd surged forward,
peasant and soldier, and snatched the shards
from the trampled mud. The commander tossed
the hilt deep into the crowd.
Smoke almost obscured Joan, but she continued
praying till the end, until finally the flames climbed
her body and she sagged against the restraints.

Joan of Arc died that fateful day in France,
but her legend and sword are reborn....

PROLOGUE

Granada, Spain, 1430

Cool palace walls offered welcome respite from the thick August heat. Dusty air clogged at the back of Garin Braden's throat. While journeying from the Christian lands of Castile to the great Muslim palace of Alhambra the two men had stopped frequently and rested much.

His master's horse was a fourteen-hand destrier of Arabian blood, but bred more for battle than long-distance travel.

Garin's own mount was a pale rouncey dusted with red clay from the roads, on its last legs, surely. Their greater destination of Rouen, France—his master had been called to protect the Maid of Orléans—would not be achieved with this horse.

Tugging the hood from his head, the young man wandered down a tiled aisle that stretched along a vast pool of indigo water. He could feel the coolness rise from the surface. The water did not stink, which he would expect from so large a pool.

Resisting a dive into the water would be a trial, but he'd

been warned to exercise his best behavior in the palace. The sultan did not take kindly to interlopers.

They'd been given a brief tour, and left to linger in this, the serrallo, which his master, the Frenchman, had mentioned was built less than a hundred years earlier. Elaborately detailed carvings on the walls arabesqued in precise wooden curves. Hand-painted colors were vivid jewels set into the design. The courtyard was open to the sky and bright morning light illuminated everything as if under a thousand candles. It was blinding.

Garin had never before seen such a blatant display of riches. He did appreciate what coin and barter could bring a man. Someday he would have riches of his own.

They'd come to visit an alchemist his master had met a decade earlier during a previous visit to Spain. His master had taken Garin under his wing as an apprentice. The elder man's methods of teaching were brusque and not always pain free.

Garin missed his father, a German knight. But the man had never so much time for him as Roux offered. Roux, he followed everywhere. Roux was master, teacher, reluctant friend and—rarely—father. Garin learned much during their travels. He thought he would never cease to marvel at all the world, and its riches, could offer.

Yet he looked forward to a future with no master.

"Ahead," Roux said in his curt manner.

Inside, a long hallway edged the courtyard. The men's boot heels clicked dully. Here in the shade it was much cooler. A man could seek the liquid shadows and garner relief.

Garin looked at the walls, his eyes traveling high to marvel over the intricate arabesque work carved into fine, varnished woods. It was a style he'd not seen before traveling to Spain. It was decadent and pleased him to look upon it.

He favored this land of dark-skinned Moors. They were tall, brave men who decorated their clothing with opulent metals and their blades more grandly with jewels and religious carvings. They prayed all hours of the day and bore a regal mien as if a birthright.

"Ah!" Roux hastened his steps, but Garin meandered behind him at his own pace. "Alphonso!"

The two men exchanged kisses to the cheeks while Garin hung back. Even when Roux walked in through the long strands of beaded wood to the alchemist's lab, he did not gesture for him to follow. He merely expected Garin would.

And the young man did, because he knew it was expected.

"Someday," he muttered under his breath. "Someday I will not follow you, old man."

Introductions were made. Alphonso de Castaña impressed Garin little. He hardly believed in men who claimed to change lead into gold, and cure all disease with an elixir of life.

The alchemist gestured for Garin to have a seat on a wicker chaise padded with damask fabric, or even look about if he desired. He and Roux had matters to discuss.

That suited Garin well and fine, though he did wish for something to drink. He was parched. A glance about convinced him the discolored liquids in the assorted vials, alembics and glass pitchers were likely not consumable. He didn't want to look too closely at the one—was that a skinned creature inside? It had…fingers?

Garin averted his eyes from the shelves.

The room was compact, yet the ceiling high and vaulted, so it gave the illusion of a grand yet intimate area. It was packed to every wall with items of interest. More than four walls—Garin counted six. Interesting.

Dusty vases, stacks of leathered books and globes of thin

glass covered every available space. Intricate metal devices must calibrate and measure, he decided. Wooden bowls and animal skins hobbled and propped here and there. Books open everywhere, some marked with a shard of bone, others tilting nearly off a table.

Garin glanced across the room where the two men spoke in low tones. His master studied a kris blade with a bejeweled ivory handle. A glint of ruby caught sunlight beaming through a grilled window. Roux did like unique weapons.

Garin stroked his fingers over a folded cloth run through with silver threading. Curious things. Unnecessary to him, but still, they were something to behold.

Only last night he'd run his fingers along the shabby torn cloth of a serving wench's skirts upstairs in the tavern where they'd stopped to eat. She, too, had been something to behold.

But his master had been eager to find a more suitable resting spot, so Garin had left the wench with but a kiss and a remorseful sigh.

He could appreciate all his master had done for him, shown him the way and taught him skills for defense and survival. But he did not fool himself that someday he would break free and be on his own. He deserved freedom. He was no man to answer to another.

A small brass key tied through with a shimmery pink ribbon went untouched, for something marvelous caught Garin's attention. He reached carefully behind a stack of leather-bound books and palmed the curved shape of a skull.

It was not a man's skull, for it fit upon his palm. A child's?

It looked like the many other skulls he had seen as he and Roux ambled over the highroads for days without end. Skulls attached to skeletons and hanging from a gallows or tree; lying roadside, detached from the neck as if fallen from a bone collector's pack; or sitting upon a desk or windowsill in declaration of the dark arts.

The bone was creamy pale and smooth. The scalp was delineated into sections and the pieces were held together by some kind of dirty plaster. The eye sockets were large in comparison to the skull, and the jaw quite small. It was missing the lower jawbone.

It surely belonged to an infant.

Did the alchemist practice the dark arts?

Garin glanced again at the two men. De Castaña wore a white turban and his skin was brown, yet paler than most Moors. His voice was kind. He gestured gracefully with long fingers as he spoke.

Roux had mentioned something about de Castaña having angels and demons at his beckon. What foul deeds men got their hands to, Garin thought.

He turned the skull on his palm, smoothing his fingers over the slick bone. Poking two fingers into the eye sockets, he did it only because of curiosity. Hooked upon his fingers, he turned the skull and found the tiny hole at the base where it must attach to the spine.

Compelled for no reason other than it was what his hands next decided to do, he lifted the upturned skull to his ear. Slithery, silver tones clattered within. A voice without words.

"What have you there, boy?" His master fit the kris blade into the leather belt at his waist and glanced at his charge.

"Ah! No!" The alchemist clapped his hands twice over his head. "Put that down, boy. Its secrets are not for you to know."

Roux cast him the fierce eye. Not a look Garin ever wished to challenge. He set the skull on the books, yet his fingers lingered. As did Roux's gaze upon the skull.

"It whispers to me," Garin said with all due fascination.

"Ah, ah." The alchemist leaned in and snatched the skull from its perch and gave it a smart toss, catching it on his palm. "Not yet, boy, not yet."

"But—"

There was nothing more to say. His master shuffled him toward the stringed wooden beads marking the entrance. "Take yourself out to the serrallo, apprentice. I'll follow directly."

Casting the skull a desirous glance, Garin licked his lips. He met the alchemist's eyes and thought sure he'd seen a star blink in the center of each dark orb.

"Someday, perhaps?" the alchemist said with a slippery grin. "Someday, all good things."

Garin rushed outside. The open-air serrallo beamed brilliant white sun upon his face, altering his mood for the better. Moments later he was joined by his master. Roux laid out plans to ride to the city and find a meal. Fine and well. Yet all the day, Garin's thoughts tried to form sense of the mysterious whispers from the skull.

All good things, he finally decided. Someday.

1

Desperation had prompted him to contact a stranger. Annja didn't know him. Had never met him, save through a couple e-mails.

So why agree to meet him?

Others had helped her out of desperate situations. And this is what she did. She didn't sit at home lazing before the television. She seized what the day offered.

And today's offering was too good to resist.

The season's first snow smacked Annja's cheek with a sharp bite. It melted on her warm skin. Glad she'd the forethought to tug on a ski cap and warm jacket, she stalked onto the Carroll Street Bridge. One of the oldest retractile bridges in the country, this sweet little bridge was about one hundred and twenty years old.

The traffic was sparse. Few cars crossed the Gowanus Canal at this bridge. Annja glanced up and read the antique sign hanging overhead on the steel girders.

Ordinance of the City: Any Person Driving Over this Bridge Faster than a Walk Will Be Subject to a Penalty of Five Dollars per Offense.

You gotta love New York, she thought.

Peering over the bridge railing, recently painted a fresh coat of bold green, she decided the water in the Gowanus Canal wasn't so lavender as rumors claimed. The city had gone to remarkable efforts to clean the grungy, putrid stretch of water. A flushing tunnel was also supposed to clean out the raw sewage more often.

The effect of snow falling around her as she looked over the water produced an eerie hyperspace vibe.

"It ain't like dustin' crops, boy," she said in her best Han Solo imitation.

So she could geek out with the best of them.

"Not interested in a swim tonight," she muttered. "Not without my hazmat bikini."

Turning her hips against the bridge railing, and shoving her hands in her pockets, she switched her gaze skyward. There weren't a lot of stars to be seen with the ambient light from buildings and street lamps blasting the heavens. At least there was a sky to see. One of many advantages of living in Brooklyn was the lack of skyscrapers. The Cuban cuisine wasn't too shabby, either.

Somewhere, she gauged maybe half a mile off, a siren shrilled. Horns honked, announcing the bar crowd as they scattered to various haunts. The snow was heavy, but not enough to make the road slippery.

Annja had walked from her loft. Passing cars had lodged muddy spittle onto her hiking boots. A quick walk in brisk weather always lifted her spirits. Until the chill set in. And it was nippy tonight.

Staying home with a cup of hot chocolate in hand, and watching her latest favorite TV show on DVD, sounded a much warmer plan. But she was not one to resist a mystery when it involved an artifact.

Only that afternoon Annja had received a desperate e-mail from Sneak. She didn't know the person, just suspected he was a *he*. He'd followed her conversations at alt.archaeology.esoterica, and felt she could give him some answers about something he'd found—a skull.

Skulls were more common than gold coins in the archaeological world. There was a skull in every myth, every legend, every thrilling adventure tale told. Skulls granting wishes, skulls promising fortune, skulls bringing about the end of the world.

Plain old skull skulls that could be anything from some peasant who'd died of a heart attack working the fields to some deranged serial killer's leftovers.

What was so special about this one?

Sneak hadn't sent a picture, claiming his digital camera had been broken in a recent fall. But his mention of a dig in Spain grabbed Annja's attention. He claimed to have apprenticed during the summers, though he'd abandoned his desire to dig for bones two years earlier.

Annja related to a fellow archaeologist, even if he wasn't official.

He thought he held an important artifact, yet also feared people wanted to take it from him. Why? Had he stolen it from a dig? He couldn't possibly know its value enough to cause worry.

Annja held no favor for those who raided archeological digs. She'd had run-ins with more than her share of pothunters. They were unscrupulous and weren't beyond putting a bullet in the back of someone's head to clear their escape with a valuable artifact.

Sneak claimed he was a fan of *Chasing History's Monsters,* and quoted a lot of Annja's schtick from the show in his e-mail.

Proved nothing. He could have watched the DVDs, researching her. If she'd learned anything over the past few years it was to trust no one. Everyone played the game; the goal was to win.

But she had a gut feeling about this guy. He wasn't trying to pull something on her. She sensed no malice. And she was really curious about the artifact, which he'd only said was rumored to be twelfth century and mystical.

A nine-hundred-year-old skull? Cool. No way was Annja going to let this one slip out of her hands.

"Miss Creed?"

Taken off guard, Annja twisted at the waist. She hated being caught out unawares.

A tall, slender man strode down the plank sidewalk hugging the bridge, which served only eastbound traffic. Dressed in close-fitted black, the straps and buckles about his upper thighs and ankles gave his attire a militant look. She didn't see any weapons.

Just because she couldn't see any didn't mean he wasn't carrying.

Hands loose at her sides—but ready to call her sword to hand—Annja waited for him to approach her. They'd agreed to meet here, a quiet spot easily accessed by both parties.

"Thank you for meeting me." His voice was whispery low, yet he gasped as if he'd been running. "We must be quick."

She put up a hand as he approached. Stay out of my personal zone. You wouldn't like the result if you put me to guard, she thought.

"You think someone followed you?" she asked. "Why?"

"I can't be sure, but better safe than not." He wore a black ski cap tugged down to his dark eyebrows. A black turtleneck peeked from his jacket and climbed up under his narrow jaw. "I'm glad you came, Annja. I wasn't sure you would. I didn't want to give any information over the Internet."

"Except that you found a skull?"

She glanced around as a silver Honda crept slowly past—obviously not wanting to risk the hardship of the five-dollar fine—but still marking her to the ankle with muddy water.

"You're not going to pull it out right here?" she cautioned. "There's a café a couple of blocks from the west end of the bridge."

His eyes scanned their periphery. Sneak's fingers clutched at his backpack straps nervously.

Annja didn't like the vibes he was giving off. At once she sensed a strange tingle to the air. More so than the toxic fumes rising from the canal. It was the man's weird anxiety, she told herself. It was bleeding off him and onto her.

Just be cool. Who could be watching?

Unless he was a thief, as suspected, and really had stolen this from a dig.

"Tell me how you obtained the thing," she prompted. Putting her back to the street, she paralleled him, and looked out over the water.

"That's not important. But I can tell you this."

He leaned forward. Annja stepped closer because she couldn't hear well with the water slapping against the canal walls. They stood shoulder to shoulder. His cologne was strong but not offensive.

"I was hired to pass this along to a specific individual. It is what I do."

Thieves passed things along to others. Annja coiled her fingers, imagining the sword in her grip, but did not call it forth.

"But I have a terrible feeling about this job," the man said. "Something isn't right. That's why I wanted your opinion. Maybe you can identify—"

His head shot up from their close stance. Annja followed his gaze as it soared through the iron bridge girders and traced the line of buildings edging the river.

She didn't see anything to cause alarm. Darkness softened the edges of buildings and parking lots. Moonlight glinted on a few windows high along the perimeter. All seemed calm. Strange, but not for this part of Brooklyn. It was a quiet, old neighborhood.

The man's sudden exhalation startled her. He grunted, as if punched. His shoulder jerked against hers. He gripped blindly, his fingers slapping across her shoulder.

He stumbled backward. Annja spied the hole in his forehead. Blood trickled from the small circle. Sniper shot. It could be nothing else.

Instincts igniting, she knew when there was one shot, there could be another. Grabbing him by the shoulder, she directed his staggering movement to swing around her body and stand before her as a defensive wall.

Ice burned along Annja's neck. She knew the distinct slice of metal to flesh well enough. She'd been hit. But it didn't slow her down.

Leaning backward over the railing, she slapped both arms about the man's shoulders. Eyes closed, his head lolled. The dead weight of him toppled her. For a moment, she felt the sensation of air at her back, with no support to catch her, dizzied.

And then she pushed from the sidewalk with her feet.

2

Annja's belt loops dragged over the bridge railing, but didn't catch. The man was heavier than she'd expected from such a slender frame.

Bracing air tugged off her ski cap and bruised over her scalp. It hissed through her too-thin-for-winter jacket as she fell, headfirst and backward, toward the water.

With less than twenty feet from railing to water, she worked quickly.

Twisting in midair, still maintaining a death grip on the man, she managed to kick and aim his legs downward. Now she fell over him, positioned as if she'd stepped up to put her arms around his shoulders for a hug.

Impact loosened her fingers from his body, but she scrambled to grip the slippery coat fabric. His horizontal body broke the surface of water and slowed his descent, while Annja's body crashed hard against his. It felt as if she'd landed on the ground, belly first, after a daring leap from a backyard trampoline.

At least she was making comparisons and not pushing up daisies, she realized.

The water was only slighter warmer than frozen. Some summer heat must yet be trapped in the depths. Or a toxic boil.

Their bodies submerged and Annja immediately struggled with the backpack straps. The first one proved difficult. She couldn't get the tight strap over the man's shoulder.

Breath spilling from her faster than she wished, she stopped herself before a frustrating cry would see her swallowing water. As it was, she'd snorted a healthy dose upon submersion and it wasn't the finest vintage she'd tasted. If she did survive drowning, the toxic cocktail she sucked down her throat would surely kill her, if not at least make her glow electric green in the dark.

With thoughts of hypothermia storming her thinning brain waves, Annja jerked on the backpack strap and tugged it from the man's arm. His body felt twice as heavy now. He was sinking fast, taking her with him. The canal wasn't deep—perhaps fifteen to twenty feet—but a person could drown in less than a foot of water.

Utilizing a death grip on the backpack strap, she struggled to release his other lifeless arm.

A wince let out her last ounce of breath. Thanks to some trapped air, the backpack floated and Annja hooked it over an arm and bent her elbow. Kicking, she headed toward the surface, but quickly decided to change course for the murky shadows to her right.

Surfacing under the bridge, she gasped. The icy air pierced like needles at the back of her throat. Spitting out water, she sucked in just as much. Sputtering, she bit on a nasty piece of something she didn't care to identify.

A kick of her legs slammed her against the slimy log bulkhead hugging the bridge girder.

Shivering, she pushed the hair from her eyes. She wanted to climb out, but didn't know if the sniper would still be watching. Of course he would. Whoever he was. Was he allied with Sneak? If so, then someone wasn't playing nice.

She couldn't risk the chance of emerging in plain sight. She'd have to swim downstream as far as possible.

"Should have stayed home and popped in an episode of *Supernatural*," she grumbled.

A cup of hot chocolate sounded too good to be true right now.

Her words stuttered from the cold. But the sound of her voice reassured in a strange way. The sting on her neck had subsided. The bullet must have only skimmed flesh. She was alive, which is what mattered.

Submerging was a difficult choice, but she took a deep breath and let her body drop into the dark, muffling depths.

The murky water and her position under the bridge made it impossible to see. But she didn't need to see. It wasn't as though she'd run into a boat or shark down here. Though a whale had been trapped in the canal a few years back. It wasn't so much taking a bite from a fish that Annja worried about, as the raw sewage in the water.

A slight lightening in the waters signaled she'd cleared the bridge. Keeping close to what she felt was the shore, though her shoes didn't touch bottom, she kicked swiftly and stroked with her free right arm, while maintaining a secure clutch on the backpack with her left.

A muffled horn honked as a car passed over the bridge. Annja was surprised to hear sound at all. The reminder the real world was so close again bolstered her confidence and made kicking in the cold waters easier.

A branch snagged her ankle. She kicked frantically, briefly panicking. Bubbles of air escaped, and she had to surface to gasp in air. She didn't bring up her shoulders, only the top of her face. Sucking in the cold November air, she then inhaled deeply and went under.

While she hadn't planned for an adventure swimming the depths this evening, Annja could only fault herself for not expecting it. When did the world just leave her alone and allow her a normal day?

Finding a surprise smile, she soared forward, turning in the water, to tilt her face to the surface. The world could mess with her all it liked. She was up for the challenge.

Paddling her hands near her thighs to keep her body under as much as possible, she managed to break the surface with only her face. A scan above the lumber edging the shore spied rooftops where she guessed the sniper had shot from.

A gulp of air, and she again submerged. She was on the wrong side of the river. But she wasn't about to cross it. The current would carry her the way she'd come. Which meant she'd have to go another hundred yards at least, to put her out of sight of the buildings.

What seemed like an hour in the water was probably more like fifteen minutes. It was fourteen minutes too long.

Emerging, she dragged herself up along a mooring of old timbers lashed together with slimy rope. Slipping around behind the mooring put her next to a dock. The backpack no longer floated. It snagged on a branch—no, it was a hook of iron rebar.

Annja tugged, but the rebar held her prize securely. It was close to the surface. Deciding to get out from the water, and struggle with the backpack then, she heaved herself up. Using the rope wrapped about the moorings, she managed to slap a hand onto the dock.

The sting of a warm leather-gloved hand gripped her wrist, and reeled her in as if a giant fish. She was able to stand—for two seconds.

A fist to her gut forced up a hacking cough of water. Annja stumbled backward. Her soggy boots slipped on the wet plank dock. She went down. The landing might have hurt worse if she had feeling in her body. The cold did a number on that.

Kicking at the man who leaned over her, she managed a boot to the side of his face. He yowled. The hood of his jacket fell away to reveal a bald head.

She hadn't the mental dexterity, or warm enough muscles, to exercise a judo kick or to pull out her Krav Maga moves.

Annja turned and pushed to her knees. Swinging out her right hand, she willed the sword into her grip. It arrived from the otherwhere, solid and weighted perfectly to her hold.

Not completely focused, her brain felt half-frozen. She blindly swung backward. Contact. The hilt struck his temple.

The attacker went down in silence. Must not have expected the fish to bite back.

Annja whipped the sword into the otherwhere. Moving as quickly as her numb limbs would allow, she crawled to the water's edge and dipped a hand into the canal glimmering with oily residue. Her fingers hooked the backpack strap. It came free of the rebar with a tug.

Her cheek settled on a thin layer of snowflakes. Lying sprawled, her hand gripping the heavy backpack, she closed her eyes.

Did other women spend their Saturday nights like this? She must be doing something wrong. What did a girl have to do to meet a nice guy who wasn't either set on killing her or being hunted himself?

Standing, her body shivering and her steps moving her in zigzags across the ground, Annja didn't look back.

If the man lying on the ground was the sniper, she wanted to get out of his range before he came to.

Her lungs thudded like heavy chunks of ice against her ribs, and the muscles in her legs felt as if they'd been stretched like taffy. She wasn't far from home.

Forcing herself to wander through the debris-littered back lot of a warehouse, she found the street and trudged onward.

When a cab pulled alongside her, Annja hugged the icy yellow vehicle before crawling into the backseat.

"GOOD GIRL, ANNJA. You got the prize."

Dropping the sniper scope, the tall dark-haired man quickly crossed the cement floor and descended the iron stairs. Each footstep clanked loudly. He wasn't concerned with stealth.

He'd almost been too late. Hadn't been able to stop the first shot. But the second he'd altered the course. Not much, but enough to save the girl.

Now, to see what she did with the prize.

HARRIS LET THE PHONE ring six times before hanging up. The sniper had agreed to contact him with details of the skull's whereabouts, and keep him posted about each move Cooke made.

He wasn't supposed to fire a shot unless the man holding the skull looked as though he would hand it over to someone else. Cooke hadn't even gotten the thing out of his backpack. Harris, from his vantage point on a building half a mile down the canal, bit back a growl as the pair went over the railing, taking the skull with them.

"Idiot," he muttered. "Ravenscroft must have hired the sniper. That man knows so little about fieldwork!"

Tucking the cell phone inside his jacket, Harris eyed the brick-fronted warehouse where he knew the sniper had been positioned. The shooter should be long gone.

Five minutes later, Harris topped the fourth-floor stairs in the abandoned warehouse. His shoes crunched across debris of broken glass and Sheetrock. An icy breeze whipped up his collar and froze his face. At the far end of the warehouse he saw the M-16 rifle, still set upon a tripod.

He rushed through the darkness and stopped before he tripped over a man's body.

"What the hell?"

Inspection found no ID on the body. He wore black leather gloves and shooting glasses. The sniper. He was dead. No blood evidence. Looked as if someone had broken his neck.

Harris stretched his gaze through the hazy darkness in a circle around him. Whoever had taken out the sniper could still be lurking.

Why had this happened? Had Ravenscroft sent his own backup?

It made no sense at all. This was merely a surveillance job. Keep an eye on Cooke, and make sure he doesn't do anything rash between the time he landed in New York and met Ravenscroft for the handoff.

Harris scrubbed a hand over his scalp. Anything and everything had gone wrong.

"Ravenscroft is not going to like this one bit."

3

The cabbie had argued fiercely for a generous tip after he'd seen Annja was dripping wet and smelled like something he'd dumped out of his rain gutter last week. Good thing the twenty she'd stuffed in her back pocket had survived the swim.

Much as Annja wanted to unzip the backpack and discover what she'd almost drowned for, the call of a hot shower denied that curious need.

Dropping the backpack inside the door of her loft, Annja made a beeline through the living room for the bathroom. Twisting the spigot, she would let the shower run for a few minutes to warm up.

Stripping away her wet clothes, she caught a glance of herself in the vanity mirror. Her lips were blue, as was the fine skin under her eyes. Tilting her head up she stroked the bruised skin on her neck. An abrasion tormented the base of her earlobe. The bullet had skimmed her flesh, but hadn't drawn blood.

"Lucky girl."

To touch it hurt worse than actually getting the wound.

She pressed a palm over her gut. She could still feel the bald guy's knuckles there. He'd packed a force. But she'd gotten lucky when the hilt had clocked him on the temple. A blow to that sweet spot joggled a man's brain inside his skull and instantly knocked him out.

"Should have searched him for ID," she said to her sodden reflection. "You weren't thinking straight, Creed." Due to her frozen brain. "Who was watching us that would rather kill the one who holds the artifact than see it retrieved?"

Because the shooter had to have known if he did kill one or the both of them, the backpack would be irretrievable.

Had Sneak expected a tail? He'd been nervous. Probably a thief. Might explain why someone was following him.

Twisting the water faucet adjusted the temperature and she climbed into the shower, but was too weak to stand any longer. Settling into the tub in a self-hug, she let the warmth spill over her aching half-frozen muscles.

Annja had learned long ago comfort was never freely given. If she needed a hug or a reassuring word, it had to come from herself. She was fine with that. If you couldn't pick yourself up after a trying challenge, then you'd better get out of the game because life wasn't designed for sissies or wimps. Mostly.

She laughed into her elbow. "You must still have brain freeze. The game? Whatever."

A half hour later, with a mug of hot chocolate in hand and some warm flannel pajama bottoms and her Dodgers sweatshirt on, the final shivers tickled her spine.

Annja squatted on the floor before the waterlogged backpack. It reeked of things she'd rather not consider. Things she had washed down the shower drain. Toxins in the Gowanus Canal? Big-time.

This is a complete loss, she said to herself. Good thing it wasn't hers.

Setting the mug on the hardwood floor, she then unzipped the pack. Water dripped out from the inside, but not a lot. Inspecting the tag on the outer rim of the zipper teeth she read it was designed for hiking and was waterproof.

"Good deal."

Tools and a metal-edged leather box were tucked inside. The tools she took out and examined, placing them on the floor in a line. Not like carpenter's tools. A small screwdriver slightly larger than something a person would use to fix eyeglasses was the only one she thought fit for a house builder.

The assortment included a handheld drill with a battery pack dripping water. A glass cutter. A few flash drives. A wide-blade utility knife. Soft cotton gloves, only slightly wet. A stethoscope. And a small set of lock picks in a folding black leather case.

She blew on the flash drives, wondering if they would dry out enough to attempt to read. She wasn't sure she wanted to risk an electrical failure by inserting the memory sticks into her laptop.

"Who would use stuff like this?"

She looked over the array on the floor. An interesting mix. An archaeologist might use the gloves, but she preferred latex gloves herself. Never left home without a pair.

Instinct said *thief.* But why would a thief steal something like an ancient skull if they had little idea of its value?

Though Sneak had said he'd been hired to bring this to someone. And he feared that someone.

Too tired to push her reasoning beyond simple deductions, Annja decided to sleep on it. But not until she'd opened the box. She'd sucked in half the Gowanus Canal to get the thing and had taken a bullet. Kind of. It sounded more dramatic than it was, she admitted to herself.

Secured with a small padlock, the box was made of a hardwood edged in thin metal. The wood was covered with pounded black leather, impressed with a houndstooth design. It didn't look old, only expensive. It resembled a reliquary, though on the plain side.

Annja eyed the lock picks tucked inside the leather pouch. She'd never used anything like them before, but had read a few Internet articles on how to manipulate the pins inside a lock with a pick. A girl could use a set like this. Definitely something to hang on to.

The padlock was simple enough, though it was heavy, made of stacked steel plates. She might fiddle around with the picks, but would get nowhere.

The wood box was hard, like ironwood, and she was glad for that. Hopefully it had kept the water from seeping inside.

Foregoing any burgeoning lock-picking skills, she picked up the knife and rocked the tip of it around the metal edging. Small finishing nails secured each end of the metal strips. She managed to pry off two sides, and another, until the entire top square of wood could be removed.

"So much for the security of a padlock."

A fluff of sheep's wool poufed out of the open box.

"Good," she muttered. "Still dry."

Carefully plucking out the packing revealed the top of a skull. Annja drew it out and held it upon both palms. The eye sockets observed her curiosity without judgment.

Immediately aware of what she held, Annja gasped. "An infant's skull."

It wasn't uncommon to unearth infants' and children's skulls on a dig. She did it all the time. But it didn't make holding something so small, and so precious—obviously dead before it had a chance to live—less agonizing.

Switching to the analytical and less emotional side of her brain, Annja inspected the prize. The bone had a nice polish to it. The cranium was overlarge compared to the facial bones, as infant skulls were. Large eye sockets mastered the face. The lower jaw bone, the mandible, was not intact.

The parietal and frontal bones, normally fused with various sutures, were instead joined by thin strips of gold placed between them, much like glue, to hold it together. The anterior and posterior fontanels were also joined with those sutures. Each fontanel, normally the soft spot on an infant's skull, was smooth and shiny gold.

"Fancy. I wonder whose living room shelf this has gone missing from?"

Turning it over and taking her time, Annja smoothed her fingers over the surface, feeling for abrasions or gouges. There were no markings on the exterior bone that she could find. Sometimes knife marks remained after a ceremonial removing of the scalp. The gold lining the plates was fascinating enough.

No dirt. It didn't smell as if it had been freshly unearthed. It was musty but clean.

It looked an average skull, stained with age enough she'd place it a few centuries old, at the least. There were no teeth in the upper maxilla, nor did it look as though there ever had been teeth. Could it be newborn?

"So sad," she muttered.

And yet, the elaborate gold decoration might prove it was an important person. Perhaps a child born to a royal or great warrior.

Retrieving a digital camera from the catastrophe she called a desktop, Annja then placed the skull on top of a stack of hardcover research books. She snapped shots of the skull from all angles. When the flash caught the small gold triangular posterior fontanel section, she noticed the anomaly in the smooth metal.

"So there is a mark."

Sneak had mentioned a curious marking in his e-mail. Holding the skull close to the desk light, she squinted to view the small impression in the shiny gold.

"A cross? Looks familiar."

She had seen it many times researching renaissance and medieval battles, religions and even jewelry.

A cross pattée was impressed in the gold. It was a square cross capped with triangular ends. An oft-used symbol in medieval times. It did not always signify a religious connection, and some even associated it with fairies or pirates. The Knights Templar had worn a similar cross on their tabards.

The cross pattée was more a Teutonic symbol than Templar, she knew that. The Templar's red cross on white background tended to vary in design. That set her original guess of a few centuries back, perhaps to the thirteenth or fourteenth century.

Sneak had thought it twelfth century. It was possible, she acknowledged.

Hell, the skull could be contemporary. She wouldn't know until she could get it properly dated. And Annja knew the professor who could help. But first, she'd send out feelers to her own network. If the skull had been stolen from a dig, someone would be looking for it.

Powering up her laptop, she inserted the digital card from the camera into the card reader to load the photos she'd taken.

As she waited for the program to open, Annja wondered again about the man on the bridge. Dead now. Yet, a part of his life sat scattered beside a puddle on her floor. A foul-smelling puddle. That canal water was something else.

At the time, she'd suspected he'd been frightened. But now she altered that assessment to worried. Fear would have kept him from approaching her. Worry had kept his eyes shifting about, wondering what, if anything, could go wrong.

Had he been aware he was being watched? By a sniper? Perhaps by the buyer who didn't trust the thief would bring the prize right to him?

What about the bald man who must have followed her swim through the waters and waited for her to surface? Same guy as the sniper? Or an ally tracking the target by foot? Was he allied with the sniper or Sneak?

Something Sneak said now niggled at her. He'd been hired to hand this over to—how had he put it?—*a specific individual,* and had a bad feeling about it.

So who was Sneak? An archaeologist? He'd only claimed to work on digs over summers, and that was part-time. Could have just been a lark, joining friends to see if he liked the job. He hadn't struck her as someone in the know. If he had rudimentary knowledge on skulls, such as she, he could have puzzled its origins out.

Maybe. She hadn't figured the thing out yet, so what made her believe anyone else could?

Online, Sneak had sounded like a layman who stumbled across an artifact while hiking with friends near a defunct dig site in Spain. And yet, that explanation didn't feel right to Annja.

Add to the leery feeling the fact a lock-pick kit, drill and glass cutter had been on his person…

Annja knew when people hired others to handle artifacts and hand them over it was never on the up-and-up. Whoever had hired the sneaky guy may have also killed him.

But why? If the sniper had known the man carried the artifact on him, why then kill him and risk losing the skull in the river?

Annja envisioned a body found floating in the Gowanus Canal come morning. It wasn't as though it never happened. Heck, the canal was rumored to have once been the Mafia's favorite dumping grounds. But it had been cleaned up quite a bit since the Mafia's heydays.

Annja considered her options.

Bart McGilly was a friend who served on the NYPD as a detective. He knew trouble followed Annja far more closely than she desired, and was accustomed to calls from her at odd hours of the night.

He didn't know everything about her. Like at certain times she could be found defending herself with a kick-ass medieval sword. And after successfully dispatching the threat, the sword would then simply disappear into a strange otherwhere Annja still couldn't describe or place.

What was it about the sword? Since she'd taken claim to it, weird stuff happened to knock on her door weekly. It was as if the sword attracted things to her. Things she needed to change. Things that required investigation. Things that could not always be determined good or evil, but, Annja knew innately, mustn't be allowed to fall into the wrong hands.

It was as if she'd become the crusader for lost artifacts and weird occurrences. World-changing occurrences. And that put a heavy weight on her shoulders.

Bart was also unaware she really could use a good hug every once in a while. With the sword came challenge and hard work and, oftentimes, danger. Survival and strength could only be maintained with good old-fashioned friendship. Of which, she had a few, but not a single person she could call a BFF.

Did she need a BFF? Probably not. Then again, probably.

With a sigh, Annja retrieved her mug from the floor and took a sip. Cold. But still, it was chocolate. Propping a hand at her flannel-covered hip, she leaned over the laptop.

The photo program allowed her to choose a few good shots of the anterior and lateral views, and close-ups of the gold on the fontanels. She cropped them to remove the background. Didn't need anyone knowing her curtains were badly in need of dusting or that her desk was a disaster.

Signing on to her favorite archaeology site, Annja posted the pictures along with a note about a friend showing her the skull. She wouldn't make up a story about finding it on a dig, because that could get her in trouble. She had no idea where this had come from, and if she guessed a wrong location, well, then.

She'd check back in the morning.

Before signing off, she searched the Carroll Street Bridge to see if it had security cameras. It didn't. Which wouldn't help her sleuth out who she'd spoken to, but proved excellent should the sniper want to track her.

On the other hand, if the sniper and the bald guy were indeed two different people, the sniper may have tracked her home.

Flicking aside the curtain, Annja scanned the street below. Car headlights blurred in the snow that had turned to sleet and rain. No mysterious figures lurking.

She picked up the phone to call Bart. It was past midnight, but she dialed, anyway. Bart's answering machine took her cryptic message about swimming the canal with a stranger. He'd call her in the morning, for sure.

With one last inspection over the skull, she decided to forego doing an Internet search on random skulls. That would bring up more hits than her sleepy eyelids could manage.

Instead, she flicked off the desk light and wandered into her bedroom. It hadn't felt so good to crawl between warm blankets in a long time. Annja dropped instantly to Nod.

4

In the meeting room attached to a fiftieth-floor corner office overlooking Central Park, a crew of three cameramen noisily went about setting up for a photo shoot. A top business magazine had declared Benjamin Ravenscroft CEO of the year. They wanted to flash his mug across their pages, and he was obliged to agree.

He'd gotten an e-mail that morning regarding the Fortune 500 list. Another photo shoot was imminent.

The entrepreneur's company, RavensTech, had risen from the detritus of struggling dot coms over the past year. CNN had crowned him Master of the Intangible Assets. Ravens-Tech now held weekly cyber auctions for intellectual property rights, such as patents, trademarks and copyrights. They'd netted six hundred million dollars last year, and this year looked to double that figure.

Just goes to show what a little roll-up-your-sleeves ingenuity can do for a man. And the proper connections, he thought as he waited to be photographed.

"Ten minutes and we'll be ready for you, Mr. Raven-scroft," the photographer said.

Ravenscroft waved a slim black clove cigarette at the pho-tographer, who then disappeared inside the meeting room.

Leaning against the edge of his granite-topped desk, ankles crossed and whistling the first few bars of *Eine Kleine Nachtmusic,* the businessman tucked the grit between his lips and inhaled. It made a faint popping sound.

He had the cigarettes imported from Indonesia. He pre-ferred them over regular cigarettes for their intense scent. He'd become addicted to them during his college days when he'd sit through the night, eyes glued to the computer monitor as he shopped his way through available domain names.

He'd made millions nabbing domains. Another intangible. He loved buying and selling things a person could not physi-cally hold, touch or see.

He tapped the calendar on his iPhone. He verified two meetings that afternoon: Accountant and Marketing. Both would be a breeze.

Another tap. The plans for the Berlin office were due to arrive before noon by courier. Where the hell were they?

He eyed his secretary's desk through the glass wall that separated their offices. With a touch of a button on his desk the electrochromic glass would turn white, granting privacy. A necessary amenity.

Rebecca was on the phone; her red hair spilled over one satin-clad shoulder. She would notify him as soon as the Berlin plans arrived. Lunch with her in the meeting room—her legs hooked over his shoulders—was scheduled for twelve-fifteen.

He hadn't scheduled Harris in, but he expected him before noon, as well. Not the best time to arrive, with the photog-rapher in the next room, but Ben was anxious to get his hands on what Harris had retrieved.

He twisted and eyed the blurry photograph on the desktop. The skull had been removed from a glass display case, and a glare from the glass blurred part of the photo.

"Good things," he muttered. "Soon."

But the day would give him a migraine if he didn't dose on Imitrex before facing the camera's bright lights.

And tonight he had to leave the office early to arrive home in time to tuck his daughter in for bed. He and his wife had agreed he'd make a concerted effort to be home at least twice a week to do so.

He hadn't tucked Rachel in for more than a month.

He sent a text message to his secretary. Send flowers to wife. White roses, two dozen. As he hit Send, Rebecca buzzed on the intercom. Her voice made him want to dash the damned schedule and today's commitments and lift the frilled red skirt above her hips and take her right now.

"Mr. Harris is here for you, Ben—er, sir."

"Thank you, Rebecca, send him in."

Stepping over to assure the photographer he'd be right in, Ben closed the meeting room door and strolled to his desk. He snubbed out the cigarette in an ashtray, inhaling the clove fumes deeply.

He settled into the leather chair that had put him out a mere ten grand. It heated the lumbar area and massaged overall. It also included a heart monitor and blood pressure cuff. It had been worth every penny. A man could forget his whole family sitting in this thing.

But never Rebecca. That's where the ultravibrating function came in handy.

Lifting his feet, he propped them on the ottoman he kept to the left side of his desk. The slight elevation kept his legs from clotting. He'd spent his early twenties running marathons, pushing his body to the limit. His desk job reminded him daily how quickly the body degenerates without exercise. Hell, he was only forty-two.

He made a mental note to have Rebecca check into treadmills. Then he ditched the idea. He had no time for extracurricular activity. Lunch dates with Rebecca would have to serve as his exercise.

Time was more precious than gold to Ben. But he'd learned to control it. He controlled all aspects of his life. Save the one. Rachel. And that frustrated him no end.

Harris entered the massive office and offered a respectful bow, hands pressed together before his mouth like some kind of besuited samurai. The heavy oak door closed slowly on hydraulics behind him. The white-haired behemoth looked completely out of his element in the ill-fitted navy-blue suit and red tie.

He did not carry a briefcase or box.

Ben leaned forward, waving a hand frantically. "Where is it?"

"Sir."

Harris bowed again. He fingered the gaudy red tie strangling his thick neck. His glance around the room, as if checking for trespassers hidden behind the potted cactus or narrowed behind the blinds, revealed his anxiety.

"There was an altercation," he said cautiously.

"I don't like the sound of that, Harris. Either Cooke was apprehended or he was not. I don't see anything on your person which would indicate you retrieved the artifact, so I'm going to go out on a limb and guess you failed me."

"Sir, there was a woman."

Ben raised his eyebrows. An exhale settled him in the comfortable chair. Relaxation was far from his mind.

"Before or after you began to trail Cooke?" he asked. "I don't need to hear about your amorous liaisons, Harris. And

I certainly hope you were not entertaining the flavor of the week on my time."

"I would never, Mr. Ravenscroft. Cooke didn't go immediately home from the airport. He met a woman on the old Carroll Street Bridge. He must have arranged for them to meet before arriving in the States."

Cooke going behind his back with the goods? The bastard had come highly recommended after Serge had worked his magic. Ben did not tolerate those who tried to screw with him.

"The sniper followed the backup plan, as discussed," Harris said.

"Good." The backup plan did not allow for Cooke to live.

"The artifact, unfortunately, was sacrificed in the process."

"Damn!" Ben slammed a fist onto the desktop.

Harris flinched, tugged at his tie.

Ben tried not to get his hands dirty. He remained invisible in any business transaction. A liaison had been necessary to meet Cooke. He'd sent out an idiot when he should have taken care of this himself.

"The sniper got this." Harris approached the desk and reached inside his suit coat. He placed a black-and-white photograph on Ben's desk. "He sent it to me on my cell phone. Then I, er, lost contact with him."

Not picking it up, but instead drawing the slightly curved photo toward him with the edge of his thumb, Ben leaned over the image. It was blurred, but some details showed on the two faces. He recognized Cooke from the one meeting he'd arranged during an art exhibit at a gallery in the Village.

There was enough clarity to ascertain the figure talking to Cooke was indeed a woman. A dark ski cap hugged her head. Prominent cheekbones suggested beauty. Mouth open, as if talking, she couldn't have known her conversation was being observed.

Tilting his head to reduce the glare on the photo, Ben sought more in the grainy depths of her eyes. Something about her was familiar. But he couldn't recall seeing her in person. He attended so many damned parties he felt sure he'd slapped palms with half of New York over the past year alone. If he ever wanted to pursue politics, he'd certainly gotten flesh-pressing down pat.

The door to his right opened. The photographer shoved his head through. "Ready, Mr. Ravenscroft."

"Five minutes," he said. When the door closed, the clicking sound of the mechanics bit at the base of Ben's skull, threatening the imminent migraine. "What happened?"

Watching the door with wary suspicion, Harris finally decided the coast was clear.

"After the sniper shots they went over the bridge railing."

"He got them *both?*"

"We're still waiting to verify bodies, sir."

Ben rolled his eyes and pushed back in the chair. Again, he propped his feet up and clasped his hands on his lap. He didn't look at Harris. To give him any regard was more than the man deserved right now.

Bodies. He didn't do bodies. What a fiasco.

"And the sniper is gone?" he asked.

"No, uh…"

"What the hell is it, man?"

"I went looking for him."

Ben picked up on the man's increasing anxiety. More so than when he'd initially entered the office. The rancid sweat from Harris's armpits blasted over any lingering waves of clove.

"Why would you go looking for him? Didn't you maintain radio contact?"

"He didn't contact me as arranged. I found him…dead."

"How?"

"Broken neck. His weapon was still in place. Nothing was removed from the body. I have no idea who did it. I'm sorry, sir."

"Sorry?" Ben shook his head and glanced out the window. He saw nothing. Not the clear winter-white sky, nor the acres of steel skyscrapers.

The sniper was dead. That was good. One less witness. And yet, an unknown had gone after *his* sniper? That was not good. Add one unidentified witness to the list.

Had Cooke placed his own man on the scene? He couldn't have, or else why would he kill him?

Ben calmed his racing thoughts.

"You disappoint me, Harris. The operation was thoroughly botched. And not even an artifact in hand."

"I'm unsure if the exchange was made."

"You say exchange." Ben studied the bead of sweat running down Harris's forehead. "*Was* there an exchange?"

"I feel it was intended, but the sniper reported nothing was exchanged before they went over the bridge railing."

"What about after, do you suppose?"

"After?" Harris sputtered. "Difficult to imagine either survived. Two shots were fired. Both found their mark. If the bullet didn't do it, the toxic sludge would have smothered them, surely."

"The canal is a hell of a lot cleaner than most believe. Men have fallen in before, and emerged with nothing more than a case of hepatitis A."

Ben took the photo and tapped the edge sharply on the stone desktop. So it all ended right here?

No. There was too much at stake. And now with the unknown who'd taken out the sniper, the risk in not following through could prove deadly. Someone had too much information.

He needed that skull. A life depended on it. He wasn't about to let it be swept under the carpet until he'd heard confirmation of two bodies. And when the bodies were found, would the skull also be found?

"Do we have a man on the inside?"

"The inside, sir?"

"The police. We need someone on location at the NYPD when the bodies are found. The artifact mustn't wind up shelved in the municipal evidence closet, never to be claimed or seen again."

"I'll ensure it happens."

"Do so. Did you remove the sniper's weapon?"

"I did."

"No clue whatsoever to our mystery killer?"

"No, sir, but I'm looking into it."

"I want a lead within eight hours. That will be all."

Harris bowed and turned sharply to leave the office.

Ben tucked the photo inside his suit coat. He drew out his phone and tapped Serge's number.

"No." He set the phone on the desk. "Not yet."

He didn't want the man involved until the right moment.

Ben gazed at the phone. Could Serge be the mystery man who took out the sniper? What reason would he have to do so? If he guessed Ben was tracking the skull, he would have gone directly after it. To imagine Serge killing a sniper was difficult. It just didn't fit. He had no knowledge of weapons, as far as Ben knew. He was a big man, but one of those wouldn't-hurt-a-fly sorts.

The meeting room door opened again.

"On my way," Ben called.

He pulled open the bottom drawer of his desk and took

out a syringe. Tugging his shirt out from his trousers, he grabbed a wodge of middle-age bulge. The autoinjector pierced the flesh. His skin warmed and tingled.

What a way to start the day.

5

Annja took the subway stairs two at a time to emerge a few blocks away from Columbia University. She spied the Olive Tree Deli and made a note not to forget to eat today. She'd forgone breakfast in lieu of excitement over her current find. The skull, tucked in the reassembled box and nestled in its lamb's wool, joggled in the pack on her back.

Her cell phone rang and Bart McGilly's name flashed on the screen.

He started right in. "Annja, one of these days your messages are not going to be funny anymore. You were joking about swimming in the Gowanus Canal. What kind of monsters do your producers think you'll find in that filthy water?"

"Sorry, Bart. I wasn't kidding. I've still the lingering scum in my bathtub to prove it. I don't know what's in that water—and please, if you know, don't tell me—but it certainly wasn't a day at the beach. And it had nothing to do with *Chasing History's Monsters.*"

"Seriously? Annja, don't do this to me. So there's a body? For real?"

"Young. Probably late twenties would be my guess. Male. Dark hair and slender."

"How'd he end up in the canal?"

"Sniper shot to the brain."

His silence could be interpreted as surprise, but Annja pictured Bart grasping his throat and shaking his head. *There she goes again,* his silent thoughts broadcast loudly over the greater consciousness.

"It's not like I seek out these sorts of situations, Bart."

"Oh, really? Because with your record a guy would be inclined to believe that is exactly what you do. What, do you listen to the police scanner? Track nefarious transactions online?"

"Is that possible?" she wondered curiously as she stepped onto the university grounds and followed the sidewalk south.

"Annja." Bart sighed.

"I got an e-mail from a guy with an artifact he wanted me to look at."

"So anytime a stranger pings wanting to show you something, you just make a date? Wait. Don't answer that one. I don't want to know. I'll send a team out to check the canal. Do you know who the victim is? Who was shooting at—hell, the *both* of you? Are you okay?"

"It's just an abrasion, but I almost got a pierced ear out of the deal." She spoke quickly to alleviate his gasping protest. "After the first bullet, I thought it wisest to get the hell out of there. Down was the only way I could come up with at the time. As for the dead man, his Internet ID was Sneak. At least in the archaeology forum where he found me it is. I don't know who he is. Didn't have any ID in his backpack."

"In his—you removed evidence from the body?"

Bart groaned. Annja imagined him clenching his fists in frustration.

"Had to, Bart. I'm not going to let a valuable artifact get

flushed through the canal like a hunk of sewage. Speaking of which—no, I don't even want to know. A skull was in his backpack, along with a bunch of funky tools. I'm thinking he was a thief because there was a stethoscope and some kind of hand drill. Oh, and lock-pick tools."

"I need to take a look at the tools, Annja. All of them are evidence. Have you touched them? Of course you have."

"Sorry."

"How did you meet this guy?"

"Online."

"Right. At the Dangerous Dating Depot?"

"Oh, Bart, you made a funny."

"No, I'm trying to fit myself into the strange world you seem to navigate with startling ease. You said there was a skull?"

"It's why I agreed to meet the guy in the first place." Annja turned down a tree-lined sidewalk toward Schermerhorn Hall.

"So you have the skull. What are you doing with it now? Or do I want to know?"

"I'm an archaeologist, Bart. Skulls are our thing. Don't you know we bone botherers like to tote around various bits and bones to keep us company?"

Another groan. She was having far too much fun teasing him when she knew the situation was serious. A dead thief could account for that.

"I'm taking it to a professor at Columbia right now. Going to have him date it and see if I can begin to place it on a historical time line. If I can do that I might be able to track it to a point of origin. And then we'll have an M.O. on the thief. Maybe."

"What makes you think your alleged thief isn't just a

wacko? A killer? What if it's a random skull? Annja, what if it's from one of his kills?"

"You surprise me, Bart. I didn't think you jumped to conclusions so easily. And why would someone kill for a random skull?"

"Why would someone kill and *not* go after said random skull?"

Annja glanced over her shoulder. She was sure she hadn't been followed because she kept a keen eye to her periphery. No snow today; in fact, it was warmer by fifteen degrees, so it felt almost tropical. In a thirty-degree kind of way.

"It's pretty hard to go after something sitting at the bottom of the canal. Besides, it's an infant skull."

"A baby? Christ, Annja, it doesn't add up."

"It does from my end of the stick. It's an artifact, Bart, not a victim. At least, not from this century."

"I hate working on crimes against children. It's so sad. Fine. I'm heading out to the canal. You keep an eye over your shoulder. And please, promise me, you won't meet any more strangers without having them vetted by me first?"

"I can't promise…"

"Woman, you are going to give me a heart attack."

"Hey, that reminds me, we haven't had a decent meal out lately."

"Because you're always trekking across the world, posing for TV cameras and sticking your nose in danger."

"You love me for it, admit it."

Bart's sigh made her smile. She'd successfully redirected him from her dangerous dabbling with the criminal mien.

"Give me a call after you've talked to the professor, will you? I've got some time tomorrow night. We can meet and you can bring along the evidence you've contaminated. How about Tito's?"

"Sounds like a plan. Me and my contaminants can make it."

Tito's was one of their favorite places to meet over a plate of Cuban pulled pork with sweet plantains.

Bart was one of few friends Annja had in the city, and she valued that friendship tremendously. Though she couldn't deny he was also a handsome single man who, on more than a few occasions, sat closer to her than a friend should, stared into her eyes longer than a friend should and made her think of him much more than the average friend should.

The redbrick front of Schermerhorn Hall popped into view through a line of lindens. "I'll talk to you later. Thanks, Bart."

6

Schermerhorn Hall, a four-story colonial redbrick building, sat just off Amsterdam Avenue. Annja liked the street name. How cool would it have been to live in the seventeenth century when New York was New Amsterdam?

"Not as cool as you wish," she admonished.

While it was interesting to conjecture a life lived in a previous century, the appeal of it only lasted until Annja reminded herself of lacking plumbing, sanitation, medicine and the Internet.

The building was quiet as she entered. Classes must be in session, she thought. As she passed various classrooms the doors were open to reveal dark quiet rooms. No one about. Odd.

Professor Danzinger was the rock star of the Sociology and Anthropology department. At least in the minds of the attending females. Pushing sixty, the man was still in fine form. Tall, slender and with a head full of curly salt-and-pepper hair, a quick glance would place him onstage, guitar in hand. Closer observation—perhaps a genial handshake, as well—would discover he would have to play backup for Mick Jagger, for the lines creasing his face.

Annja recalled he actually did play guitar—sometimes during class—which only made the girls swoon all the more.

An excellent teacher, most students claimed to learn more from one semester of Practical Archaeology than they did all year during some of the more advanced classes. Danzinger frequently guest taught at universities across the country, and Annja had been lucky to have him for a semester herself in her undergrad days.

She remembered him fondly, and she'd had the requisite crush on him, too. But she'd never dated him, as some of her classmates had.

She peeked inside the open doorway to the anthropology lab and found him bent over a high-powered microscope. Curly hair spiraled down the side of his face. A tatter-sleeved T-shirt revealed thin yet muscular arms. He was wearing brown leather pants so worn they looked like the cow wouldn't take them back. And bare feet.

"Annja, don't stare, it isn't polite."

She entered the lab, swinging the box containing the skull like a bright-eyed schoolgirl dangling her purse as she watched the football star walk by.

Plopping the box on the lab table with a clunk helped to chase away the silliness in her. So she had her goofball moments. Sue her.

"Fancy little box." Professor Danzinger pushed from the counter and gave her a wink. He moved in an erratic, over-caffeinated, no-time-to-sit-still motion that made her wonder if he didn't moonlight in a band on weekends. "Is that the newest fashion in purses for hip, young archaeologists?"

"No, I prefer my backpack. And it's not mine. It belongs to the thief who gave it to me."

"Ah, a thief."

"Alleged thief."

The professor leaned a hip against the counter, propping an elbow and crossing his legs at the ankle. He signaled beyond her. "Where is he?"

"Dead. His body is floating somewhere in the Gowanus Canal."

"Too bad. Drowned?"

"No, bullet."

That got a lift of brow from him. She respected him too much to make up a story, and he was one of those who could take anything a person said as if it were merely a weather report. "Truth earned respect" was one of his favorite mantras.

"Annja, you do have an interesting assortment of acquaintances. I seem to recall a nervous junior movie producer tagging along with you last time we met. Doogie something or other?"

"Doug Morrell. Television producer, and jumpy hyperactive is his normal state. I'd hate to see him on caffeine."

"He produces your show?"

"It's not *my* show, but yes, he does."

"I saw the show a few months ago. Who's the bimbo?"

"Why? You interested?"

Flash of white teeth. "Always."

"Good ol' Professor Danzinger. Always on the make."

"Sleeping with the professor won't get you an *A,* but it does promise a night to remember."

She felt a blush rise in her cheeks. Annja glanced about the room, unconcerned for the stacked femurs or plaster casts of hands and faces. Just don't let him see my red face, she thought.

Danzinger, blessedly nonchalant, nodded toward the box.

"So let's take a look, because I know my flirtations will get me nowhere with you."

"Oh, they might," she said, trying to sound blasé.

"Really?" He tugged the box toward him and leaned over the counter, bringing him closer to her. So close she could smell the spicy cologne and wonder why she never did invest in the extracurricular extra credit the professor had offered.

"Probably not," she decided with a sigh. "I'm much too busy most of the time. And running about like a mad woman the rest of the time."

"No time for a love life? Annja." He shook his head. "What did I teach you about taking time for yourself?"

"The enslaved soul dies. Or something like that."

"Close enough. You need to take care of yourself, is what it boils down to. All work and no play, well, you know how that one goes."

She did. But somehow, even when Annja finagled a little vacation time, it managed to become work. Or adventure. Or both—with bullets.

She had to laugh at her life sometimes. It was either that or scream.

The professor pried off the box top and let out a whistle. "Standard skull enhanced with decorative gold. You seen one, you've seen a million. Small though. Newborn. What's so special about this one, Annja?"

"I'm not sure."

She was surprised at his dismissive assessment of the skull. Though his focus was on sociology as opposed to anthropology, which went a little way in explaining his lacking interest.

"As I've said, someone has already been killed for it. The guy I got this from was able to tell me he was afraid someone wanted to take it away from him before he was shot."

"Such a life you live. Puts my world-crossing shenanigans to shame."

She doubted that one. Annja did dodge a bullet or two more often than most. But she had nowhere near as many notches on her bedpost as this man.

The professor fished out a magnifying glass from a drawer by his hip and studied the gold creeping along the sutures. "Cross pattée. Teutonic? The gold was added much later than this baby died."

"You think? What's your guess on age?"

"Haven't a clue. Though Teutonic is thirteenth century— formed at the end of the twelfth. That means little. We don't have the supplies in the lab to properly date it. We don't have a department dedicated to archaeology, as you know. Though perhaps Lamont might have the carbon-14 equipment. They do dendrochronology—dating tree rings—so they could probably take a look at this skull."

Annja knew all the earth and environmental science people were located at Lamont.

Danzinger turned the skull upside down to peek inside the hole on the occipital bone at the skull base where the spinal cord normally ran through.

"There's something inside. Carvings?" he asked.

"What?" Annja was caught off guard.

"You didn't notice the interior designs? Looks like carvings. I'll need a scope."

He tucked the skull against his rib cage and wandered to a cabinet on the wall. Rooting around like a mechanic who sorts through a toolbox, he produced an articulated snake light from a scatter of tools and returned to the lab table with it.

The end of the snake light had a USB connection. He plugged it into his computer. It opened a program that, Annja realized, streamed video from the light.

"It's a little camera on the end?" she asked.

"Cool, huh? Isn't technology a marvel?"

He poked the device inside the skull. Carved designs appeared on the computer monitor.

"Wow." Annja inspected the image. His movements were jerky and she could only make out lines here and there. "Stop. Let me look at this. You think those were carved? But how? That would take a pretty precise instrument to work through such a small hole, and these are very elaborate carvings."

"Unless the skull sections were pried away for the carvings and then the sutures were resealed with the gold."

"No, it hasn't been separated like that. The skull is intact."

"Annja, you think it came this way? Or rather, it was born this way?"

It was a silly conjecture, she realized. "Let me see."

He handed her the skull and camera, but she only took the skull.

Poking a finger inside the hole, she traced it along a carved line and dug in her fingernail to test the depth. It was shallow and the edges were smooth. It felt natural, as if the lines had existed since the skull had, well, been born.

It was utterly ridiculous. Human skulls were not embedded with a worm's nest of interconnecting carvings. The designs had to be manmade, and the gold supported that guess.

Still, she smoothed the pad of her finger over the designs. It was remarkable no sharp edges appeared that would give a clue the lines had been carved. Of course time would soften all knife edges and chisel marks. But even on the inside?

"Can you leave this here with me overnight?" Danzinger asked. "With patience I might be able to map the interior with the camera."

"So you're interested now? It's no longer just another skull?"

"Hey, with the holiday this weekend the building is serene. It's difficult to leave when there's not a soul to bother me. I've got a few hours to spare tonight. Joleen broke our date."

"I don't even want to know." She caught his sly wink. "What holiday?"

"Seriously? Annja, it's Thanksgiving in two days."

"Oh, right. I don't pay much attention to the calendar." She tapped the skull. "I'll leave it. I'd love to see what's going on inside this thing."

He took the skull and nestled it carefully in the lamb's wool. "Cool. I will call you as soon as I have something."

She scribbled her cell phone number on a piece of paper and he tucked it in his pants pocket.

"So, Annja, if you ever need an expert on classic electric guitars for the show, you know where to find me."

"You'll be the first I ask. What a pair you and Kristie would make on the screen. They'd have to do up posters and send you to fan conventions to sign them."

"You think?"

She smirked, and shook his hand. "Thanks, Professor. Call me as soon as you have something."

ANNJA STOPPED in the lobby below her loft and chatted with Wally, the building's superintendent, while she sipped coffee. The building's residents were all on friendly terms. She liked the small community and felt safer for it.

The connection to people who didn't necessarily know her well, but well enough to smile at sight of her and offer a few friendly words, was something she cherished. A girl who had grown up in an orphanage will take all the camaraderie she can get.

Climbing the fourth-floor stairs, she was glad for the residents' rule of no elevator after-hours because the thing was creaky and loud. Who needed an elevator when the exercise felt great?

Tugging the thief's backpack from her shoulder, she swung its empty weight by her side as she took the stairs.

A strange touch of grief suddenly shivered inside her rib cage. She hadn't known the guy at the bridge. They'd had a few online conversations, shared some common knowledge and a fascination for old skulls. Yet he'd died standing right next to her. She had used his body as a shield to break the water during their fall.

As much as she'd encountered death in her life—and it had increased tenfold over the past few years—Annja would never become so used to it that it didn't at least make her wonder about the life lost. It was the archaeologist in her.

If some goon were intent on killing her, and she had to take his life to save her own, the regret was minimal. But innocents caught in the line of fire? That was tough to deal with.

Had Sneak been innocent? Bart suspected he might be a thief from the description she'd given him of the tools. Yet, if he were a thief, why bring the booty to her? Wouldn't he have his own network of experts to authenticate an artifact?

Unless he was just forming that network, and he'd neglected to mention she had been chosen as his expert archaeologist.

What nest of vipers had she stepped into by meeting the man and claiming the skull?

Whoever had killed the thief had gotten a look at her, surely, through the rifle scope. She hadn't looked her best last night with a ski cap pulled to her ears and bundled against the cold so, hopefully, whatever look the sniper had gotten hadn't been enough to pick her out from a crowd. With her face flashed across the TV screen on occasional Thursday nights it wasn't easy going incognito.

She pushed open the fourth-floor stairway door. The sudden awareness that something was not right made her pause before her loft door labeled with 4A. She held her palm over the knob, not touching it.

The door wasn't open, but she sensed a weird vibe in the air. Intuition had always been good to her.

Had someone been here while she was gone?

"Paranoia does not suit you, Annja," she muttered, and twisted the knob.

Apparently paranoia fit this time.

Her loft had been ransacked. The messy desktop was now clear save the laptop. Books, papers, manuscripts, pens and small artifacts were spread haphazardly across the floor. One sweep of an arm had cleared them from the desk.

Curtains were pulled from the rod and heaped on the floor. So much for dusting them. Couch cushions were tossed against the wall and the couch overturned. The filming setup in the corner of her living room was trashed. The green screen coiled on the floor, and the camera sprawled on top of that.

Everything had been touched. She didn't want to venture into the kitchen. She got a glimpse of a cracked peanut-butter jar from the doorway.

The reason Annja didn't rush into the kitchen sat on the desk chair before her. As if waiting for her return.

Annja lowered her body into a ready crouch, but she did not summon her sword to her grip. She didn't know who he was, but she wasn't so quick to reveal her secrets before she learned the secrets of others.

Besides, he didn't jump her, nor did he have a pistol aimed on any important body parts.

The man was bald, seeming tall from his seated position and his broad shoulders and dressed in a dark suit with a black tie. He looked up from his canted bow through his lashes, which made him seem more sinister than the business suit could ever manage.

Could he be the man who'd pulled her from the canal? That man had been bald.

"Annja Creed," he said calmly. "I've been waiting for you."

7

He sounded Russian. The voice was deep but the tones were even and he didn't sound threatening.

What was she thinking? The man had destroyed her home. And she had a pretty good idea what he must have been looking for.

"You know my name. It's only polite I learn yours." Still in defensive mode, Annja kept the open door behind her in case a quick escape was needed.

"Serge," he said, putting a Slavic lilt on the second syllable. "You know what I am here for, Miss Creed."

"I have no idea. How about you tell me? That is, after you apologize for tearing my place apart. You've tossed valuable artifacts about as if toys."

"Unfortunately, not the valuable artifact I seek. You slipped through my fingers last night."

So he was the guy at the canal. That explained the bruise at the corner of his left eye. Points for the half-frozen chick.

"I know you have it. I saw the pictures you posted online."

Crap. For as many times as she'd posted photos—and said postings had resulted in cluing the bad guys to finding her—she would never learn. And yet…

"How did you find me? I cover my tracks well online. My Internet profile is secure. You couldn't have traced me."

"I have my ways."

She chuffed, then thought better of angering the guy who had turned over her heavy leather couch. His *ways* may simply include following her cab home last night. She only took it eight blocks. And she had been out of her head, not thinking clearly.

On the other hand, she'd left him flat on his back. He couldn't possibly have followed her.

"So you knew the man I spoke to last night *before* you shot him?"

"I fired no weapons last evening."

That supported her theory on the existence of both the sniper and her attacker.

"So, you and the sniper work together?"

The man looked aside, breaking eye contact, but he didn't drop his dead calm. He reconnected with her gaze immediately. "No," he said quietly.

Interesting. So if this one had been tracking the thief for the skull, then what stake had the sniper in the whole thing? How many parties were involved? She counted three so far—the thief, the sniper and this lunk.

"I've spent an hour going through your things," he said. "It's not here."

"I could have told you that, if you'd been polite enough to simply ask."

Her *things?* That implied something so personal. Things that were meant for her eyes only. The idea of this creepy bald guy shuffling through her underwear sent a shiver up Annja's spine. He didn't look the sort who would linger over silky things.

Then again, crazy never did look crazy until it was too late.

"News of the skull's emergence pleased me." The slow calm of his speech made her wonder if he thought out his words before releasing them into the ether. "It is quite the prize. I thought to have it in hand last night. But then the contact you know as Sneak switched things. I was unaware of your clandestine meeting on the bridge."

That meant Serge had been tracking the thief. Or the sniper, Annja thought.

Emergence? That might rule out the possibility of it being taken from a dig sight.

"I still cannot understand why he would give it to *you*," Serge said.

Well, he didn't have to make it sound as if she were a distasteful tangle of octopus sitting on a plate of greens, she thought. She said nothing in response.

"I have studied you, Annja. On your own computer."

That explained the laptop on the desk, powered up and open to Google. Nice of him to spare that expensive piece of equipment. The green screen and camera, on the other hand, were definitely a loss.

"You're a television personality." His grimace was accompanied by strange wonder. "As well, an archaeologist. But you're no one special, Miss Creed. You are common. Your schooling is common. Your expertise not equal to the world's foremost in your field. Why would he give the skull to *you?*"

She shrugged. "I'm cuter than you are?"

The man tilted a malevolent frown at her.

What did he expect after that berating put-down? Common? She'd show him common. And he wouldn't see it coming.

He stood in one smooth motion. The dark navy suit was

tailored to his body. It revealed thick biceps and a broad chest. She couldn't detect any sign of a shoulder holster for a gun bulging under the arm.

He didn't approach her. Annja maintained her ready position by the door. Knees slightly bent, hips aligned with her shoulders. Fluttering her fingers, she thought of the sword. It was right at her grasp with a beckon—but she didn't call it.

If he was willing to talk, she'd get what information from him she was able. Then she'd show him how very uncommon she could be.

"It's not here," she offered.

She wasn't about to give directions to Danzinger or Columbia, because she could guess how that would end. One body last night was enough for her.

"I believe you," Serge said. "You don't have it on your person, either, because you entered with nothing but that empty backpack."

She'd dropped it inside the doorway.

"Do you work for Benjamin?" he asked.

"Benjamin?" Annja cursed silently. If she'd played that one right, she could have danced around, tried to finagle exactly who Benjamin was. The name meant nothing to her.

Serge nodded, picking up on her lacking knowledge.

He toed a thin steel lock pick that had scattered during his melee. "You don't know what you've been given, do you, Miss Creed?"

Held by his pale gray gaze, she stared at him as if to dig the answer out from his expression. Phrenology was the science of determining character and personality from skull shape. She wondered what a big, rugged cranium meant.

The longer she looked into his eyes, the more she felt creepy crawlies skitter up her spine.

"No, I have no idea what it is." She looked aside at the mess, then caught movement in her peripheral vision.

Serge reached inside his suit coat and drew out a blade.

Any previous reluctance to calling out her sword fled.

With a lunge to her right, Annja dipped low. She summoned the battle sword. It emerged from the otherwhere in an instant. It fit into her palm with a sure grip. She hoped she'd made it seem as though she were plucking the sword from the floor behind the couch. With a bend of her knee she thrust toward Serge.

With minimum movement, he flicked his wrist, blocking her stab with the edge of his bowie knife. A nod acknowledged her challenge. His dark eyes narrowed.

Annja swung low, seeing if she could get a rise out of the guy. He had only to step back, then forward, as the sword swept past his thigh.

He retaliated with swift grace. The knife passed near her cheek, but didn't cut flesh. His reach was long and surprisingly agile for one so large and bulky.

"I don't know how you think fighting me is going to help you find the skull," she said. A twist of shoulder and a double step backward put her out of reach from his next swipe. Annja slashed her sword across Serge's shoulder, opening the seam of his suit coat. "I don't have it," she said.

"But you had it. Which means, you know where it is now."

She didn't answer. Couldn't. A knife to the thigh sliced out a painful chirp from her. It cut through her jeans and a couple of layers of skin. Score one for the bald guy.

Annja countered by spinning and putting her shoulder to his. She twisted and gripped his knife wrist. Releasing the sword she grabbed his sleeve. A twist moved Serge into a spin and he wobbled and fell. The force of landing popped the bowie from his grip. The knife flipped in the air and hit the wall with a clank, dropping onto a stray couch cushion.

He slapped a hand over her throat and shoved her off him. Annja's hips connected with the desk. Turning and rolling across the desk she came to her feet with sword again in hand.

Serge stood, hands near his shoulders. He was not surrendering by any means, just making nice. "Proficient sword work. I didn't notice the weapon earlier."

"Because you were so busy throwing things about."

He blocked her thrust with a jerk of his elbow, the flat of Annja's blade sliding along the suit fabric. Serge gripped her left wrist, twisting it. Annja had to duck forward, bringing her sword arm down and away from attack. Moving with the twist, she spun under his arm, but came up to meet his fist. A backhand slap put her on the floor, arms spread and legs landing on a sofa cushion.

Serge leaned over her. Annja twisted her head to the side. Knuckles cracked the hardwood floor.

In no position to deliver a masterful riposte of sword, Annja thrust blindly. The sword slashed across his back. He didn't cry out. Hell, she had only cut through his suit again. Must be some kind of Kevlar-reinforced stuff.

Before she could lever herself to stand, Serge gripped her hair and tugged her upright. She met the wall with her palms, dropping her sword. It slipped into the otherwhere, the sound of steel hitting floor lacking.

Knuckles bruised into the base of her spine. No knife? So he didn't want her dead. Or maybe he liked to play before he did real damage.

"You like doing things the hard way?" she grunted.

He didn't wait for her answer. A slam from his knuckles at the back of her head crushed her cheek into the brick wall. Blood spilled into Annja's mouth.

"I have been doing it the hard way for longer than you can imagine. It's my game, baby. And I can play it all night."

Baby? Oy.

She coughed on the blood trickling down her throat. Blood from her nose. The sword's image formed in her mind, but then streams of blood spilled over that image and Annja quickly lost the idea of summoning it.

Her body slung about, shoulders impacted against the brick wall. Serge grabbed her left wrist and smashed the back of her hand high on the wall over her head.

Seconds stretched as he peered into her eyes. His gray irises were wide, the pupil too small in the centers. Demonic, Annja thought. But she didn't believe in demons. There were logical explanations to all things supernatural. And Serge was just a man.

"I'll give you twenty-four hours to bring the skull to me. If you do not comply, at precisely five minutes beyond the twenty-four hour mark, I will kill you. Got it?"

She nodded. To argue might earn a broken nose. "How am I supposed to find you?"

He reached inside his coat. Would he pluck out a business card? Why did the hard edges of his jaw go all fuzzy? Damn, she was losing consciousness.

The flash of bright steel summoned her to a semiconscious state. He held some kind of weapon. He hadn't been in position to retrieve the bowie.

Serge leaned close and hissed in her ear. "The Linden Hill Cemetery off Starr Street. Tomorrow morning, this time."

"A graveyard? Swell," she mumbled.

Something sharp pricked her wrist. And the pain only increased. The stab became a searing poker. Annja let out a yelp as what felt like a knife entered her flesh and, with a forceful shove, traveled through to bone.

Serge gave the instrument a twist. Annja screamed. He tugged it out with a gruff exhale.

Agony felled Annja to her knees. Serge stepped back.

Struggling to maintain consciousness, and looking up to see the weird tubelike blade he tucked inside his coat, Annja reached out—for what, she didn't know. It seemed as though…*something* should come to her hand. Something that could protect her.

Instead, she fell forward and blacked out.

8

So far as apartments went, it was unassuming and quiet. Tucked in a dark corner of Lower Manhattan, in winter it got about an hour's worth of sunlight around two in the afternoon, but grew dark before four due to the surrounding tall buildings.

The most crime the neighborhood saw was old lady Simpson going after the postman with her cane, or the occasional burglary. A diminutive Russian market stood three blocks west and sold dozens of varieties of caviar, and a homemade borscht that tasted excellent served with heaps of sour cream.

Serge closed the door, sliding the chain lock deftly behind his back. The room was dark. Peaceful. He breathed in and exhaled. Palming the smooth hematite globe sitting on the key table near the door, he released anxiety, ego and any anger the outside world had put upon him.

He tapped the globe once.

Moving around behind the black leather sofa with the low back, he scanned the living room's cool shadows. There was but the sofa and a coffee table sitting before the slate-tiled hearth he used every night in winter. No nooks for anyone to hide.

Assured he was alone, he paused before the entry to the spartan kitchen and placed his palm upon the second hematite globe he kept on a hip-high iron stand. The cool stone took him farther from the world—into sanctity.

A glance assured the kitchen was empty. The short narrow aisle down the center was bare. Doorless cupboards revealed glassware and plates. A grocery list stuck to the refrigerator awaited Serge's precise scribbles for the next trip to market.

Two taps to the hematite globe.

He crossed before the window looking over a chain-link fenced-in yard behind a textile factory but did not look outside. His sleeve brushed the cheap shades that had been in the apartment when he'd assumed rent. He liked the sound the thin tin strips made when agitated.

As with the kitchen, there was no bedroom door. It was a small, efficient room he used only for sleeping. He did not bring women home; sanctuary would be lost. Though certainly, he did go home with a woman when opportunity arose. His shoes creaked the fifth board on the floor, reminding Serge he had yet to pick up finishing nails to fix the squeak.

A queen-size bed was covered by a taut black bedspread and two pillows encased in matching black cotton covers. Beside the bed on the nightstand, the white lilies he'd purchased two days earlier from the Russian market were beginning to wilt.

Serge touched a bedpost. A smooth hematite globe. He tapped it three times. The next post received four taps.

Shrugging off his suit coat, he tossed it on the bed. He wasn't a neatnik, but his home did remain pristine. He didn't spend much time here. Since setting foot on American soil a year earlier he'd been kept busy. He liked to be busy.

But a busy mind was not always favorable. Distilling, releasing the outside world upon arrival home, was always important.

A shower felt necessary after picking through the Creed woman's home. How one person could collect so much material stuff and jam it all into the small loft was beyond him. Though it had been an interesting collection of things. The artifacts and books had clashed oddly with the baseball team pendants and pink ruffled pillows.

Inspecting the shine on his loafers he inadvertently noticed a streak of peanut butter on one of his shirt cuffs. He rubbed at it but it smeared. He should tend it with an ice cube and some spot cleaner. The dry cleaner never pressed his shirts the way he preferred, with the collars creased.

Unhooking his cuff links, he then unbuttoned the crisp white shirt and discarded it on the suit coat. Unbuttoning his pants, he let them hang loosely at his hips. Starting for the shower, he remembered, and swung around to probe the inner pocket of his coat.

He drew out the biopsy tool and inspected the bloodied tip. The stainless-steel blade was curved, curled the length much like the large cheese corer he'd used as a child. A bone extractor. A tool of his trade.

The contents—skin, blood and bone—were still intact.

Foregoing a shower, he pushed open the closet door—the only door in his small apartment beyond the front entrance—and padded inside. Groping through the darkness, his fingers snagged a hanging chain and tugged. A fluorescent light beamed across the interior. The closet was as large as the bedroom. Two suits hung from the bar just inside to the right.

The walls were paneled in bamboo. A sisal mat stretched before a small dark wood shrine, bare right now.

At the far side of the room a stainless-steel counter

stretched three feet along the wall. Above it a glass shelf held many vials, syringes and jars. His work area.

On the topmost shelf he kept a small library of grimoires and herbal references. It had cost a pretty penny to have these precious items shipped overseas. Yet shipping expenses had been covered. Not exactly a perk of his job, more like a necessary evil.

Touching a flat switch set above the counter focused a spotlight on the table. Thumbing a box of small waxed papers, he drew one out. The *snick* of paper leaving cardboard pleased him.

Serge tapped the blade handle against the steel counter. The tiny bit of Annja Creed dislodged and landed on the small rectangle of waxed paper.

Using surgical tweezers and looking through a magnifying lens, Serge separated flesh and muscle from bone. He used his forefinger to swipe away the blood and marrow from the bone. It was a good sample. It didn't crumble as some did. Sickness, age and addiction tended to weaken human bone, which was made of minerals, collagen and water.

"Strong bone structure."

He was impressed. In his experience, women generally had honeycomblike bones, especially those living in the United States. The American female's diet was atrocious. Copious sugar and caffeine, and never enough calcium. Of course, this woman was still young and, judging from her physical skills—and ignoring her kitchen inventory—took good care of her body.

He tapped a few drops of alcohol onto the pencil-erasersize sample to clean it. It wasn't necessary to sanitize it. He just needed the bone clean. A small wet tissue cleared away the remaining flesh and blood. He would deposit the bone in a mortar and crush it—

The cell phone vibrating in his pants pocket disturbed his concentration. Serge reached for a glass vial and coaxed the bone into it. A rubber stopper closed it securely.

He answered on the fourth ring. He did not say his name. Only one person in the city—the entire country—had this number.

"Serge, I'll need you in the office by three. I've got a necessary task. You're not busy?"

For a moment Serge stared at the phone. That was an odd question. Busy? When had the caller ever been concerned with his private life? For that matter, the caller was his only employer; he should know if he were busy.

Did he suspect?

"Serge?"

"I'll be there."

He hung up. Something wasn't right.

9

Annja woke on her living room floor. Something smelled off. Her wrist pulsed with pain. Rolling to her side, she was startled to see the drops of blood beneath her left hand. For a puncture wound, she'd lost a lot of blood.

She examined the wound. It no longer bled. Skin tissue had puckered around the tiny entry circle on the underside of her wrist. She didn't want to probe it. It hadn't gone through and out the other side, though it had damn well felt as if it had.

Serge, her less than welcome guest, had shoved something deep into the bone. And he'd twisted.

"Like taking a freaking core sample or something," she said, testing her voice.

She sat up, cradling her wrist, and blinked away the wooziness still toying with clear thinking. The light in the room was dull, which told her she'd passed out for some time. It must be late afternoon. It started getting dark early this time of year.

"Not smart, Annja. Why didn't you pull the sword on him?"

Because when he'd slammed her against the wall, impact

had stolen the senses from her. She hadn't been thinking clearly.

Looking around she saw her door was still open. "Oh, man."

Dragging herself to a half-conscious stagger, she closed the door. Her neighbor across the hall hadn't noticed? The guy was a night owl. He was probably still sleeping. It was very likely he hadn't heard a thing when Serge had been tossing bits of her life around.

With a glance at the carnage of said life, Annja shook her head. Earlier she'd only been worried about dusting. Now she was going to need a bobcat with a loader on the front.

She wandered into the bathroom to clean her wound. Shampoo bottles, face cream and tubes of toothpaste and athletic rub were splayed across the floor. The towels she kept tucked beneath the sink cupboard were strewn, half of them landing in the tub. There wasn't much in here she worried about getting broken or damaged.

She didn't want to look at the green screen setup. That had cost her a few grand. Though she received money from royalties on her books, and *Chasing History's Monsters* paid her a nice fee, Annja was a penny pincher. And it was never a day at the park explaining things like this to the insurance company. She'd have to report a break-in again. But she couldn't tell anyone about Serge if she wanted the insurance check.

If the guy had been looking for a skull why would he open her toothpaste and squeeze that out? This vandalism was just plain malicious.

Clearing out the sink, she turned on the hot water, then some cold. The phone rang while the water was running. Watching the pink blood trickle over her wrist, Annja vacillated whether or not to answer.

Remembering her call to Bart last night she dashed for it, spraying water across the bathroom floor.

She picked up on the fifth ring. "Hello?"

"Annja, we got an ID on the body lifted from the canal this morning," Bart said.

"That was quick." She stepped across a scatter of books, noting the volume on Scythian metalwork was cracked down the spine. Stupid Serge. Even if insurance did cover it, she'd never find another; it was irreplaceable.

"Who and, more important, *what* was he?"

"Marcus Cooke," Bart said. "He also goes by the alias Travis Traine, and a few others. He's a thief, Annja, and a damn good one. He's hit museums in the States, Europe and a few royal caches in Germany and Poland. The guy likes colored stuff, rubies and emeralds. Interpol has been after him for years."

"Big-time thief. So why was he interested in a crusty old skull?"

"Exactly. Jewel thieves don't usually go in for anything they can't immediately fence."

Annja leaned against the desk. "There is gold on the skull, but I doubt that would amount to any more than a few hundred bucks in value."

"You didn't mention gold before. An infant's skull with gold on it? I'd have to stretch the definition of *colored stuff* to think it would interest a thief who has only stolen jewels."

"Maybe he was hard up? When was his last big job?"

"That we know of? In 2003. It's been years, which means little. The man could have changed his M.O. So if we allow he's changed his habits, or had just added artifacts to his repertoire, there's still one question. Why do you think Marcus Cooke chose to contact you, Annja? Have you ever heard of this guy or come in contact with him before last night?"

She remembered Serge expressing his surprise the thief had come to her. *You're just an archaeologist.*

Just. As in no better than any other.

It was true. Just because she hosted a TV show didn't make her better than half the archaeologists who devoted all their time to their passion. But the way Serge had muttered it had offended her. And she didn't upset easily.

"He saw me on TV and probably thought I looked trust-worthy."

"Professional thieves do not fence stolen goods with television personalities, Annja."

"Oh, so now I'm a fence?" She toed a plastic file of recipe cards detailing notes from a dig in Wales that had toppled on the floor. "Bart, please. Like I told you, I exchanged a few e-mails with the guy, then bam."

"You always arrange to meet strangers?"

"Not always. Sometimes they arrange to meet me." Or she found them waiting in her living room with nasty tools and a taste for bone. "You know I can't resist a mysterious artifact, Bart. A skull to me is like a cache of stolen credit cards to you. Yes?"

"I hate credit-card scams. So much paperwork involved. All right, so we'll agree the answer to why the thief chose you will never be solved. And he probably didn't intend to make you a fence, just wanted your opinion on its value."

"Agreed."

"You get a clue on the skull yet? Someone killed for it. Is it made completely of gold?"

"There is some decorative gold between the cranial sutures. Total? Probably less than a few ounces. I left it with Professor Danzinger at Columbia this morning. He's unable to date the thing because they don't have the proper equip-ment at the university, but he did find some interesting markings on the skull interior."

"Inside it? How does a person get anything inside a skull?"

"Very carefully."

Should she tell him about Serge's visit?

Annja was always cautious about telling Bart too much about the fiascos she found herself involved in. But she wasn't stupid. If having a detective back her up would advance the case, and she read Bart's mood as helpful, she'd ask.

She wasn't sure if police involvement was wise at this point in the game. It may hinder her by requiring she turn over the skull as evidence.

On the other hand, Serge had hurt her. The stab wound still pulsed with a dull ache. But what had he been trying to accomplish with the weird instrument?

She'd have to see if she could find a match on the Internet. If she knew who used a tool like that, and what for, that may give clue to who the heck Serge was. But what would she look under? Bone core samples? Bone biopsy tools?

She did not like knowing someone was walking around the city with a literal piece of her. Her DNA. The last time someone had gotten a piece of her DNA she'd come close to being cloned.

"I need a look at the evidence you have, Annja."

"Of course. I'll pack up the tools and get them to you."

"What about the skull?"

"Not in my hands at the moment."

"So you're going to sit tight until you get word from the professor?" Bart asked. "Or do I sense you've already formed a plan to track the origins of this thing? Something that'll see you in more trouble than a pretty young woman like you should be in?"

Pretty? Had he ever called her pretty? Maybe, but if so, she'd never noticed. Hmm, she'd take the compliment. Lately, they were few and far between.

"Bart, please." She sat on the floor and tugged a pillow to her lap. "I'm so not like that."

His chuckle tweaked her to smile. All right, she was exactly like that. And that Bart knew as much meant a lot to her.

She did have other friends. Some. There were the women on the *Chasing History's Monsters* crew. And Doug Morrell was a friend. An irritating one, but that's what friends were for, to irritate.

"I'll keep you updated," she said to him. "Let me know if you learn more about the thief. Like where he's been the past few days. You can track his movements, can't you?"

"Possibly. But I'll need more reason to do so than curiosity. I may need a certain skull as evidence to trace to its origins. Would you turn it over if you did have it in hand?"

"Probably not."

"Annja."

"Bart, don't press on this one. You handle the police business. Let me follow the skull's trail."

"Annja, you were shot at last night. So I am going to press. I'm getting a sense that you're only telling me half of what's going on. And why is that not unusual?"

He cared about her; she knew that. It felt great. Sometimes too great. Because the moment she let down her staunch defenses and let her innate neediness rise, then look out. Sometimes a girl had to resist what she wanted most. A pat on the back, a compliment.

Yeah, too risky.

"So you'll let me know if you come up with more info on Marcus Cooke?" she asked, avoiding his accusing question. "Anything that can point me to where the skull was found, unearthed and/or stolen is going to help me a lot."

"What if it's just another skull?"

"Men don't kill for just another skull, Bart. I've had a look

at it. There are some amazing carvings inside. It's special—
I can feel it. But it will help to know if it was taken from a
dig, or a museum, or a private collection."

She made a mental note to get online and do a search for
infant skulls.

"Hey, Annja?"

"What?"

"Are we still going to dinner tomorrow night?"

"Uh…"

"Annja? How else will you hand off the tools to me?"

"It's a date. And not even because of business. I want to
see you, Bart. It's been too long. Talk to you soon."

She'd hand over the thief's tools but there was no way
she'd give Bart the skull.

She hung up and went to bandage her wrist. She kept an
arsenal of medical supplies stored in her medicine cabinet—
which were presently strewn all over the floor.

"He was looking for a skull. It couldn't possibly fit it in
this narrow cabinet. This wasn't necessary," she muttered.

Minutes later, she'd dabbed the wound with alcohol and
bandaged it with medical tape. It had stopped bleeding. She'd
be fine. Heck, she took bullets and knife slashes all the time.
This was nothing.

"You are so not the Rambo you sometimes think you are,
Annja," she reminded herself.

Thoughts to start picking up her trashed loft were coun-
terattacked by the rumbling reminder from her gut that she
hadn't eaten yet. Picking through the debris on the kitchen
floor and over the counters, she found a box of cereal Serge
hadn't emptied onto the floor. That he had emptied others and
unscrewed all the jars astounded her.

"Who's going to hide a skull in a cereal box?" she
muttered as she poured the cereal into one of two bowls re-

maining in the cupboard. "Really. Did the guy think he'd find the prize at the bottom of the box?"

The fridge was relatively undisturbed. She knew that was because she hadn't gotten groceries lately, and there wasn't much to toss around. She poured milk over the chunks of colored sugar and fortified whole grain, plucked a spoon from a pile of scattered flatware and padded into the living room to sit before her now-clean desk and looked at her laptop.

"And to think I was complaining about how messy this desk was. Guy did me a favor. Too bad he doesn't dust."

The cereal was a rough go at first. Her aching jaw reminded her she'd taken a few more punches than she'd delivered.

Pressing the spoon over the cereal so it sank deeper into the milk and would become soggy and easier to chew, she moused her way to the archaeological site and found a few replies to her post.

BestMan573 wrote, You've seen one skull, you've seen them all. Though it does resemble that of a newborn. Where'd you say you found this? By the way, love the online pic!

"Must not be an anthropologist," she commented on his blasé dismissal of skulls. "And no, I'm not going to tell anyone I found this in some dead man's backpack. Online pic? Must have seen my bio at the *Chasing* site."

In that picture, taken on a lavender-streaked Scottish moor, she wore a boonie hat, cargo shorts and hiking boots. Not at all sexy. But indicative of her true self.

PinkRibbonGirl started by saying she was only in the seventh grade. Annja worked the numbers and figured she must be about twelve years old.

Hi! I'm so excited to be talking to you. I think you have the Skull of Sidon. I just found out about it a week ago, and thought it would be an awesome idea for my history report. I handed the outline in to my teacher and she nixed the idea. Said I couldn't write about necrophilia in middle school. It wasn't very becoming of a young girl. I didn't even know what necrophilia was until I looked it up. Eww!

"What comes out of kids' mouths today," Annja said. "The poor teachers. If it isn't bad enough they have to deal with gangs and cell phones and ADHD, there's the class brain in the front row writing about necrophilia."

She chuckled and clicked on the next e-mail.

NewBattleRider commented on the various skulls in history.

There are many black magic rituals involving skulls. Blood is drunk from the cranium to gain immortality. In medieval Cathay, rituals to honor gods involved skull bowls lined with brass or copper that blood was drank out of. The Knights Templar used to worship heads, which could be construed as a skull. That would jive with the cross pattée on the gold.

None of them felt right. The cross pattée felt like a red herring. A common marking. Could have been a goldsmith's mark or some kind of freemasonry symbol, Annja thought.

She reconsidered the Knights Templar. Head worshipping?

Annja had cursory knowledge of the monks who had taken vows of chastity and promised to protect helpless peasants who traveled the highroads from thieves. Didn't ring any bells to her, though, regarding skulls. The Templars were a few centuries earlier than her favorite research period.

She reread NewBattleRider's e-mail.

"I don't know. Worth a look," she said.

She moused to Google and typed in *head worshippers*. The search brought up references to trepanning, which was carving a hole in the skull to give a swollen brain room or air. The ancient Greeks had used trepanning frequently. Macabre circular hand-cranked drills had been used to cut through the patient's bone. Anesthesia was little more than some crushed herbs in those days.

The whole thing gave Annja a headache.

She typed in *ancient skulls,* which brought up more entries than her tired brain could manage. If she wasn't careful she'd need trepanning to give her gray matter room for expansion.

"All right, so I won't rule out the Knights Templar."

She couldn't get behind the idea. There were so many grail myths, she didn't want to get drawn into that muck of rumor, legend and hearsay.

Worship of gods made more sense to her. And her skull did have decorative metal.

Going back to the archaeology list, she posted a quick note, asking if anyone had a skull that had recently gone missing. Not the one attached to your head, she added in parentheses.

She didn't list specifics, beyond that it was possibly newborn and medieval. For sure she'd get lots of inquiries about missing skulls. But she never knew what might be found in the detritus.

Shoveling down spoonfuls of cereal, she dripped milk onto the keyboard. Swiping the milk from the space bar, she winced at the tug beneath the bandage about her wrist.

"Talk about the sword attracting danger. Can I just be a normal archaeologist for one day?"

Since she'd come into possession of Joan of Arc's sword normal days were few and far between. And Annja realized she enjoyed the adventure, even the danger. But not the pain.

"My kingdom for an aspirin." Annja swung around and winced at the mess in her loft. "If I can find one."

She decided she wouldn't get anywhere, or think clearly, until she'd done some major cleaning.

10

"You're looking well, Serge."

Serge Karpenko nodded an acknowledgment, but maintained a stare over the top of Benjamin Ravenscroft's head. The businessman's nose leveled at the center of Serge's chest. He wasn't short; Serge was tall. He could crush the ineffectual pencil pusher easily. But he would never do it.

Some men garnered power over others by manipulating reality—not the spiritual, as Serge was capable. Ben was a master at making things happen—or not. And Serge cherished his present reality, only because the alternative was unacceptable.

From what Serge understood, Ben sold nothing. And people bought those nothings. Things that could not be touched, held or looked at. It made little sense to Serge, and he hated that he could not wrap his mind around the concept. Should not a business have a tangible asset to show prospective buyers? It was like selling air!

Over the past year, he'd sought any means to crack open

his employer's psyche and begin to understand what made the cogs turn in his brain. Thus far, he'd been unsuccessful.

"Are you unhappy with your circumstances here in America, Serge?"

The tone of Ravenscroft's voice wasn't so much curious as delving. Serge knew better than to provide too much information. Or rather, he had learned a hard lesson regarding letting others know what you valued and what could make you do things you'd rather not.

"Very pleased, Mr. Ravenscroft. Is there a problem?"

"No problem. I just wanted to ensure I'm treating you well. I know the culture shock was initially difficult for you, but you seem to function with ease in the city."

Function meant serving this man. It wasn't as though Serge had a social life beyond his service to Ben. He wasn't sure he wanted one. How to begin? He knew a few local merchants in the neighborhood. The dry cleaner, the old man at the Russian market, the cheery young girl who worked Mondays and Thursdays at the all-night video store.

"The apartment still satisfactory?"

"It is."

"That's a fine piece of real estate, Serge. Apartments in Lower Manhattan are hard to come by."

"I have no complaints. The place is clean and quiet."

"Your stipend is seeing you well fed and comfortable?"

"Yes, sir."

"Good, then." Ben tilted his head, studying Serge's face. It was a stoic visage Serge had practiced all his life. There were so many reasons not to show emotion. Especially when one communicated with spirits and passed along messages to the living.

Exhaling, Ben shrugged and gestured to the door at his right.

"The summoning room has been prepared for you. I'll need information on the Tokyo funds listed in last week's dossier. I've left a copy of the file for you to study. Spirits this afternoon?"

Serge nodded. "They are most open to the future. The one I contact on your behalf seems to enjoy this field you work in. The untouchables."

"That's intangibles, Serge. I'd like to meet the spirit some day."

"Impossible. It does not come to corporeal form, as I've explained."

"Yes, just voices in your head, eh?" A curious smirk stretched Ben's stubbled cheek. "You're a marvel, man. You possess a remarkable skill."

"I was born this way." He'd previously explained his skills.

It was not so remarkable really. Many could commune with the dimension beyond this living realm, but few in the rushed, chaotic modern world took the time to notice that innate intuition.

Serge bowed and crossed the shiny black marble floor to the hidden door in the wall Ben had pointed to. He pressed the wall and the panel slid an inch inward. The action never ceased to amaze him.

Before entering the private room, he bowed his head and looked aside. Ben stared out the window at the view of Central Park below. He'd lit a clove cigarette, yet the smell didn't cross the room.

"And all is well with you, sir? Your…daughter?" Serge asked.

Ben stopped midinhale. A wisp of thick white smoke wavered from his nostrils. He didn't turn to Serge. The tension stiffening his shoulders became apparent.

"Measures must be taken, Serge. We'll discuss it soon."

Serge nodded and entered the low-lit room. They'd already discussed measures. Serge did not have the power to give Ben what he most wanted.

And when the man was again denied, what then would he do to Serge's family?

BEN STRUGGLED to control his anger. The insolent man dared to bring up his daughter.

Did he think to pit Ben's family against his own? The man could not conceive the move Ben could make against his family. They would be obliterated before Serge could remember the name of Ben's daughter.

The Ukrainian peasant denied Ben something he *must* be able to control. The man communed with the dead regarding the future. Why not help his daughter? Had he no compassion?

"I need that skull," Ben muttered. "But where is it?"

Could he ask Serge to send out spiritual feelers for the skull?

No, he didn't want the man to have any more advantage when the playing field was so unbalanced right now.

11

There were better things to tend to than necromancing for Benjamin Ravenscroft. Like researching Annja Creed. With her bone sample at home, Serge could easily track her footsteps over the past weeks. It was as simple as attaching a bloodhound spirit to her aura.

But he had to focus. Ben squeezed the Karpenko family's lives in his greedy corporate hands. And since Serge had bound himself to the man, he could do no harm against him. Powerless, he could only look to freedom.

Soon enough.

Bent over the crushed bone, sweet smoke curled into Serge's nostrils. He drew in the odor, surrendering to its intoxication.

Almost.

The Creed woman prodded his thoughts. She hadn't been the least unsettled to find him waiting in her home. A home he'd trashed. The skull had not been there.

Why hadn't he run across the battle sword while creating that havoc?

When she'd brought it out, it had given him momentary surprise. He feared very little. No skinny woman with a big sword was going to intimidate him. He may not have martial arts in his arsenal—such a rudimentary grasp at self-defense—yet he could easily exercise enough brute strength to overwhelm and attack.

Since he'd begun necromancing as a young boy Serge had always felt protective forces about him. He thought of them as a sort of force field against evil and negativity. Yet even that force field could not stop Serge from agreeing to help when a man asked kindly and promised to secure his family's future.

There were times Serge had ignored his intuition. It was foolish of him. For if he'd listened to his heart a year ago, he'd still be living on the small farm north of Odessa with his family. He'd be struggling to survive, but happier with those he loved in no danger.

He owed a call to his father and would stop by a phone booth on the way home. Serge no longer used the fancy cell phone Ben had gifted him. After a few strange clicks and tones during his first calls to his family, he became suspicious Ben was listening in or tracking his contacts.

Serge knew little about technology, but he was getting over that deficit quickly. Every Saturday he spent five hours at the New Amsterdam branch library. The class on Surfing the Internet for Fun and Profit had taught him about search engines, and how to go deeper for information worth having. It was how he found information on the woman he'd pulled from the Gowanus Canal.

Who would have thought the one television show playing in the café two blocks west of the canal, where he'd stopped for eggs and toast after that encounter with the woman, would be showing *Chasing History's Monsters*. It was dumb luck.

Or rather, Serge's intuition had been working strongly after it had failed him at the canal. It had led him the direction he needed.

He thought he should have processed her bone right away. Began to summon with it. See what the Greater All had to give him about her. He'd do so later, when he returned home.

Of course, he could wait. In the morning she'd bring the skull to him. If she wished to live. And who would not?

Annja Creed had impressed him with her defensive skills, and hadn't backed down from him no matter the fight he'd given her. Serge knew he was imposing. He stuck out like a bull in a daisy patch when walking the streets of Brooklyn.

He was very patient. But his patience was growing thin with Benjamin's unrelenting demands. The man kept insisting Serge could conjure a spirit to save the girl. He could not. A necromancer had no power over life and death. Such was ineffable.

He could but contact spirits and use them to manipulate the will of mortals, such as convincing them to turn right into traffic instead of left across a safe intersection. He could use spirits to cause illusions, either visible to all or but a figment in a man's mind. If he wished, he could drive a man to insanity—but he had no such malicious desires.

He most frequently contacted spirits. The spirits, unattached to this mortal realm or its constraints of time, provided him knowledge both from past and future.

Such knowledge was what Benjamin paid for. How certain stocks would perform, and those patents he bought and sold as if candy. Serge did not understand the man's business, but he did not have to. The spirit he contacted understood completely, and took greedy delight in providing details. It was demonic, the vibe Serge felt when he conjured.

Rarely did he summon demons, though they had their uses.

Remembering what he was doing, Serge gave his head a shake. He'd fallen out of trance. He'd never get this right if he couldn't concentrate.

He was so close to holding the skull. It would give him good things.

He felt it in his bones.

SHE'D BE AT TITO'S in less than ten minutes. Annja couldn't walk fast enough. She shoved a hand in her coat pocket to retrieve her jingling cell phone.

Professor Danzinger started in without introduction. She had to chuckle at his enthusiasm.

"It's quite incredible, Annja. I know I was initially reluctant about looking over another skull, but those carvings… Well, I don't believe they are actual carvings."

She paused on the street corner, waiting for a green light. The thief's backpack, with tools intact, was slung over her shoulder. "What could they be, if not carved?"

"I don't know! It's as if—well, you'll think me crazy."

"That's a word I've never heard associated with the rock-and-roll Danzinger."

"You tease, Annja. But the markings inside the skull? It's as if it was *born* that way. As if the brain's many convolutions had somehow made the impressions on the skull's interior. They are not carved, it is a reverse imprint."

The light turned green. She was bustled across at the head of a crowd of pedestrians. "Born that way? Professor, what have you been smoking?"

"Nothing! Yet. Heh."

Again she chuckled and skipped across the street to the restaurant.

"I'm mapping out the interior with the snake camera, but

it's a slow go. I stayed most of the night. It's so incredible, I didn't want to leave it alone."

"Huh. Then maybe we really have something there. Do the markings give any indication to provenance? Year? Nationality?"

"Who can know? And I'm no anthropologist, so I haven't a clue to begin assigning nationality or even sex from bone structure. It's difficult enough with an infant's skull. I haven't had the opportunity to research online for anything like this. I never do trust the Internet. Not sure I'll find time to run over to the library, either. There won't be many researchers around because of the holiday break."

"Right, I forgot, it's Thanksgiving weekend."

"I take it that means you've no family plans?"

"Nope, just me and the Macy's Parade on TV."

"I'd invite you to share the day with me, but all I can offer is turkey TV dinners."

"Sounds like heaven. Tomorrow?"

"It's a date. But I will be here all evening pouring over this incredible skull. Can I keep it until our date?"

Should he have termed it a date? She was not going to sleep with the man. Seriously. She was no longer a blushing college girl.

"Certainly. You know of anyone in the area who can date it for us?"

"I'll give Lamont a call. Not sure if they have the equipment, but it's worth a shot. That is, if anyone is around and not packed off over the river and through the woods to grandmother's house. Annja, I must let you go. I got another clear shot from inside. I'm starting to paste things together to get the big picture."

"Call me when it's finished. Thanks, Professor."

Annja slid the phone into her pocket, and entered Tito's.

The hostess knew her and directed her to a table near the back. Born that way? Incredible, she thought.

But nothing—as the holder of Joan of Arc's sword should know—was impossible.

"I ordered for you," Bart said as she slid into a booth. "I know you like the pulled pork with sofrito."

"Mmm, all those peppers and onions. Thanks for agreeing to meet me today."

She rubbed her hands together and blew on them to bring up the warmth. "Wine, too? You spoil me, Bart."

"It's on the house."

The owner, Maria, knew them both and always made sure they were well fed and happy. This wasn't the first time she'd gifted Annja and Bart with wine. It was almost as if she wanted to play matchmaker, designing a romantic setting with wine and food.

"Is that the evidence?" he asked.

She nudged the backpack toward his feet under the table. "All intact, save one very interesting skull. I just talked to the professor. He's very excited about the inner carvings."

"Sorry, I can't relate to anything old and dusty like you do, Annja."

"Sure you can. You must study cold evidence? Bones dug up from backyards? Old bloodstains? It's all the same."

"I leave that for forensics."

Dinner arrived. Tito's served generous portions designed to feed a small crowd or, at the very least, a hungry archaeologist.

"I'm so glad we changed our plans, Bart. I'm starving." Annja dug in. The plantains nestled beneath the tender pork were sweet and, combined with the savory meat, absolutely sang on her palate.

Arms crossed on the table, Bart looked her over, smiling.

A tiny scar at the right of his eye gave him a heroic visage, yet Annja knew it was from falling off the swing when he was seven. He'd been trying to jump higher than the cute neighborhood girl, and had failed miserably.

"You look great, Annja. I haven't seen you in a while. Really good," he drew out the compliment.

"Thanks." She shoveled two more forkfuls and a hearty swallow of water.

"And famished. Pace yourself, or we'll need another bottle of wine before you get to dessert."

"Nothing wrong with that. I'm no connoisseur, but this stuff is excellent."

"It is better than anything I've had lately." He dodged his glance from the wine to her face. "Is that a bruise?"

She rubbed her jaw. "Slipped on a dig."

"I doubt it."

Annja shrugged and sipped the white wine. The man was a detective and possessed remarkable deduction skills. She couldn't put a lie past him if she tried. So back to redirection. "This stuff is great. I wonder if I could get another order just to take home for lunch tomorrow?"

"Avoiding the subject as usual."

Setting down her fork and settling against the hard chair back, Annja relented. "What *is* the subject?"

"You and your current death-defying adventure. And me and my worries."

"I'm a big girl, Bart."

"You are. But big girls don't swim in the Gowanus Canal with dead men."

"I thought this was a reunion, not an interrogation."

"Okay, let's eat. But don't fault me for caring about you."

"I would never." She drank more wine because it was easier when she had something to do with her hands than just sitting dumbly, open, allowing him into her personal space with his delving gaze. "So how's it with the NYPD?"

"Great. Couldn't be happier. Well, I could, but that's personal."

"Personal stuff! It's about time. I want to hear some dirt. No girlfriends?"

"Not lately. You?"

"Girlfriend? Nope, I don't swing that way."

Bart chuckled. "I'm glad I got you out tonight."

"I am, too." She held up her wine and Bart matched the move. "To good friends."

"Who worry about each other," he said.

By the time they'd finished the meal and the bottle of wine Annja had learned Bart was considering online dating. Just to check it out. To learn the scene, he'd used the excuse, in case it ever came up on a case.

Why a good-looking guy like Bart had to resort to finding a woman online was beyond her. It must have something to do with his broken engagement. It had hurt him, she could sense. Bart was doing the rebound thing, looking for a replacement for his fiancée. Rebounds never worked out. Even he confessed that much.

So he was basically looking to get laid, though he'd never say it outright like that. She could understand. Who didn't want a little human contact now and then?

They stepped outside into a light flutter of snow. Before Annja could say anything, Bart pulled her in for a hug. A good hug. Not flirtatious, yet it warmed every part of her body. She clung to his shoulders before gently moving away.

"How'd you know I needed one of those?"

"Really? That one was for me." He winked as a snowflake dashed his eyelid. "This one is for you."

The second hug was even better than the first. Yet Annja couldn't enjoy it completely because, much as the close contact appealed, she did not want to be Bart's rebound girl.

12

"Daddy!"

Ben swung his briefcase into the maid's waiting arms and glided into the living room to greet his daughter. She didn't rise to hug him. Instead, her attention was glued on the television.

"You got home early tonight, Daddy," Rachel announced, without looking from the plasma screen.

"I wanted to spend some time with the most beautiful girl in the world."

"Mommy?"

"No, you, silly." He settled on the sofa next to her, and tucked the end of the pink scarf she wore tied about her scalp behind her ear. "Where is Mommy?"

"Upstairs, taking a bath. She put supper in the microwave for you. We had beets." Rachel managed a second away from the TV to comment on supper with a distasteful wrinkle of her nose.

"Maybe I'll forget they're in there?" he teased. "I had salad again today. I think we need a new cafeteria at the office. It's either salad or cold roast-beef sandwiches."

"Mommy said to say good-night to you."

She always did deliver that morsel through Rachel.

Attention still fixed on the television, Rachel asked, "Why does Mommy always go upstairs as soon as she hears you drive into the garage?"

He couldn't explain that he and Mommy were not on best of terms lately. Linda blamed him for the impossible.

Ben glanced over the back of the couch. The box of roses sat on the kitchen table, unopened. Great. Not as if he hadn't expected that reaction, though.

"Mommy gets tired early." He summoned the lie easily because it had become rote. "I see her when I go upstairs after you've gone to bed." As I grab my shirt and suit coat from the closet for tomorrow and sneak into the guest bedroom.

"Uh-huh."

Behold, the idiot box's remarkable power. Ben wondered if Rachel's teachers had ever captured her attention as easily as a six-foot plasma TV. This "coming home early to tuck the kid in" thing was going over like a boulder tossed in a pond.

"How you feeling tonight, sweetie?"

"Good. Not sick."

"Not sick is always good."

He stroked his fingers over the soft blond hair that snuck out from under her scarf and kissed the crown of her head. The hair had begun to grow back in superfine strands.

Rachel wrinkled her nose but snuggled in closer to him. "You smell good, Daddy. What's the spice again?"

"Cloves. And you smell—" he sniffed her hair "—like a purple dinosaur."

"It's groovy grape! I love that shampoo. It's so mummy I could eat it."

Ben propped his heels on the coffee table and nestled beside his daughter's warm yet frail body.

The past two months she'd been through radiation therapy.

Yet even with radiation, the chordoma tumor the doctors had removed from the base of her skull could grow back. In fact, the oncologist had seemed sure of it. The relentless cancer could lie in hiding for as long as ten years, and then suddenly strike again.

Rachel had lost weight and hair—but not hope. He worried he'd break her if he hugged her too tightly.

"What are you watching that has your attention so rapt?"

"*Chasing History's Monsters*. What's 'rapt'?"

"Rapt is what you are right now. Glued to the set. Immersed in the screen. Can't bother to give your dad a real hug. *Chasing History's Monsters?* Sounds creepy."

"It's not, Daddy. It's got this really pretty woman who stalks through caves and forests and tries to find monsters. She's really smart, too. Not like the other woman with the big knockers."

"Knockers? Rachel, where did you pick up a word like that?"

"Tracy says her dad calls them knockers."

"That's not an appropriate word for little girls to use."

And did they still use that word nowadays? Apparently so.

"Mom calls them boobs. What do you call them, Daddy?"

Ben pointed to the TV to avoid the topic. "Is that her? The one with the, er…"

"No, she's the smart one I like."

The chestnut-haired woman on the screen held some bit of pottery and pointed out the crack in it. Her voice commanded with a good solid tone. Droll, but punctuated with real enthusiasm. She was obviously very learned and passionate, even about some crud-encrusted bit of vase.

"She is very pretty," he agreed.

"Her name's Annja Creed, and she travels everywhere," Rachel explained. "I want to be like Annja Creed someday."

"Host of a television show?"

"No, silly, an archaeologist," she said, indicating he was a dunderhead for not getting it straight.

"That woman's an archaeologist? Huh."

He had no idea pothunters were so physically appealing. And so what if her knockers weren't so big, she was a nice package—brains, looks and confidence.

The show broke for commercial and Rachel said, "I e-mailed her the other day."

"Who? The lady on the television?"

"Yep. It was about the Skull of Sidon."

Ben's heartbeat suddenly raced. How could she possibly know? "Rachel, what do you know about the Skull of Sidon?"

"Well, not much until I did research. I saw it scribbled on one of your work papers last week, Daddy. Don't *you* know about it?"

"Yes, but it was just…" A stupid mistake to put questionable information out there for his daughter to find. That made him as inept as the men he'd hired to track Cooke. "It must have been something I heard on a television show. It was just a scribble, sweetie."

"Yeah, well, I thought it would be perfect for my history report, so I researched it online and wrote an outline for my teacher. She was not happy."

Ben rubbed a palm over his face. He wasn't sure how much Rachel could have dug up on the skull, but if the teacher hadn't been pleased…

"She didn't want me writing about necrophilia! Do you know what that is, Daddy? Gross."

"Yes, Rachel, sorry. It's another of those things kids your

age shouldn't have to worry about. You should have asked me about it before going to your teacher with it."

"Why are you studying old skulls and all that gross stuff?"

"I'm not, sweetie. Like I said, it was just something that caught my ear, and I wrote it down. Nonsense stuff. You know Daddy is always taking notes in case he gets ideas for work. So did the lady on TV write back to you?"

"Nah. She's probably really busy. Too busy for a kid, I'm sure." Rachel sighed. "I really like Annja Creed. Wish she would have wrote back to me."

She finally shuffled in for a proper hug and Ben squeezed her gently. "It's about time. I was beginning to wonder if you'd forgotten how to hug. Want me to tuck you in?"

"Can I watch the end of the show first?"

"I don't think so. Isn't Mommy taking you to the zoo tomorrow afternoon? You'll need your rest for that."

She gave him the patented pouty face, but Ben knew it wasn't for real because she followed with a yawn. Poor thing. She'd missed two days of school this week thanks to stomach flu. Last week it had been radiation sickness.

"All right, I'll go to bed. But will you carry me?"

Ben leaned forward and slapped his back. "Climb on, pardner."

He secured his daughter's legs with both arms and pounced through the living room, down the hall and up the stairs to tuck her in. He moved swiftly, because more important things than good-night kisses and wishes for sweet dreams must be tended.

On his way back down to the living room, Ben got side-tracked. The master bedroom door was open. Low light glowed across his wife's shoulders. It had been too many months since he'd seen her bare skin. He couldn't remember when he'd last touched it.

Pausing in the doorway, he admired Linda as she pulled the brush through her long blonde hair.

Admittedly, Rachel's cancer had been tougher on his wife. She was the one who had to bring their daughter to her doctors' appointments and radiation treatments. It had changed Linda. Made her harder. Distant.

Ben didn't know how to crack that hardened exterior. So he did not try. Instead, he sought acceptance from others. Rebecca's exterior was soft and lush and always giving. And she never blamed him for things he could not control.

Linda's tearful tirade still lived fresh and so punishing in his memory. Two months earlier, Ben had been watching Rachel at the park. He'd wanted her to have a fun afternoon before her doctor's appointment that day. He and Linda had been concerned about Rachel's frequent verbal slurs and loss of equilibrium.

He'd had a lot to do that day, as usual, and had spent more time on his BlackBerry than he had watching his daughter. He'd lost her for one heart-wrenching harrowing hour.

Linda had been out of her mind by the time the Central Park police had found Rachel huddled at the base of an oak tree, oblivious to her parents' fears as she'd chatted with her Barbie dolls.

An hour later, the oncologist diagnosed Rachel's bone cancer.

That night, her face red with anger and tears, Linda had beat her fists against Ben's chest and blamed him. If he had been paying attention, Rachel would be safe now.

Not sick, had been the unspoken implication.

"What are you staring at?"

Shaken from his distressing thoughts, Ben staggered into the room and crossed the floor to his dresser. "Nothing, sorry." He dug out a T-shirt and boxer shorts to sleep in.

"You were late."

"Rachel was still awake. I got to kiss her good-night and tuck her in. I thought that was what you wanted from me?"

Her reply was a snort.

"It's hard on me, too, Linda."

"Yes, I suppose prancing about in your five-thousand-dollar business suits and lunching with executives is rather trying. And when you're not working late at the office you're hanging around with that sinister Russian guy."

"He's Ukrainian."

The brush slammed on the vanity. Ben felt the clatter in his bones.

"You never have time for family!"

"I'm *always* thinking of Rachel, and don't you dare take that from me."

Linda stared at him in the mirror. Rarely did he garner such focused attention from her. Not that he looked for it, because it always ended like this—in an argument.

She could never comprehend that he simply needed attention. Appreciation. He worked long hours to support his family and pay the medical bills. Did she not understand he had a heart, too, and it broke into more pieces every time he looked at Rachel?

"What are you involved in, Ben?"

He gaped. Then assumed calm. Always, she talked around the subject of their daughter. "I've been building a successful business, if you haven't noticed."

Ben clutched his things and strode toward the door. It was easier to avoid an argument. And he didn't want Rachel overhearing.

Pausing in the doorway, he said, "I see you got the roses."

"Your secretary has almost got your signature perfected."

"A simple thank-you would have sufficed. Good night, Linda."

Five minutes later, Ben was able to shuck off the chill of Linda and remembered his conversation with Rachel about the skull. He settled onto the couch.

The show was just ending. The woman detailed her findings and, though they hadn't located vampires in the Carpathian mountains, implied that anything was possible.

He could sense the sarcasm in her voice as she spoke of vampires, but also sensed she knew what bolstered the ratings.

Rachel was right. She was pretty. And *familiar.* He'd never seen this show before. It was rare for him to watch anything other than CNN. Where had he seen her?

He plucked the picture Harris had given him earlier from his pocket.

Leaning forward, he compared it to the face on the screen. The sniper photo was grainy but the jawline and nose were similar.

It was the same woman, he was sure of it.

But really? Some television hostess had met with Cooke about the skull? Had she been meeting him in the capacity of an archaeologist or a buyer? Or with intent to feature the skull on her show?

Had the thief been thinking of handing the skull over to her? Or had he merely wanted details on it only an archaeologist could provide? What interest did Cooke have in the skull? He'd been employed simply to obtain it, and deliver it directly to Ben.

And now the one man who could give Ben hope was dead because the shooter he'd hired had an itchy trigger finger.

And the Creed woman?

"The sniper couldn't have killed them both," Ben muttered as he tapped the photo against his lower lip. "Maybe."

If Annja Creed was dead wouldn't the show feature some kind of memorial? The producers wouldn't run the episode with a dead star. Or would they?

13

Annja! I never knew. Great assets.

Annja clicked the Internet link in the e-mail from a fan. It landed on a page titled "Celebrity Skin." And there was her head, capped by the boonie hat she wore for her biography picture. From shoulders down she was naked.

"Oh, no. Really?"

She clicked the picture and it opened a page devoted exclusively to her, listing all the episodes of *Chasing History's Monsters* she'd hosted, the books she'd penned and her various guest spots on *Letterman* and *Conan.* Her picture took up half the screen.

Annja cringed and looked away from the screen, but like an accident scene, she couldn't make herself look away from the carnage. "Those are not my breasts. Those just look so uncomfortable. This is not for real. Seriously. I've never posed nude in my life. And who would think I could do something like this? For that matter, who would do this to me?" Annja couldn't keep her thoughts to herself.

Her first guess was the most obvious culprit. Doug? Her producer was prone to practical jokes, but he'd never do anything to damage her reputation. Of that, Annja was confident.

So who else?

She searched the site for a contact e-mail. That wouldn't help. Annja felt sure the site would merely brush off her claims to false photographs, even if they knew the truth. Sites like this were rampant online. They likely knew the photos they featured were fakes.

Whose assets were those?

"Argh!"

She checked her watch. There was no time for tracking this down. It was an hour before Serge made good on his promise to kill her. He did know where to find her.

She wasn't going to run scared. Serge was the only one who knew anything about the skull.

"Looks like this girl has another date."

A GRAVEYARD WAS the last place Annja wanted to meet anyone. Even a friend. And Serge was no friend. But at the moment he was her only link to the skull's origins, so she wouldn't miss this meeting for the world.

Rather, she was assuming he knew about the skull. Why attempt to steal it if he didn't?

And what about that sniper? Serge had mentioned a name. "Benjamin," she muttered. "Ben who?"

Annja shivered. The temperature was a blistering fifteen degrees. The wind was whipping and she was walking into its teeth. The windchill must be chasing zero, she thought.

She should have dug out her long johns. It was prematurely cold for late November, but this was New York, after all. Six feet of snow could fall any minute now and it wouldn't be odd. It wasn't the Arctic, but New York could chill 'em with the best of them.

Before stumbling onto the "Celebrity Skin" site, she'd found a view of the Linden Hills Cemetery, and spent an inordinate amount of time playing with the street view function. It was so cool what a person could do online and with a mouse. Now if only they could get a live feed to do things like track down a sidewalk and walk into an area and look about in a three-hundred-and-sixty-degree view and she'd—well, she'd spend far too much time drooling before a computer monitor.

Clad in dark jeans and turtleneck, she tugged up the furry collar of her jacket and the hood around her head.

Perhaps she should have told Bart about where she was going today. But their dinner had been too cozy to spoil with business. And he'd left her feeling at odds about being a rebound girl. Not that he'd mentioned it, or had even been thinking about it. But she had. And much as she wanted to, she couldn't tell him about her sword or the kind of danger it seemed to draw to her.

She had fled her place quickly this morning. Though straightened and clean, Serge's intrusion had changed the feel of it. It was no longer her private retreat from the world, not while his threat was hanging over her.

Sure, she'd once had ninjas drop through the skylight and try to kidnap her. She'd returned later to find the sultan behind the scare had sent in a cleanup crew and he'd then later tried to seduce her. Weird stuff like that happened to her all the time.

But Serge was beyond weird. Disturbingly calm before the maniacal storm kind of weird. She had an aching wrist to confirm that. Had the guy purposefully wanted a piece of her? That treaded in stalker or serial killer territory. What would he do with a sample of her flesh and bone?

She didn't want to imagine.

By seeing him this morning, she could confront him in the daylight, see that he was just a man, and know he couldn't do her any more harm than he had already done. In a manner, she could take back the sanctity of her home and psyche all at once. Kill two birds, so to speak.

It was snowing again. More thick, heavy flakes. She preferred the downy stuff over the tiny sleety pebbles that made for nasty weather. Flakes collected on the grass surrounding the tightly spaced grave markers.

Annja pushed down the furred hood, and scanned the rows of tombstones. The graveyard was huge. A line of mausoleums stood south of her location. She expected Serge to pick the most out-of-the-way, least used area, maybe under some trees for privacy.

SERGE STOOD AT THE END of a long-neglected open grave sunk in around the four edges. The grave was half-filled with dirt. It could be dangerous to visitors, and had been marked off with orange cones that now lay in a pile tossed as far away as he could manage.

Open graves always came in handy.

The Creed woman stomped across the grass, her boots kicking up tufts of snow before her. *Stomp* wasn't the right word. She was graceful, as she'd been when wielding that curious sword yesterday at her loft.

He still couldn't believe he'd missed that when rummaging through her things. And then he'd forgotten to look for it before leaving.

Rangy, observant and confident, she appeared keener than the average woman. She was not the sort who preened and expected others to notice. She altered his equilibrium. It was hard to remain focused around her. She was different.

Unafraid. Not like ninety-nine percent of the females in this world.

Fearless women fascinated him. There were many here in New York—especially on the subway—but none who had prompted him to look outside his own world and wonder about hers.

If he didn't need to threaten her life, Serge imagined it might be a thrill to get to know Annja Creed.

She stopped thirty feet from him. Puffs of air fogged before her parted lips. She held out her arms to reveal she carried nothing. Not the backpack, nor could he see where she might have hidden the skull. Black leggings skimmed long legs. The jacket had many pockets, but it fit her body as if a second skin. A rim of fake fox fur on the hood dusted her ears and cheeks.

There was no three-foot-long battle sword in sight.

And no skull.

"Where is it?" he asked.

She shrugged. "I already told you I don't have it. Can't give you what I don't have. Wouldn't give it to you if I *did* have it."

Clenching his leather-gloved fists, then releasing them, Serge calmed his anger. Nothing was ever accomplished out of anger. Or violence, for that matter. Yet, more often than not, violence was the only weapon capable of opening some minds to reality.

A reality Benjamin Ravenscroft had introduced to his life, damn that man.

"I thought my warning was clear," he stated, jaw tight, more from the cold than tension.

"Crystal. But I can't give you what I don't have. Get that into your thick skull," the woman said.

Obstinate and gorgeous. The combination tormented his need to remain stoic and alert.

"Speaking of skulls…" He paced to the grave head, hands crossed before him. He should have worn a hat. He didn't like the feel of snowflakes dropping on his shaved scalp. But the snow had ceased melting and dripping down his face. The world was cold—like Benjamin Ravenscroft. "Have you learned more about what you claim not to have?"

"If I had, I wouldn't tell you," she said.

"So why did you come today, Annja?" He liked the feel of her name when he spoke it. It had Russian origins, he felt certain.

Stupid man, *concentrate.*

"To talk to you," she replied. "To figure you out."

She hooked her hands at her hips, matching him with a pacing stride. She was aware of his every movement, her body ready to dash, either into the fray or away from it.

He sensed she was more than a mere researcher who spent her days digging in the dirt. Yet he couldn't figure out what experience on television could have taught her about self-defense or the fighting skills she'd used against him yesterday.

She was a well-rounded woman. Smart and capable of protecting herself. Unlike his family. They would never see it coming when the reality of Benjamin Ravenscroft came for them.

That was why he had to settle this matter and get the skull before Ben did.

"Is figuring me out so important?" he called through the crisp air.

"I'm a curious kind of girl, Serge. A guy breaks into my loft, then stabs me with some funky tool and it makes me wonder, you know?"

"How is the wrist?"

She stopped pacing. He saw the tiny wince she made at

mention of the wound. It satisfied him. He was still in control.

"What the hell kind of weapon was that? You punched a hole right through me."

"A specialty item. Necessary to my trade."

He marveled inside as she wondered over that morsel of noninformation. She wasn't a high-heels-and-lipstick kind of female. Not easily breakable. At least, not yet. He'd give it a go, if need be.

"Let's quit with the banter," she said. Flicking her glove-less fingers over her cheek, she swiped away a few snow-flakes. "Why do you want the skull? And what is it, exactly?"

"So you have no clue. Good. It's not information you require, Annja."

Always be familiar with your enemy; it put them off guard. But was she really the enemy? he wondered.

Anyone who would keep from him what he most desired was definitely on the opposition.

"As for why I want it? Will you accept it means more to me than it ever could to you?"

"I'm an archaeologist. Old bones are like gold to us. And puzzling out their origins are the platinum sprinkles on top. If you're not going to help me, then I can't help you."

He bit off the retort, *But you would help if I did?*

That was weak. He wasn't about to cower to get what he needed. And this was more than a want; it was a *need*.

"Did you have anything to do with Marcus Cooke getting shot?" she tried.

The thief Ben had hired to obtain the skull. Serge had tracked him from the moment he'd landed in New York.

If a man thought to control him by threatening his family, then Serge made sure to keep a keen eye on that man. There wasn't a move Ben made without Serge knowing about it.

Mostly, he knew things like where Ravenscroft took his secretary for an after-work rendezvous, or at what clubs he entertained high-roller clients. Material bullshit.

But when Ben had returned from a trip to Venice and had gone to the Cloisters, a medieval museum in Manhattan, Serge had followed. He'd overheard Ben asking a curator about Sidon and a mythical skull rumored to be giver of all good things.

Could Ben possibly know what it would mean to Serge to possess the skull?

"I can honestly say I don't know the man," Serge offered. "The thief, that is."

"But you knew the sniper?"

"Again, no. That surprised me, I must say. If someone was after the skull, why shoot the man carrying it and risk losing it?"

"That's what I can't figure out, either. So why were you there? How did you know Marcus had the skull, and who else is after it?"

"I thought I was the one asking the questions?"

She shrugged. "My bad. Looks like you hauled your ass all the way out here for nothing." She scratched her head and looked at the grave markers. Puffs of breath condensed before her face. "Any family members you need to say hello to?"

"You do remember my threat, don't you, Annja?"

"I'm not much for threats. They're mostly hot air. Besides, if you've heard one threat, you've heard them all. And trust me, I get them a lot."

"I sense that you do. Not the most agreeable woman, are you?"

She didn't want to cooperate? Time to see how breakable she really was.

Serge kept a bowie knife tucked inside his coat, in a leather sheath right next to the bone biopsy tool. He did not draw it out.

This time, he wanted to see what she could do without weapons. She hadn't brought a sword. It would be fist to fist. Or rather, fist to air, as his first strike was parried by a dodge from his opponent.

"What's with you and beating on women, Serge?"

Light on her feet, she dodged another punch, and swung a return that connected with his jaw. But it wasn't hard enough to make his head jerk.

"Violence is gauche," he answered. "I would never harm a woman unless she disobeys a direct request."

"Is that so? But taking core samples from people is cool with you?"

"As a matter of fact, it is."

The heel of her boot soared through the air. Serge blocked the roundhouse with a forearm, and swung his other hand to grip her ankle. He twisted her leg, and she went down, her body spinning to land forearms and knees on the snow. But she was quick. Kicking back with her other leg, she managed to bruise the side of his knee.

Serge yelped.

The ground was slick with fresh-fallen snow. He teetered. His heel slid through the wet grass. In that moment, a kick to his ankle knocked him backward. It was humiliating to be felled by a female.

The woman landed on his chest, crouched and determined. She punched his jaw. Once. Twice. The third time, he clapped a hand about hers and kneed her in the gut.

With a ragged grunt, she spilled sideways and rolled across the snowy grass. The open grave lay nearby. She didn't move. Had he knocked her out? Not from a gut kick.

A small storm aimed for his head was blocked with a fist. The snowball clattered against his elbow. Snow wet his face.

She no longer lay on the ground, nor stood in front of him.

A heavy rubber heel to the base of his spine stung and prickled through his extremities. Serge swung back, growling. He managed to clothesline her across the back of her shoulders.

He lunged and gripped one of her ankles. A hard heel crushed the side of his face. She went down, but gripped the front of his coat. He rolled over her, clasping her in an embrace as he did. Her face landed in the snow and she snuffled. A fist to her gut, right up under the lung left her motionless.

Jumping to his feet, Serge palmed the bowie knife.

Annja groaned and rolled to her back.

She was tiring. But he hated to see her brought to her knees when he was sure she didn't have the skull. She must have handed it off to someone, or hidden it. And he wouldn't be able to follow a dead woman. So he'd end this, but not completely.

Annja pushed onto her hands and jumped to stand. A fist to her sternum, right above the center of her breasts, put her back. She wobbled, sucking for the air the punch had stolen from her.

Working swiftly, Serge landed punches to her throat, her shoulder and her jaw. She spun, arms out and groping the air.

Striking her across the back produced an agonizing moan from the woman. She lost balance and fell forward, into the grave.

Working quickly, Serge kicked the dirt over her inert body. "Sweet dreams, Annja Creed."

WHILE HER MIND GREW heavy and her lungs took on the dirt's muffling weight, Annja struggled with the idiotic situation. She'd let the man get the better of her again. And now he would bury her alive!

Why hadn't she drawn the sword? The thought to do so had tickled her brain. And then Serge had smashed it with his fist. It was as if the sword was being fickle.

Serge still needed the skull from her. So what was his deal?

She'd landed facedown. The hard dirt froze against her flesh. Dirt crumbled on her tongue. Her chest ached from the forceful punch. The earth was icy cold and numbness already thickened her fingers.

Thought about worms crept in. Worms were just wrong. They were about the only thing that could make her get up from a dig and, shuddering, wander off for a deep breath.

They would not be so high in the soil this time of year, she thought hopefully.

Fingers curling, she clawed into the cold earth. The numbness reduced her efforts to futile movements. Lifting an elbow backward to drag through the dirt was difficult. There was little give.

A heavy thud of something landed on her back and squeezed her lungs. He was seriously burying her!

Eyes closed, because her face was flush with the earth, her ears popped. Being buried felt much like drowning. Not that she'd ever drowned, but she had survived a tsunami and was an excellent diver.

The grave had not been deep. Buried three feet under? This should be a piece of cake.

Cake sounded good right now. And what the hell was she thinking? Now was no time for dessert.

An inhale sucked dirt up her nose. She snorted and choked.

Stop panicking, she coached inwardly.

If her breathing accelerated, she'd use all her air. She had recently read about a man buried in thick mud who'd survived two hours through meditation, and a small pocket of air trapped in his hard plastic safety helmet.

No helmet here. And what little air that might have been trapped in her jacket had been crushed out on impact.

To release her next breath slowly, and concentrate on the careful movement of her fingers as they worked through the earth, brought sudden calm. Almost Zen, she stretched out a finger and curled it.

Could she do this? Mediate her way out?

Sound was muffled, yet her heartbeat pounded in her ears. And it was that frantic pace that made her realize meditation was for monks.

Her next intake didn't enter her burning lungs. Stretching an arm, she thought she felt the dirt loosen. And then she felt…nothing. She'd broken through. The sheer joy of feeling the cold air on her palm ratcheted her anxiety and Annja choked, gasping for air.

When a hand slapped into hers and formed a tight grip, she was too happy to be fearful. She'd hug the bastard and then give him a taste of three feet of battle steel.

Pulled from an early grave, the dirt sucked at her limbs, wanting to pull her back, but relenting. When she was able, Annja toed the grave's edge and stepped up. The hand released her.

She wobbled and her muscles gave way. Dropping, she landed a graceless, but sitting, sprawl.

Slapping away the dirt from her clothing, she sensed she'd find dirt in strange places later when showering. Almost as an afterthought, she looked up at her rescuer. She cursed.

14

Garin Braden stood six-feet-wow, with broad shoulders and a long black leather duster coat. A fine trimmed moustache edged his mouth and connected to a dark goatee. The snow didn't touch him, seeming to fear landing on a surface that may be harder and colder than it.

Looking like some kind of devil's bounty hunter, he grinned slyly at her.

Slapping a hand on her dirt-dusted shoulder, Garin said in his deep, raspy voice, "Annja Creed, I do believe you are in over your head this time. Quite literally, it would appear."

She shoved his hand from her shoulder. "Yeah?" She shook the dirt from her hair. "When have I *not* been in over my head? It's what I do. Why should this time be any different?"

Okay, that wasn't exactly true. It wasn't what she did. She was an archaeologist with a TV show. She wasn't an avenger, a heroine who saved the world.

And yet, she'd begun to buy into the superheroine thing. So maybe it *was* what she did. Why did the guy have a problem with that? It wasn't as though he hadn't joined her on a few of her adventures. Hell, the man had the most irritating way of showing up at all the wrong times, and even some of the right ones. Like now.

Reaching back, Annja shook out the dirt from her jacket hood. She winced and squirmed when dirt sifted down her back.

"You have no idea who you are involved with, Annja. Ben Ravenscroft doesn't like to lose. Nor does the man who just buried you."

"No kidding? That guy must have been a real treat in the sandbox when he was a kid." A stomp of her leg sifted dirt tucked in the folds of her jacket to the snowy ground. "Ben Ravenscroft?"

"You don't know about him?"

"Serge mentioned the name Benjamin. I have a feeling you know everything I want to know. Which always seems to be the case with you and me. Why is that?"

"Come with me," Garin offered.

Annja followed his gesture across the cemetery. A black limo idled on the street outside the fence.

She glanced at him. Not a nice man, but fierce. A force one must reckon with. Devil's bounty hunter was an appropriate summation. Give the man a flaming chain whip and he'd ace the role.

Garin Braden was her nemesis. A nemesis who infrequently appealed but mostly disgusted. She did not trust him, yet on occasion she relied upon him. Or rather, took the generous assistance he offered because it was either that or be abandoned on a remote island or left behind to flee machine-gun fire.

She'd kissed him once—no, that wasn't right. He'd kissed her.

She was still kicking herself for that one.

And yet, the man did possess an irresistible charm. All she could figure was it was something about good girls and the bad boys they liked to change.

Not that Garin would ever change his ways. Rich, powerful and smart, he was involved in many alliances and business associations that would make Annja cringe. He played the world as if it were his to master.

He, like Roux—another five-hundred-year-old immortal who had appointed himself a sort of mentor to Annja—had insinuated himself into her life. Whether or not she liked them in it.

Both men were inscrutable. Yet the things Annja did know of them were like valued jewels she kept filed in the For Further Research section of her brain.

Of the two, she trusted Roux first, if barely.

If Annja stood in his way to getting something, Garin Braden would not stop at harming her. And she knew he desperately wanted Joan's sword.

She'd met Garin and Roux after finding the final piece of Joan of Arc's once-shattered sword, and fitting it to the other pieces to become whole again. Garin and Roux believed their immortality was tied to the sword that had remained in pieces, scattered throughout the world since Joan of Arc had been burned at the stake. Roux had spent centuries gathering the pieces together again.

Now, for reasons no one completely understood, Annja wielded the sword—in one piece. Garin believed the sword threatened him. Though there was no way to prove it. But a few years had passed since the sword had become whole. He hadn't dissolved to ash or shown negligible signs of aging or loss of strength.

And he couldn't simply take the sword from her. He'd tried, as had others. If Annja didn't want someone to touch the sword, it would disappear. Yet, if she wanted to allow someone to look at it, she could hand it over, and it would remain solid, tangible. It all seemed to be tied to who she trusted and who she did not.

For Garin to ever hold the sword intact, Annja assumed she had to gift it to him.

And that would never happen.

So, in the meantime, when he was not making her life miserable, he was pulling the rug out from under her with surprising acts of kindness.

This is what made placing him solidly on the enemy list difficult. He was so damned charming, and he knew it. The man had an international harem. He was an alpha male, arrogant and dangerous. And yet, Annja couldn't stop herself from staring at him as if he was a celebrity and she wanted his regard.

But she was not a fool. She wasn't going anywhere with him.

"Thanks, but I think I'll walk." She strode across the snow-dusted grass, feeling her shaky legs protest. They needed a good rub down to get the blood flowing through them again. The heavy, cold dirt had zapped her strength.

"You can't go home, Annja. Serge has already been there. It's not safe."

"Then I'll go to a hotel. City's full of them."

He knew Serge had been to her loft? He must have followed her here. So why hadn't he stepped in when Serge had been tucking her in for a dirt nap?

Because he had probably been amused by the whole thing.

"Let me put you up for a few days." He came to her side.

Annja spat dirt from her mouth.

"I might be able to fill in some missing information," he teased.

"At what price?"

"Annja, dearest."

"Oh, please. You know damn well, that I know damn well, the only reason you're ever nice to me is because you want something. You want the skull?"

She cringed. Oops. Had he known about the skull?

"You don't have it, so that's not going to help me much."

"Have you been following me?"

"I never reveal my methods."

"Yeah? Well, thanks for the rescue, but I'll see you later."

He *had* been following her. He did it often. The man had ways of tracking a person even she couldn't comprehend.

Annja stepped off the curb behind the limo and her ankle twisted. Slapping the trunk as she went down, her palms didn't meet the rough wet tarmac.

Garin lifted her with one arm around her gut and swung her to stand against the trunk.

"You'll never make it home on foot. And I know for a fact Ravenscroft has a man watching your loft."

"I don't even know this Ravenscroft guy. Is he the sniper?" Annja asked.

"Sniper? No. Stop being so stubborn, Annja. You don't trust me? I'll give you that. My apartment in Manhattan is large. The guest room is at one end. You don't even have to see me, if you don't want to."

Propping her palms on the trunk, she shook her head. "This is just wrong."

Yet all that man looming over her did a number on her racing heartbeat. There was something appealing about being rescued by a man who had once been a real knight.

"You can call your protector Roux," he added snidely.

"I don't need Roux's help, and I don't need yours."

"But you do need a shower. What's this?"

He plucked something from her hair and Annja closed her

eyes, cringing. "Not a worm, not a worm, please, not a worm."

He tossed the find over his shoulder.

"Was it a worm?"

His smile came across as warm, inviting. "I'll never tell. Come." His offered a broad hand, palm up. "Take a ride with the devil, if you dare."

He called it as she saw it.

But if he was right, and a man was watching her loft, she couldn't risk returning. Who was Benjamin Ravenscroft? If he wasn't the sniper, that added yet another player to the game, and she'd lost count.

Maybe a call to Roux was necessary. Not to ask him to come rescue her, but to feel him out, see if he knew what Garin was up to. Because the man never appeared in her life by accident.

"You know about the skull?" she asked.

"I may." He opened the back door and waited. "We'll talk after I've made you comfortable, yes?"

Playboy that he was, he embodied old-world manners.

And she could use a shower. Neediness reared its ugly head.

Blowing out a surrendering breath, Annja crawled into the backseat and slid across to the far door. Garin reached in to brush away the dirt left in her wake before joining her.

15

"Block my calls for the next hour, Rebecca."

Ben swiveled on his chair and pressed the button on his desk that brought up the computer screen and pushed out the slim keyboard drawer to a perfect height for typing.

After years spent working around the clock buying up domain names while in college, he'd learned a desk and chair designed to his exact measurements provided comfort and prevented nuisances like carpal tunnel syndrome.

On his desk was the sniper's photo of Annja Creed and the notes Ben had taken from the television show the previous night. He had the phone number for the television studio, but he decided to surf the Internet before calling and thus having to make up a story about wanting info on Creed.

At the Web site for *Chasing History's Monsters* he found a short bio on Annja Creed that emphasized the episodes she'd hosted regarding mythical creatures and legends. The bio downplayed her archaeological background.

"Idiots," he muttered of the show's producers.

It was obvious they felt the buxom Kristie Chatham was the real cash cow and they thought they'd add a little scholarly realism once in a while with that other chick.

Ben tapped the tracking pad. There was no eulogy, no memorial. That meant she was still alive. Most television shows would certainly capitalize on the death of one of their stars, or at the very least issue a statement regarding their sympathies to her family.

He scanned the show's masthead. Doug Morrell was listed as the producer. It boasted a skeleton crew for a show that looked pretty slick. They didn't post a phone number, but Ben highlighted and copied the e-mail contact information.

He knew they wouldn't give out Miss Creed's address to an anonymous caller. But if the caller was an elite businessman who had a proposal for a show idea featuring her?

Ben pondered what he could push as an idea, but his mind didn't function beyond stock market figures and the patent craze in Dubai and the current need to find that damned skull.

History's monsters? He wouldn't know where to begin.

Opening a new window, he searched Creed's name and it produced page after page of snippets from online chat room discussions. A quick glance determined all were archaeology sites.

Then he spotted something unusual. A site called "Celebrity Skin" was advertising exclusive nude pictures of Creed. He'd check that one later.

Clicking through the archaeology forums proved tedious. He realized it was possible Marcus Cooke had contacted her through a chat room. It was stupid—nothing online was secure—but still possible.

He scanned pages of chatter about pottery shards and gold coins. There were kudos to Miss Creed for surviving a tsunami during a dig in southern India and a few others wished to convince her that her excursion to Transylvania had damaged her credo.

Creed hadn't replied to those.

The Amazon rain forest, the jungles of Southeast Asia, Siberia, Paris, Texas, China. The woman did have adventures. How the hell had she gotten tangled up with the Skull of Sidon? The owner had kept its whereabouts quiet for decades. Hell, a few centuries, he thought.

For that matter, Ben couldn't fathom how Serge had discovered he had arranged to steal the thing. Someone was putting information out into the public arena. But who?

His thoughts averted by the disturbing idea, Ben typed in the name Maxfield Wisdom. It produced two hits. One for a used car salesman in Toledo, Ohio, the other was a small *Who's Who* bio on the man he knew.

They named Wisdom as an avid collector of eclectic ephemera from around the world, an enthusiastic philanthropist, never married, but always looking. He once garnered an entry in the record books for the most gum balls chewed at one time.

Ben didn't recall Wisdom as being so eccentric, just passionate about the oddities he'd secured for his collection. He bought everything online, of course; the man was not a world traveler due to an extreme dislike for air travel.

The bio did not mention the skull. But of course it should not.

Sitting back and huffing out a sigh, Ben twisted the chair to gaze out the window. Snow fell heavily.

How had Serge learned about the skull?

"Serge knows things normal people cannot dream to know. He's mystical. He has connections to a world we cannot imagine," he said aloud.

It was the very reason Ben had hired the man. After a trip to finalize the Berlin headquarters for RavensTech, he'd detoured east. He'd been interested in the Ukrainian farming crisis. Their assets were being mishandled. The government was all about keeping information under lock and key as opposed to actually helping their citizens thrive.

A visit to an Odessa deli had resulted in the most interesting experience.

There were only six tables in the deli, each crammed chair to chair, and topped with faded red-checked tablecloths. A smiling elderly woman had seemed to be waitress, cook and hostess. Ben had marveled over the borscht. He'd never tried it before, and though reluctant at first to taste the brilliant pink cold soup, he eventually ordered a second bowl.

On about the last spoonful of soup, Ben was startled to hear a low humming sound coming from behind the long brown wool blanket that served as a curtain between the dining room and the kitchen. It was a man's voice.

He questioned the old woman to see if someone was in pain. She clasped Ben's face with warm, pudgy palms and shook her head sweetly. "Summoning the spirits," she said. "Reading the future."

Ten minutes later, a pregnant woman emerged from behind the wool blanket, smiling and rubbing her belly. She'd obviously heard what she wanted from the fortune teller.

"You next?" the old woman asked Ben. "You want to know your future?"

Ben shook his head, trying to dismiss the request, but at the sight of the tall bald man standing behind the curtain, just a glimpse of his side view, curiosity changed Ben's negative nod to a positive.

There wasn't much difference between selling futures and telling the future, was there? he thought.

Remarkably, Serge had pinpointed Ben's need to obtain nothing. The man didn't know what that meant, only that it was what the spirits offered to him. With that, Ben knew the man was for real.

Ben had taken Serge to dinner that evening to an expensive restaurant in Odessa. The fortune teller had marveled over the waitstaff's manners and was fascinated with the linens and devoured the steak. He'd never had such a fine meal. The price of the wine alone would surely feed his family for a week.

Serge traveled to Odessa to find jobs to help his family, but unsure of navigating the city proper, always kept to the impoverished outer suburbs. He found work mostly in the back rooms of family diners or feed shops. His skills were unusual, but not questioned. The old folk believed, and those who would scoff at him didn't need his help, anyway.

He had to keep a low profile. If the Odessa police got wind of a man who conjured spirits, they would have him arrested and he'd never see his family again.

Ben had seen opportunity. He was the man who believed in things one could not see or touch. He'd made a good living buying and selling just such things. Embracing Serge's talents had come easily.

And he'd been rewarded for his beliefs.

It was possible to learn the future through spiritual contact. Ben had no idea how it worked—only that it did.

But at the moment, Serge landed second on Ben's list of persons of interest. His mole in the NYPD had reported there was nothing more than clothing and a roll of sodden twenties on Marcus Cooke when his body had been dredged from the canal. No skull.

Ben decided Annja Creed must have the skull.

What would an intrepid young archaeologist do with a

skull like that? Obviously bones and stuff were her thing. Could she know what she held? Marcus hadn't been told what it was, so he could not have clued her in.

So then, Ben thought, she must be curious about it. She'd probably search online for information about it. Likely try to date it, as he suspected archaeologists would do. She couldn't have any fancy equipment herself, so how would she do it?

"A university?" he wondered.

Turning back to his computer, he reread the bio on the television show Web site. He scanned her academic credentials. She'd spent a summer at Columbia.

"Bingo."

16

"I didn't know you had a place in New York," Annja said as Garin tapped out the entrance code on a digital pad beside the door.

"I do now. With real estate at such a delicious low, how could I resist? I do love to catch a Broadway show now and then."

Annja couldn't help but grin widely. Wonders did never cease.

"I'd give you the official 'Enter freely and of your own will,'" Garin said as he stepped inside, "but I suspect you'd reserve that statement for me."

He had that one right. She never found vampires on her trip to Transylvania. Maybe because the closest thing to one stood right before her. Immortal and hungry for blood, be it racing or spilled.

Annja entered the thirtieth-floor Manhattan apartment with reluctance. She peeked around the corner as she entered the foyer, expecting to see a half-clad nymph scrambling away like a blood-drained Renfield into the shadows. The few times Garin had called her, she'd heard feminine giggles in the background. Gentleman he may be, he wasn't discriminating by any means.

"There are no booby traps," he said as he closed the door behind her.

"Just want to steer clear from the giggle brigade."

"It's just you and me, Annja. I would never be so rude to impose on your presence by including another woman."

"I'm honored."

"You're being snarky."

"Yeah, well." A brush of her palm still sifted dirt from her jacket. It landed on the polished hardwood floor. "Where's that shower?"

"Down the hall and left is the guest room. Let me take a look at you first. Those clothes are too filthy." He drew his dark gaze up and down her body. Her coat was unzipped, and he lingered at her breasts, which should have offended, but it was just so Garin. "You're still a size six, I'd guess."

Annja nodded. "You going shopping?"

"Annja, please, I have people who do that for me."

She rolled her eyes, and twisted her hips to start down the hallway. People? The man was a real item. Tall, dark and too knowing for her own good. He'd once before arranged to have her dressed by some high-fashion name she couldn't recall.

With a reluctant nod, Annja had to admit the dress had rocked. It made her look and feel sexy. Not something she felt when mucking about on a dig or swimming through toxic canals.

That had also been the time Garin had kissed her.

She would maintain vigilance this time.

WRISTS CROSSED UPON his lap, he knelt within the circle on the bare cement floor. The circle had been painted with tar. It was wide enough for him to kneel comfortably and to work the bone powder on the floor before him.

He wore a black linen coat over his shirt. The coat was not his and it gave off a musty odor. It was once worn by the man he now conjured to help him, one of his closest spirit contacts. It was important to wear a piece of the dead subject's clothing to open the connections.

He'd crushed the bone sample taken from Annja Creed in a mortar and had placed half in a vial for later use.

Serge slipped a slim silver lighter from the coat pocket. Holding the flame low over the bone fragments he moved it to singe the particles. Wifts of smoke rose but it did not take to flame. Unnecessary.

The scent of burned bone wavered through his nostrils. Sweet, always, a scent he'd grown up with.

It had been a serendipitous accident that night his father had been burning some old junk found in the field—unearthed clothing, half a wagon wheel and a human leg bone. Serge had inhaled the smoke and the next moment had felt the presence within him. He'd been occupied by something not himself. Yet he'd been calm, leery to tell his father about it. The spirit had whispered of a lynching and his death. He'd left Serge with the idea he could learn anything he wished by contacting the dead.

Serge's very soul spoke to the dead.

After mentioning the experience to his mother, she'd brought out an old ring her deceased mother had worn. Serge hadn't been able to contact his grandmother. He needed the bones—the visceral evidence of what was once life.

Now, after years of training, he only needed an item the

spirit had once worn or treasured. But still he needed bone if he wished to summon regarding a living being.

Serge hummed, low in his throat. It vibrated in his chest and throbbed against his ribs. The space between life and death was vast and navigated with vibration. A unique trip he enjoyed making.

He bowed his head low, moving his forehead to his wrists. Closing his eyes pushed away all unnecessary thoughts from his mind.

Humming continuously, he moved up an octave, notching the tone higher in his throat. It was an ancient means of communication, taught to him by his grandfather. This language of no words was his own. It belonged to the Greater All. An All he was humbled to be a part of.

Stretching out his arms, and holding his fingers parallel to the floor, he began to keen, a high-pitched wailing that crackled in his ears and filled his sinuses.

There were a few particular spirits he worked with often. They treaded the edges of his reality, willing and oftentimes curious to communicate with the corporeal realm.

Alone in this soundproof room behind his bedroom, Serge touched the Greater All. It emerged swiftly and filled his being with presence. It tasted the burned bone and assumed the constitution of the bone's owner.

Moving throughout Serge's body the All gave him glimpses, for that is what he mentally asked to know. Glimpses from *her* eyes. The familiar walls of a loft Serge had only yesterday trashed. The screen of a laptop, scanning through text, and the photos of a skull he had found with his own search online.

Snowflakes dusted her forearms. She walked briskly. A huge building stretched before her. She stood inside. The face of a man with curly hair smiled. He accepted the skull and—the images faded.

The All left him. It gave only what he asked, and left with a painful tug to his soul.

Would he simply give it over one day? His own soul?

Not yet. Not until he was free.

With a groaning noise, Serge slapped his palms on the floor as his body shuddered back to the present. He would remain in this position for a few minutes until all was as it had been before the summoning. His heartbeat slowed.

But his thoughts raced. What was the building? It had looked like a school of sorts. Some kind of college? Where would the Creed woman study? Was there an archaeological center here in the city?

He swallowed, in need of water. Reaching for the small brush and dustpan outside the tar circle, he quickly swept up the bone fragments. When the floor was spotless, he went to the kitchen, passing the hematite bedposts in the bedroom and tapping them four, then three, times successively.

Tapping the stone before the kitchen entry, he then lifted the spigot and put his head down to drink a long drag.

A university, he decided. Somewhere in Manhattan.

17

Annja strode out from the guest bathroom. Vanilla-scented steam wafted behind her. From what she'd seen of the place so far, it was all done in gray slate tiles and gray walls with brushed-steel accents and black marble. Ultramacho.

She liked it. No lace or frills for this chick. But could a girl get a maid to stop by the loft once in a while?

A large red department store box sat on the high king-size bed. Tugging her towel tightly about her chest, she checked the bedroom doors. Closed. The curtains bunched to either side of the window did not hide any lurking forms.

"You never used to be so paranoid," she said. With the gift of Joan's sword had also come many a curse. And just plain suspicion.

The closet door was still open from when she'd entered and had done a cursory search of the room. The balcony doors were also latched.

With a resolute sigh Annja slid onto the bed and ran a hand over the glossy box. "If there's silk or some kind of lacy stuff in here I'm going to stuff it down his throat," she said, knowing it was quite possible Garin had the room bugged.

The only occasions that would see her close to dressed up were better forgotten, as far as she was concerned. High heels and nylons were not on Annja Creed's radar. And yet, one of the few times she had been wearing just that had found her dancing the tango in Garin's arms and accepting his kiss.

It was ironic the situations they found themselves in.

"That man has a way about him. A way I don't like."

On the other hand, that *way* did challenge her every time she came up against it. And she'd never walk away from a good challenge.

Taking a breath, she opened the box and exhaled with relief. Inside a folded pair of khaki pants and long-sleeved turquoise shirt sat neatly folded. Beneath the pants, a slip of black lace revealed itself.

Annja tugged out the bra and read the tag. "Hmm, French. The man knows his lingerie, I'll give him that." Much better than she did, she thought.

After dressing, and combing her wet hair into a ponytail, Annja padded barefoot down the marble hallway in search of the kitchen. She wasn't above rooting about for sustenance. Though she'd gargled plenty of water in the shower, the taste of earth still lingered in her throat.

The lack of food in the huge stainless-steel refrigerator didn't surprise her. Garin ate most meals at fine restaurants, with the requisite sexy lady by his side. And when at home, he probably ordered in.

Evian water was stocked as well as vodka and pomegranate juice. A carton of eggs and half a dozen bright red apples sat beside a 9 mm SIG Sauer P-250.

Annja smirked at the storage place. She supposed it was necessary for a man like Garin. One could never be too careful of the strangers one allowed into their bed. She might be packing, a spy sent by the enemy to take him down.

Rolling her eyes at the thought, Annja helped herself to a curvy bottle of pomegranate juice. Twisting open the plastic lid, she closed the refrigerator door.

"Make yourself at home."

She choked on the first swallow. Garin stood where the open door had been. Arms crossed high on his chest, he smirked, and delivered that patented full-body once-over he did so well. The heat rose in Annja's cheeks.

"I guessed right on the sizes, I see."

"You've had plenty of practice." Annja slid onto a high stool before the stainless-steel freestanding counter.

"I have. But if you've followed women's fashion through the ages, you'd be startled to know what passes as a size six today didn't exist decades ago. Every year the manufacturers make the sizes fit a smaller woman. You'd think if they wanted to sell out they make a size twelve a ten."

"Male logic at its finest. So, no food?"

"If you're hungry I'll order in. What's your pleasure? Chinese? Thai? Tapas?"

"Actually, I could go for a burger."

"Annja, the grease, and not to mention all that trans fat."

"Look at you, Mr. Health Conscious. Didn't think it would matter for a man who's immortal."

"As far as we know," Garin said.

Annja looked at him carefully. The man didn't look as if he'd aged much, since the sword had become whole—and hers. Of course, she had never noticed those fine creases at the corners of his eyes before.

"You thinking about investing in Botox, big boy?" she said with a laugh.

"Now that you bring it up, how *is* the sword treating you?

Keeping you from danger? From falling into coffin-size holes?" he taunted.

"It's there when I need it. There have been a few times I've wanted it, though, and maybe for lack of space, it wouldn't come to my grip."

"Interesting. So it only appears when possible. Gotta watch those empty graves, Annja."

"Yeah, so rub it in. Haven't I done you enough favors to earn amnesty from your sarcasm?"

"If you're keeping score, you'll be disappointed to know I've racked up more brownie points than you have. But I don't keep score. That's so gauche."

She was fairly certain that when the indignities she had suffered for the man's favor were measured against the times he'd helped her she would come out ahead. But Garin was right, keeping score was just wrong.

But who said it couldn't be fun? She'd take the points when she could.

"Let's talk business," Annja said. "You know about the skull and Serge. And Benjamin Ravenscroft is a name I've heard but know nothing about."

"Let's chat in the living room."

She followed him into the long main room, which was lined with windows that looked out over Central Park. Snowflakes peppered the gray sky. They were supposed to get two inches of fresh snow.

The brown leather furniture didn't overwhelm the large room. Huge ferns and a plant with a bright red flower gave it a tropical touch. Annja chose a chair, because she didn't want to share the couch with the man.

She couldn't be too cautious around Garin Braden. She just couldn't let down her guard.

Settling onto the chair, she tugged her legs to her body and conformed to the hug of the supple leather. She felt very relaxed and too comfortable.

What are you doing, Annja? He's the bad guy, remember?

Garin reclined on the couch, legs spread and arms stretched across the back. His crisp white business shirt and black trousers gave him an undeniably sensual aura. Though his features were rugged, not quite handsome, she bet most women did a double-take when this man walked by.

She hated that she struggled between despising the guy and wanting to learn more about him. But truly, there was so much to know. The man had walked through five hundred years of history. What archaeologist in her right mind would not grill him if given the chance?

"Whimsical thoughts dancing in those hazel eyes of yours, Annja?"

"Scholarly, actually." She dropped her feet to the floor and propped her elbows on her knees. "Just give me something, Garin. One little nugget of history that the books and artifacts have never revealed."

His eyes twinkled. Annja imagined that glint of mischief guarded the universe's mysteries. Indiana Jones watch out, Annja Creed was going to nab this lost treasure.

"I don't read history books, so how can I know what has been mentioned and what has not?"

"Avoid major wars, plagues or enlightenments. I want something tangible. Rumor-mill stuff."

"Gossip, eh? Very well. Name a century," he volleyed.

"Sixteenth."

"Hmm." He thumbed the corner of his mouth in thought. "Catherine of Aragon. Not so devoted to her good king husband as she wanted him to believe."

"Hmm. Don't believe it. She raged against Henry VIII's infidelities."

"As she should have. But their early married years were a struggle. Henry was quite the tightwad, and her father, King Ferdinand, refused to send Catherine money for her household. She sought compassion in the arms of a man who gave her brief love and a bit of coin to tide her through the tough times."

"If you're going to tell me that man was you…"

Garin lifted a mischievous brow. "You did ask for something salacious."

"I didn't use that word exactly. Seriously? You and Catherine of Aragon?"

He nodded. "But you didn't hear that from me. I guard my secrets well."

Okay, so that nugget weighed in his favor. Not that she believed him—entirely.

On the other hand, was it so difficult accepting the man had notched a queen on his bedpost?

Annja looked over Garin, trying to imagine him in doublet, breeches and the wool hose that were worn in the sixteenth century. She could see it. And would bet he had wielded a battle sword with cruel intention, as well.

Time travel would so rock. She gave her head a shake.

"So the skull," she said. "Tell me everything you know. And did you know about the thief?"

"The guy you met at the bridge?"

"Were you there, too?"

"Not at the bridge specifically."

"In the area? How many people know about this?"

He cleared his throat and said, "I heard about the drowned man the next morning, and sometimes it's very easy to put two and two together and come up with Annja Creed."

His easy smile kept her from tightening a fist on her lap.

"The skull," she said.

He leaned forward, propping his elbows on his knees. Noticing how he mirrored her, Annja pulled up her legs, clasping her arms around them.

"I've seen it once before in the fifteenth century, a few years before the execution."

"So the two of you were mortal at the time?" Annja asked, intrigued.

"Yes. Roux and I were on our way to France to meet the Maid of Orléans. We'd stopped by a Moorish palace in Granada. I think it was the Alhambra."

"That's a famous palace."

"Yes, isn't it? I held the skull while Roux talked to an alchemist."

"How can you know it's the same skull I've seen?"

"As far as skulls go, it is unique."

"Describe it to me."

"Small, likely belonged to an infant. Silver lines the divides between the bones."

"They're called sutures."

"Oh? I'm not up on skull terminology. Sound like the one you've held?"

"Not really." Silver and gold were two very different metals. "So you just let it get out of your hands, then?"

"I had no idea what it was. Thought it just another trinket, though I had thought to hear it whisper to me. The alchemist was convinced it was the Skull of Sidon."

"The Skull of Sidon?" Where had she recently heard that?

Garin smirked. "A legend the great archaeologist doesn't know about?"

"Is it Templar related?"

"Points for you. Yes, it is. How did you guess?"

"There was a small cross pattée on the gold edging the sutures. But it's so obvious a symbol. I placed it to Teutonic's."

"There's gold on it?" Garin rubbed his jaw. "There was silver on it in the fifteenth century."

"So you've got the wrong skull."

She took great delight in that statement. But too quickly.

"Or you do," he said.

Annja knew well and good artifacts were tampered with all the time. And if the skull had not been buried for centuries, whomever might have owned it over the years could have embellished it. Perhaps the original silver had worn away or been taken out and melted down for sale.

"It could have been added later," Garin said. "Hell, the alchemist might have put it on. He prized that skull, and felt it gave him great success. Although, he didn't have it to hand *after* we left."

"Who was the alchemist?"

"Alphonso de Castaña."

"Never heard of him."

"Nor had you heard of the Skull of Sidon."

Touché, she thought.

"Does it have the markings on the interior?" Garin asked.

She balked at giving the answer, but he read her reluctance.

"They appear as though they were there originally, yes?"

"Yes," she said on a gasp. "They don't look carved, but it's ridiculous to believe they were born into the skull as Professor Danzinger has suggested."

"Ridiculous, but not impossible. Especially if you look at the skull's origins. It's all very macabre and taboo."

"Sounds like ninety percent of my work. I love the taboo stuff. But the Skull of Sidon? I don't know the history."

"Hmm, then get comfortable, Annja. Let me tell you how the Skull of Sidon came to be."

18

"The Knights Templar, as you know, were formed after the first Crusade to police the high roads and keep the pilgrimage traveling to Jerusalem safe from thieves and cutthroats," Garin explained. "They took vows of chastity, poverty, piety and obedience."

"The cross on their robes," Annja added, "didn't that symbolize martyrdom?"

"Yes, and to die in combat was considered a great honor, a sure trip to heaven. They never surrendered in battle, unless all the Templar flags had fallen. They were a feared force of the times."

"Medieval. Twelfth and thirteenth century."

"Yes, the Templars fell in the fourteenth. Accusations of blasphemy and heresy led to their demise. They were accused of trampling and spitting on the cross. Engaging in vile sexual practices, such as homosexuality and head worshipping. Their doomsday happened on a Friday the thirteenth."

"Really? Here I thought that was Freddy's day," Annja

only half joked. "I thought I'd heard everything about the Templars. What with all the *DaVinci Code* and grail stuff in the media."

"There is much on the knights, true. But the Skull of Sidon is often overlooked by scholars as mere myth."

Garin leaned forward from where he sat on the couch, splaying his long tanned fingers before him as he explained.

"There was a Templar knight in love with a lady from Maraclea."

"*Clear waters,*" Annja said. "Isn't that what Maraclea means?"

"Yes, or simply *sea.* And then there are some scholars who will goad a person into believing it means something like *greater shining,* an allusion to the Holy Grail. Which makes the tale more interesting than not.

"The knight was actually a lord of Sidon, rumored to not only be a Templar but also a pirate. Sidon was rife with pirates at the time—the city was crawling with them. Anyway, because of his vows, the knight could not consummate his relationship with the Maraclean lady. But, after her untimely death, all vows were null. Or so he decided."

"Oh, don't tell me." Annja could guess the next part, and it couldn't be good.

Garin's wicked grin made her lean forward, anyway. "He exhumed her corpse and, well, let's say he had his way with it. Those of a certain mind would have the knight coming into the greater shining, actually gaining the grail, this means of enlightenment, through that copulation."

"Seriously?"

"It's a theory, Annja. So after the macabre act, it is said the knight heard a voice telling him to return to the grave in nine months. Which he did."

"Because one always obeys disembodied voices after committing necrophilia."

"Naturally."

The two shared a wink, and Annja looked down and aside to avoid the man's mesmerizing gaze.

"Upon returning," Garin continued, "the knight found a skull placed above the woman's crossed leg bones—which some believe is the origin for the skull and crossbones symbol. And if he was really a pirate, then all the more basis for the belief.

"Anyway, the knight took the skull and again the voice spoke. It told him to guard it well, because it would be the giver of all good things to him—become his protecting genius. That is also what the Holy Grail is supposed to do, be the giver of all good things."

"Yes, I've heard that. So he left with the skull and—?"

"When he wielded it in battle his enemies were put back, destroyed. His protecting genius granted him all good things. Or so that is the story."

Annja waited to see if he would continue. Garin rubbed his chin, eyeing her intently.

She broke out in laughter. "You're kidding me, right? Who set you up to this story? Roux? I mean, please. A skull born of a necrophilic liaison?"

He stretched his arms across the couch back and propped an ankle across his knee. "Annja, bearer of a magical sword that appears from out of nowhere at her beckon, does not believe my tale of a magical skull?"

She chuffed out another half laugh and took a swallow of pomegranate juice. Why did the immortal men always have to mention the obvious?

"I believe what I can see, touch and hear," she said. Yes, still a skeptic, and proud of it. "Giver of all good things? The skull didn't do anything particularly good when I had it. In fact, it brought a nasty bad guy to my doorstep, who proceeded to tear apart my home. He destroyed some irreplaceable research books."

"Better a book than you."

She curled her fingers about her bandaged wrist. The long sleeve hid the bandages, but Garin noticed. The fact he didn't ask about it went a long way toward his discretion.

"So that's why you want it?" she asked. "You need good things? What, that money can't buy, do you need?"

"I didn't say I wanted the skull."

"You don't have to. You never show up to help me without an ulterior motive."

"Annja, you bruise me."

"Doubtful. That ego of yours is ironclad."

"It is merely I feel you are out of your league. You don't know the maelstrom you've stepped into. You think the bone conjurer won't stalk you until your feet are bloody and you offer your own skull to get him off your back?"

"Bone conjurer?" She tucked a leg on the seat and leaned onto the overstuffed arm. "I've heard the term before. Is that what Serge is? And how do you know him?"

"I don't know him personally, but I've heard of him, or rather his kind. *Bone conjurer* is an ancient term, used since biblical times. He's a necromancer. One who summons the dead, can communicate with spirits, manipulate and redirect common mortals by utilizing revenants. Much like a modern-day medium. The term is old-world."

"Peachy. I haven't had any adventures with the dead lately."

Garin steepled his fingers before his mouth and nose. "Annja, you must take this seriously. I believe in the immense power the man holds. A necromancer can manipulate the dead to great means."

"So what good is a centuries-old skull to him?"

"I can only imagine it is a necromancer's grail. And let's just forget all the connotations to the real grail legend."

"Hallelujah. There are so many it's become comical."

"This Skull of Sidon, born of a necrophilic encounter, will no doubt serve a necromantic master incredible evils."

"I thought it gave *good* things?"

"Yes, but your perception of good may be completely opposite of what someone like Serge believes to be good. Good to him may be unspeakable to you and me."

Anything unspeakable to Garin was definitely not good. As well, to Annja. She'd seen a lot since taking Joan's sword to hand. Demons, murderers, twisted scientists intent on cloning history's monsters, even those who would create Frankenstein's monster.

"I still don't buy it. Skeletons don't give birth to skulls."

"It is said the birth was most grisly."

She laughed. "Wonder if she asked for an epidural."

"Skeptic."

"To the bone." She rubbed her wrist again. A bone conjurer had a sample of her bone? That could not be good. "But I'm willing to do some research. You got a laptop I can borrow?"

"I do. I wouldn't expect you to take my word for what it's worth."

"It's worth a trick, if you ask me. And I'm so not buying you not having an interest in the thing. Worried about little old me? Last time I believed you wanted to help me I ended up dodging machine gun fire."

"That was an oversight, Annja. Listen, I'm hungry. I'm going to order Thai. You have any requests?"

"No, just hook me up with a laptop, and feed me anything. I'm good."

"It's down the hall in my office. Second door on the right."

19

Closing the office door behind her, Annja surveyed the ultra-slick room. Everything was stainless steel and tempered glass. Nice, but cold. She had Garin figured for a more earthy kind of guy. Then again, he did like to toss around cash as if it was confetti.

This apartment was a recent acquisition. She wondered if it was a rental, or if he'd keep it. Did it matter? It wasn't as though she intended any sleepovers.

He, on the other hand, could be plotting just such a thing. She wouldn't put it past him.

She powered up the laptop. She did intend to go online and search. Not yet, though.

Annja inspected the glass desktop. Just the laptop. She checked behind the curtains and roamed her eyes along the ceiling. No security cameras.

She flexed her fingers and sat before the desk, pulling open the top drawer. It contained the usual office ephemera. No important papers. He may not have lived here long enough. Anything important may still be out in the open, she thought.

The computer was warmed up. Chancing the look, Annja checked the browser's history. It listed Web sites Garin had visited for the past week. eBay, Amazon, her show's site and a few archaeology sites she recognized.

"So he *has* been following me."

None of the sites offered a solid clue to the man's motives. She slipped her cell phone from a pocket on the pants Garin had bought her. Roux's number was on speed dial. Calling him was as precarious as walking into Garin's home. One never knew who would answer.

Annja had been surprised enough times by bubbly young female voices to not even be flustered when another answered this time. Roux and Garin were two of an old and distinct kind. They may not use the term *playboy,* but it's the first word that came to her mind.

The woman on the phone called loudly to Roux. The phone receiver dropped with a *clunk*.

What must it be like for them to never age and have an entire world of women at their beck and call? she wondered.

Heck, to have a single date would please her immensely. Dating was looking as precarious as the polar bear lately. If she didn't start paying attention to it, it was going to disappear altogether.

Bart was on her radar, and she knew she was on his. Since his broken engagement he'd been more open to her.

"Don't be the rebound girl," she murmured. "You're better than that."

Tito's had been fun. But was she interested in risking a great friendship for something more?

At the moment, extracurricular activity would have to take a backseat. She needed to figure out who was who and why they all wanted the skull. She should have asked Garin to tell her about Benjamin Ravenscroft.

Shaking her head, she lifted her feet over the glass desktop, then changed her mind and dropped them to the floor.

"Good evening, Annja." Roux's voice held a feather of his French accent, and it always sounded old-worldly to her. She liked it. "To what do I owe the pleasure?" he said.

"Sorry to interrupt," she started.

"Nonsense. The girls are out enjoying the pool."

Girls. And probably not much older than legal, if she guessed correctly.

"So what can I do for you?" he asked.

"I'm here at Garin's Manhattan apartment." She paused to catch his reaction. He didn't disappoint.

"Did you call to joke with me, Annja? You shouldn't do that with an old man."

"You may be old, but you've the attitude and physique of a fifty-year-old."

"Fifty? Annja, you wound me."

Well, she wasn't going any lower. He looked a nice healthy fifty, if truth were told. An attractive, healthy fifty. Man, she did need to start dating if the two oldest men in the world turned her head so easily.

"Garin pulled me out of a grave this morning as I was breathing my last breath."

"Sporting of him. Why the sleep with the worms?"

She flinched at the mention of worms. Garin had plucked one from her hair, she was sure of it.

"I've found a new friend who wants to kill me if I don't hand over a fancy skull given to me by an anonymous—and now dead—thief."

"Ah, adventure again. I do love to live vicariously through you, Annja. You may think I've lived a dangerous life, but you, you do defy even my best adventures. What's the skull about? I'm assuming Garin wants to get his hands on it?"

"That's my guess, but he's playing Mr. Nice Guy right now. Claims he wants to protect me from a necromancer. He called it the Skull of Sidon. I'm just sitting down to research it right now."

At that, she typed it in at Google. Roux's sudden intake of breath caught her attention. "You've heard of it?" she asked.

Google brought up ten pages of matches. The first flashed Knights Templar in the blurb, along with mention of the Lady of Maraclea.

"Annja, Garin's right. I don't want you going near the necromancer. Those bastards are bad news."

"Yeah? What about the skull?"

There was a long pause, and then, "It's as bad news as is the necromancer."

"So you believe in a skull born from a necrophilic liaison?" Just saying it made her want to spit, as if her mouth were still full of dirt.

"I do. But more so, I believe in the necromancer's power. And if you've got something he wants, he'll kill to get it. I take it he's the one who put you in the grave?"

"Yes. But I don't think he was trying to kill me. Just give me a scare. He has to keep me alive. I don't have the skull at the moment, and I am the only one who knows where it is."

"He'll find it."

"I don't know how he can. I was very careful not to be followed."

"If he's got something of yours, he can track you. A strand of hair, a piece of clothing."

She turned her wrist up and the bandage sneaked below the sleeve hem. Annja swallowed. "What about a bone sample?"

"What? You're not serious!" he shouted.

Annja flinched at his vehemence. "We had a scuffle, and he had this sharp instrument that took a chunk out of my wrist like a core sample from a tree."

"Goddamn it! Annja, bone is the necromancer's primary weapon. He can summon ghosts and all sorts of dark and twisted things with it."

It was rare Roux used foul language with her. Annja pushed the laptop aside. Garin stood in the doorway, listening. He filled the whole doorway with his wide shoulders and a stare so intense it could burn out her irises.

"Did you tell Garin?"

"No." She tried to look away from the man's gaze, but he had her locked in the crosshairs. She hadn't noticed him approach. He could have been listening to the whole conversation. "I don't think I told him."

"Tell him. Curse the gods, let me talk to him."

Now that was an interesting request. Roux and Garin were to odds more often than allies. While she tried to put the two as a father and son pair, they constantly proved to her they were more enemies than relatives. Certainly no common blood ran in their veins.

Annja handed her cell phone toward the man occupying the doorway. "It's Roux."

Garin took the phone and, before speaking, narrowed his eyes at her. Nope, not going to give him a clue. She'd leave the verbal combat to the big boys.

"Roux?"

While the men spoke Annja tapped the keyboard, bringing up the first site that featured a photo of a skeleton laying repose in situ at a dig sight. The leg bones were crossed, and a smaller skull sat at the hip bones. It was not an actual photo of the Maraclean woman's remains, it warned, just a reenactment of the legend.

That was the thing. Annja didn't know how to believe something so wild until she could trace it to the original dig. Where was the skull discovered? How had it made its way to the fifteenth-century alchemist Garin had told her about? Had it *ever* been buried, or had it always been tucked away somewhere, like in an alchemist's lab?

Garin had said something about the alchemist *not* having it after they left. What was that about?

If Marcus Cooke was still alive he would have the answer to where the skull had last been.

Why did the skull and necromancer freak out Roux so much? That man was cooler than cool. He'd stood against bullets, RPGs, grenades, swords and so much more, Annja felt sure, than to let one man scare him.

A necromancer? She'd come against greater opponents in the past few months. Ninjas, bio-pirates, mad scientists, tomb raiders and just plain nasty killers.

Sure, Serge was big, strong and powerful. While he didn't seem to exercise any particular martial skills, he could no doubt snap her like a twig if he got her in the right hold. He might even give Garin a challenge physically, but she would lay wagers on that match. They were about the same height and build. And she knew Garin would not hesitate before exacting punishment in his own defense.

Serge, on the other hand, had not proven murderous. Yet.

And if he did possess some supernatural power, wouldn't he have used it on her by now?

Maybe his power wasn't like zapping lightning bolts out from his fingers. It had to be conjured. Focused through the spirits Roux had said necromancers use.

He did have a piece of her bone. He could be working some mojo on her as she sat here. But ghosts? Didn't she have to *be* a ghost for him to discover something about her?

Typing in *necromancy,* Annja waited as Google searched. The trouble with the Internet is you couldn't tell it you only wanted to search scholarly articles about any given request. The search brought up Web page after Web page about necromancers—all gaming sites.

"Not what I want," she muttered.

Garin snapped the phone shut and set it on the glass desktop. He pressed his knuckles to it and hissed sharply, "He has your bone sample?"

It wasn't a friendly question. In fact, the accusation admonished with a slice.

"I thought it was a freaky kind of weapon." She tugged up her sleeve to reveal the bandage. "It's healing fine, thank you very much. Though it still hurts like a mother."

Garin gripped a fist before him, then released it. "This is not good, Annja. With a piece of your bone the conjurer can—"

"Can what?"

"I don't know specifics. Necromancers can do nasty, macabre stuff. It's not pretty. But I do know you're up shit creek. We've got to get the skull."

"It's at the university with Professor Danzinger. I left it for him to authenticate. What time is it?"

"Nine."

"I'm sure he's left for the day."

"We can't take the chance the skull will be left unattended. Let's go."

"But Roux thinks I should stay out of this."

He swung to face her in the doorway. A lift of dark brow challenged sardonically. "You always do what Roux asks of you?"

"No." But neither did she want Garin to lead her around.

"How will having the skull in hand protect me from Serge? Won't it just draw him right to me?"

"It'll keep him back. It is the giver of all good things. Trust me on this one, Annja."

He touched her chin with a finger and held her gaze. His eyes were intense. A lot of history lived there. History she was hungry to learn.

"You've witnessed the skull's power before, haven't you?" she asked.

He made to leave, but she gripped his sleeve. Garin slid into the doorway, closing their distance to but a breath.

"Tell me about it," she said. "Give me proof this skull is worth the worry."

20

Granada, Spain, 1430

Garin glanced over his shoulder toward the distant Alhambra Palace. It sat like a jewel perched atop the red hills. The setting sun glinted across the palace, catching glass and metal in a twinkle.

"No time for dawdle, apprentice."

Roux reined his mount near Garin's and nodded north. They'd crossed the Darro River an hour earlier. It was a fine time for dawdling. The night moved upon them with a surprising chill. The goshawk circling above had left them for her nest, no doubt to settle for the night.

Exhausted from the journey, Garin was ready to make camp. Ahead, a grove of trees edged a field of some crop he couldn't guess at, perhaps wheat. The trees would provide shelter for camp.

"We will rest soon?" he wondered, but expected the answer.

"No."

His master reined closer and Garin could see the old man's pale irises. "Listen," Roux said.

To what? The sound of his belly grumbling for lacking food?

Dropping his tight hold on the reins allowed the horse freedom to graze. Garin tilted his head, eyeing Roux as he listened. The old man held his gaze fiercely.

The rustle of leaves tempted. Almond trees, thick with white blossoms. Could a man eat the nut straight from the tree?

Yet there, yes, he heard something. Rather, he felt vibrations touch his bones with a wicked warning.

Garin pulled rein. His unspoken fear was met with a nod from Roux.

"They've been following since Granada," Roux said. "Six or more, I'm sure."

Now the horses picked up the vibrations and lifted their heads. Ears twitched. They walked, heads bobbing, ready to gallop. Garin let his mount follow Roux's lead as he heeled his to action.

"Why?" Garin called, as their meander into the night became a blood-racing gallop.

"I may have something they want," Roux called back. "Head for the trees. We can use them as defense."

Defense. Garin shook his head. "Here we go again."

The old man did have a manner to him. He attracted a skirmish no matter where he traveled. It was good training for Garin, and he never minded a chase followed by the clash of swords.

WIELDING LEATHER SHIELDS and helmets, six warriors entered the grove of almond trees full speed. Swords to the ready, they were quiet, no voices heard amidst the thunder of hooves.

"Moors," Roux whispered to Garin. "From the palace. Must be de Castaña's guards."

"The alchemist? Why would he send men after us? Did you not pay for the dagger?"

"Oh, indeed." Roux patted his hip where he'd sheathed the kris dagger.

He jumped from his mount—ridiculous to do so when the warriors were so close. Opening a flap on the saddlebag Roux dipped in his hand.

"I may have forgotten to pay for this, though."

He drew out the small skull Garin had marveled over in the alchemist's lab. A wink from Roux seemed ridiculous, yet Garin could only laugh. His master wasn't one to take no for an answer. If the alchemist had refused to sell the skull, well, then.

"Will it be worth it—" Garin drew out his saber "—when our heads are on the ground separated from our bodies?"

"There's but six of them, boy."

Indeed. Those were good odds.

Heeling his mount, Garin charged the vanguard. The first slash of his saber cut across the lead rider's face. Hot blood spattered Garin's wool cloak and chin. He swung low and right, sliding his back along the horse's flank to avoid the swing of a curved saber. His forehead skimmed the bark of an almond tree. Better that than the cut of a blade.

Night had fallen and navigating the grove was tricky. Garin let his rouncey take the ground where it wished. He had only to direct it toward the cavalcade.

A Moor's saber cut down his mount's neck. Slashing his blade, Garin cut off a hand. The horse's withers tensed. Garin sensed it would rear and try to shed him. So he jumped down and put his back to a narrow tree trunk.

Listening, Garin tried to locate Roux. What was the old man up to? Huddled in some tree trunk caressing his prize?

No, the guttural cry of triumph told him Roux had taken

down a rider. He may be getting on in age, but his master loved a fight as much as he.

The horse's tail snapped his cheek as if an iron-tipped whip. Garin dodged to avoid a hoof and swung around with a wide lunge toward the rider gaining him. His blade cut across the leather shield.

Swinging his shoulders, Garin used his free hand and hooked it in a stirrup. A tug mastered the rider's equilibrium. He was tossed from the saddle and, flying over Garin's head, landed on the hard red dirt with a yelp.

"Behind me, boy!"

Stabbing quickly, Garin pushed his blade into the fallen Moor's chest. It passed through mail and bone. Blood scent imbued the air. Then he ran toward Roux's voice. The air thundered. No, that was the ground.

More warriors. Dozens entered the grove. Hooting cries and slashes of blade littered the darkness. The soft touch of white almond blossom petals rained upon Garin's skin.

"So many?" Garin said as he crashed against Roux's side. Back to back, they held position in the night. "For a skull?"

"Time to see if it will give us the good things it promises."

He had no idea what the old man babbled about. Garin swung and caught a rider across the shoulder. The taste of blood was vile.

"Back toward the tree," Roux directed. "And stay behind me."

Stumbling over a fallen body, Garin wasn't willing to put himself in a position to be surrounded by the enemy. But Roux had never led him astray without then either teaching him a means to overcome, or outright crashing their way through, the melee.

He was still alive after a dozen years with the man. He

trusted he had a good dozen more at the very least. This would not be his night to die.

Garin's shoulder bruised against the tree. The scent of sweet almond oil stirred amongst the froth of heated horse-flesh and dust.

"Give us good things," Roux recited.

He held the skull before him with both hands, high and as if an offering to the moon.

A thump within his heart unsteadied Garin on his feet. Or had it been a physical movement beneath him? The earth had pulsed. Men cried out. Horses whinnied and hooves trampled the ground.

Almond blossoms were unleashed from their tethers in a storm.

Amidst a swirl of petals the melee was put back. Riders fell from their mounts and landed on the ground, arms splayed. As if cut through the heart, their chests opened wide. Blood gurgled up. The ground grew muddy from human blood. They did not rise and advance upon Roux and Garin.

Gaping, Garin clung to the tree trunk.

It was as though some unseen force had blasted through the air and killed them all at once. What supernatural force had been unleashed? He whispered a prayer to his God.

Another pulse blew the trees bare of blossoms. Garin clutched Roux's shoulders, but found he was neither toppled nor injured.

"What is it? How is this happening?"

"I would call that good," Roux said. He slapped a hand on the skull's top. "This marvel just killed all our enemies."

"It is evil," Garin gasped. Blood rushed through his veins. The old man was surely the wizard rumors claimed him to be.

"Evil it may be, but it saved our sorry asses."

Roux strode past the bodies toward his Andalusian. He did

not seem to take measure of the startling event that had just occurred. Mounting and tucking the skull at his hip, he nodded to a warrior's horse that had not been stripped of flesh or fled.

"You've been wanting a new mount, boy."

A guttural sound warbled from Garin's mouth. Numbly, he grabbed the reins of a Moor's mount.

"Good things?" he muttered. "God in heaven, forgive and watch over me."

THEY MADE MEDINA Sidonia by sunrise. Garin could not think of sleep, for the itchy dust crowded his eyes, nostrils and the back of his throat. He'd yet to take his gaze from the skull Roux held as if a child. Nestled at his hip, the white bone taunted.

It had power. A power that frightened Garin. He'd seen wonders since Roux had taken him as an apprentice. Babies birthed and giants of men fallen. Dying men cured with magic potions, and there was the man in London whose heart was exposed for all to see. Garin had seen a live heart beating.

Last night had put all those wonders to shame.

They cantered toward the village, which was just waking to the new day. Ahead were women busy at a stone well with their wash.

Forget about the battle in the grove. They would find food and rest and be on to France with no more discussion of the skull.

The truth was, he wanted Roux to be rid of the thing. The occult scared him.

A young boy, no higher than a grown man's hip, rushed out from a stone home and toward Roux. Arms wide and eyes bright, he could not know the approaching rider. Such childish innocence. It gave Garin a smile.

The boy was lifted from his feet and flung through the air. His frail body collided with the red tile roof and slid. The tiles clattered sickly. The body dropped to the ground with a thud.

Dead.

Garin heeled his mount to parallel his master. "What have you done? It is that damned thing!"

"I did not—" Shaken, Roux inspected the skull. "It was not my doing!"

"The boy is dead! By supernatural means. Be rid of the thing!"

Roux turned the eye sockets away and lifted it high.

The women gathered around the well stood and screamed.

"Put it away!" Garin cried. "Destroy it!"

Blood streamed across white fabric, spilling from ears and eyes. The women clutched at their hair and stumbled. Wash buckets overturned, washing the flowing blood into runnels of dirt.

"Turn it away from them!" Garin shouted.

But the old man was too shocked to understand what was happening. The skull was destroying more than their enemies. It was taking away life in an attempt to clear their paths.

ANNJA BREATHED OUT. The room, very still, felt heavy with an ineffable pain. Garin's regret. His fear of the skull. Roux's naïveté of its power.

"It murders?" she asked.

"It does not seem to discern murder as wrong. It gives the holder what it believes to be good. Putting back our enemies. Clearing a path through the village for us to pass."

"What did you do with the skull? How did you stop it?"

"Roux tried to crush it under his boot. It was as if forged from steel. Finally, I had him throw it down the well. It was too late for the laundresses. And half a dozen strong men who rushed to stop us."

"What did the villagers do to you?"

"We didn't stick around for the fireworks. While the village frenzied and wondered at what had happened, we fled."

Garin stroked his goatee, his gaze lost somewhere out the window on the dreary New York skyline.

It occurred to Annja that a man who lived five centuries must pay a price no mortal man could conceive. Sure, there were riches and supernatural healing and all the travel and parties. But a darkness she had but glimpsed accompanied both Roux and Garin.

It softened her to his hardened exterior. A man like Garin had to wear some kind of protection against the world. But she wondered if he wore the same protection around his heart and mind? It would be impossible not to.

"I'm no saint, Annja."

That she knew.

"So in the hands of a necromancer," she said, "the skull could do some wicked damage."

"I don't want to begin to imagine. We need to get that skull."

"I'll give Professor Danzinger a call."

21

Eric Danzinger liked spending late hours at the university. The desk lamp tossed gold light across the granite lab tables as if splashed out from a miner's pan. Hundreds of skulls observed from shelves. The *tick-tick* of the radiator kept a syncopated beat that reminded of a slow jazz tune. A man just didn't get atmosphere like this in his stuffy little Bronx apartment. It was also neater than his home, which was covered wall-to-wall with rock-and-roll memorabilia.

Humming a Rolling Stones tune, he sorted through the guitar strings coiled upon the granite lab table for the high E string. Threading the clear nylon string through the baseboard, he formed a nifty twist to keep it secure, then stretched it along the neck to poke through the tuning peg. He twisted it tight, then leaned aside to tap the computer keyboard.

Freaky Tuner was a shareware program that played notes to tune virtually any instrument. One tap of the return key played a steady acoustic guitar E note. He twisted the tuning peg, and plucked the string until the vibrations wavered to nothing and the notes matched.

The B string was next. He went through the same motions, smiling bemusedly at the skull upon the stuffing in the little box Annja had delivered it in. It seemed to approve of the musical break he'd decided to indulge.

"Wonder what kind of music you listened to. I bet if you had ears, you'd bow in worship to Keith Richards, too."

On the other hand, it was an infant's skull. Best save the rock and roll a few more years.

The professor had taken dozens of photographs of the skull's interior. The computer was cobbling them all together as he waited. The program amazed him as to how it could piece photos together without overlapping. The interior map was about fifty percent complete.

The gold lining the skull sutures sparkled after a soft polishing with a little water, some ammonia and dishwashing soap.

Though he couldn't guess at the original date without proper dating equipment, he did have a good idea that the gold had been added later. Certainly the thing hadn't been born that way. It was very common to find altered artifacts, especially those of unknown origin.

Skull modification wasn't his thing. Though he was aware it had been prevalent in early Mayan cultures. He should give Sharon in Anthropology a jingle and see what she could make of the skull. The woman got more turned on by bones than sex. Not that he hadn't tried to alter her perceptions regarding a night well spent. Man, had he tried.

He tightened the B string, wondering if it was too late to call Annja to come take a look at the interior map. A woman like her probably had an insane schedule. Darting from dig to dig, hosting a television show, writing books and appearing on *Letterman.*

Yeah, he'd like it if she could find a place for him to at

least guest as a researcher on the show. He didn't mind the spotlight at all. And if it meant he could meet Kristie Chatham, well, then.

It was almost ten. Annja was likely still awake, but he'd wait until morning. The music wanted his attention.

HIS RUBBER-SOLED RUNNING shoes made no sound on the old tiled floor in Schermerhorn Hall. It was dark, save for a few lights toward the end of the hall, two coming from consecutive doorways, another across the hall from the first.

Ravenscroft's orders had been clear. He'd likely find this strange skull in the anthropology building. He'd found a name of a teacher associated with the TV chick and had tracked his teaching schedule.

The building should be empty of students as well as professors, especially with the holiday weekend. But Jones had been given the all-clear to take matters into hand should he run into anyone wanting to ask questions.

Sliding his leather-gloved fingers inside his jacket, Jones drew them the length of the knife tucked inside a narrow pocket.

As each step drew him closer to the lighted rooms, he got a sense for the one on the left. Just a feeling. Must be like that intuition his girlfriend was always yapping about.

Stopping at the first door on the left, he read the syllabus taped outside on the wall. It was signed by Professor Danzinger. Bingo.

He knocked lightly. The door, not completely closed, swung inward.

"Professor Danzinger?"

He entered the quiet room. A bright lamp beamed over a lab table. A computer, textbooks and various tools and papers scattered messily across the stretch.

And a skull. Sitting there on an open box with tufts of wool cradling the small cranium.

Ravenscroft had said he might need to mention a woman's name. "I was given your name by Annja Creed."

"Yes, Miss Creed." The professor removed his glasses and set them on the countertop. An acoustic guitar lay on the table before him, the neck propped by a textbook, one unwound string coiled at the base by the sound hole. "And you are?"

"Jones," he offered. "Bill Jones. I'm a colleague of Miss Creed's. I see you've got the skull. Annja and I are eager to learn what you've discovered about it."

"Yes, well, the interior mapping isn't finished. As for the date…" He leaned over the skull and tapped the thin gold tracing around one eye socket. "I'd give it a good millennium. Perhaps. I'm no expert, more a fascinated learner."

"That's intriguing." Jones moved to the professor's side. When the man straightened and looked him over, he placed a gentle palm to his shoulder. "Looks like just another skull. What's so special about this one?"

He felt the man's muscles tighten under his testing touch. "How did you say you know Annja? She didn't mention—"

"I'm surprised she didn't mention me, but then Annja is always so busy."

"Yes, with her show."

Show? Jones filed that one away. "I'll bring it back to her."

"But I said I'm not finished yet. Maybe I should give Annja a call?"

"Sure, certainly. You play, Professor?"

Jones stroked the guitar neck. Three strings were strung.

"Since I was a boy. You like guitar music?" Danzinger asked.

Jones picked up one of the thicker, bronze-wrapped

strings and unwound it curiously. "Music is not one of my talents."

"You don't need to be able to play to appreciate. I've got a phone in the office. If you'll give me a minute—"

Fitting his arms over the man's head and tugging the guitar string, Jones choked off the man's protest. The wire dug into flesh. He pulled hard, sawing it slightly until he smelled blood.

As he felt the man's weight sag, Jones decided he couldn't wait. Taking the professor's head between his palms, he gave it a smart jerk, separating the spinal disks. The spinal cord severed, the body slumped and dropped.

Jones stepped back, dragging his feet from under the professor's sprawled limbs. He dropped the bloody string across his chest. Leather pants and a shimmery leopard-print shirt? What kind of professor dresses like an aging rock star?

Dismissing the thought, Jones bent forward, bringing himself eye level with the skull.

"Kinda ugly, if you ask me. The thing's cranium is bigger than its face. Must be deformed. But is that gold?"

He grabbed the skull, and when it wouldn't fit inside his pocket, he tucked it in the box filled with wooly stuff.

22

"Wait!"

Annja rushed ahead of Garin's long strides down the hallway of the Schermerhorn building. She pressed a hand to his shoulder, feeling resistance in his straining muscles. He was in too big a hurry for this to feel right.

"Right here," she said, pointing to her eyes. "Look at me."

He tilted his head and met her gaze. Dark, emotionless eyes. Not at all kind as he'd displayed earlier at his penthouse. That's what Annja was afraid of. The man tended to alter his alliances faster than she could blink.

"Tell me this isn't a trick. That as soon as you see the skull, you're not going to push me out a window and take off with the thing."

"I would never push you out a window, Annja."

"Yeah? Not unless it served your purposes. Just tell me the truth. Right now. I already know what the answer is, but I want to hear it from you."

The imposing man pressed his knuckles to his hips, widening his stance. And his gaze didn't get any less fierce.

"You think you know me? You think I'll harm anyone, *kill,* to get what I desire?"

"I do," she offered, sure of it, though it pained her to believe such truths.

Garin tilted his head. Then, swiping a palm over his mouth, he shook his head. "Isn't everyone out to protect number one? Since you've come into my world, Annja, the game has changed. I have…uncertainties. I want to make them certain once again."

"Then why not go after the sword?"

"Because I like you, Annja. Believe it or not. And, as you are aware, the sword is not an attainable goal. So until you hand it to me, with blessings and tied with a bow, then I've got to resort to other means."

Aha. He'd just, in a roundabout way, confirmed her suspicions. He was after the skull. Though what it could do for him was beyond her imagining. *If* it possessed power.

His story about he and Roux holding it in fifteenth-century Spain was believable enough, but really, he had no proof. It had killed. Didn't sound like a giver of all good things to her. And if it did grant some magical wishes, didn't Garin already have it all? And what he didn't have, he could buy.

Unless *good things* somehow meant giving him access to her sword. In which case, she should, and would, fight to the finish for this skull.

Swinging about, she took the lead down the hallway. With Garin hot on her heels, she couldn't reach the anthropology lab fast enough. She was going to lead him directly to the skull. Was there any other choice? She'd known from the moment he'd pulled her from the grave he possessed ulterior motives.

The lab door was open. Annja's heart dropped to her gut. Rushing inside, the room was empty, but the light was on over the professor's worktable.

"Professor?" Annja didn't track the room for the skull.

Garin prowled in behind her. He would do that search. "Oh, hell."

An arm stretched across the floor behind the freestanding counter. Blood spattered the professor's face and the front of his leopard-print shirt. It had begun to pool beside his cheek and shoulder.

"He's dead," she said.

"Ya think?"

She cast Garin a sneer.

He put up his palms. "Sorry. Is he still warm?"

As Garin shuffled glass jars and books about, Annja bowed her head and pressed her open palm to the professor's cheek. "Yes."

She hadn't known him that well, but had considered him a friend. A tear trickled down the side of her nose. At once it felt right, a small gesture for the man's lost life, yet it felt stupid to show emotion in front of Garin.

Using that complex twist of battling emotions, Annja was able to look over the professor's body for clues, but cautioned herself not to touch him or any of his clothes. Didn't want to leave fingerprints.

A bloody guitar string, and the dark maroon line around his neck, answered the method-of-death question. Poor guy. He'd loved that guitar.

"Wonder how long he's been like this?" she muttered.

There had been no other lights on in the surrounding classrooms. This wing of the hall was empty.

She had to report this. She'd call Bart. Much wiser than alerting campus security, who wouldn't know her history of always showing up at crime scenes at the wrong time.

"It's not in here. Was it in a case of some kind?" Garin's insistence cut at the back of her neck. He acted oblivious to the fact a dead man lay on the floor.

Annja pounded the counter with a fist. "Back off, will you?"

Garin put up his palms to placate her. "You knew him well?"

"He was a friend. Not close, but he deserves respect."

"You can go to his funeral. Right now, we are in a race to find that thing before the bone conjurer starts to use it. You can be sure that's who took the thing."

Right. The professor wasn't dead for no reason. The skull had been the motivation. Serge had some kind of power both Garin and Roux were in awe of.

Annja twisted to study the path from the professor to the door. There were no bloody shoe tracks. And as for picking up a shoe print, she had probably walked over the murderer's tracks.

"He's still warm, so Serge couldn't be too far ahead of us. Wait." She noticed the computer screen, and stood, being careful not to step in blood or on the professor's leg. "What's this?"

A completion bar superimposed over a screenwide picture showed one hundred percent. Annja slid the mouse and the bar disappeared. "It's the inside. A map of the interior."

"Annja."

"What?" Without pulling her attention from the screen, she tapped the mouse to copy the file to the USB flash drive plugged in the side of the computer.

Garin leaned in close so she had to meet his eyes. "Dead body? Scene of the crime. We need to get out of here now."

"Let me copy this first."

"We don't have time."

"Garin, chill. It's not as if there are a lot of people here so late at night."

"What about the janitor?"

"From my experience with labs and classrooms, it can be days before a janitor shows to clean. Professor Danzinger might be on the floor for days— Oh, that's so wrong. I have to call Bart right away, or the professor could seriously be here for days before he's found."

"Bart?"

"NYPD detective. A friend of mine."

"Great. Give us five minutes to clear the scene, will you?" Garin, with one last sweep of the room, strode out.

Annja grabbed the flash drive, tucked it in the front pocket of her pants and followed.

This was personal now. She didn't know what Serge could do with a skull like that, but it didn't matter. He wasn't going to get away with Professor Danzinger's murder.

She flipped open her cell phone and dialed Bart as Garin stalked outside into the dark night. Bart didn't answer, so she left another "guess what, I found another dead body" message for him.

"You know what I don't buy about this whole Knights Templar legend of the skull?"

Annja sat on the passenger side of Garin's black Escalade. They'd driven it to the college and now cruised around the building, scouting the periphery. She suspected Serge had killed the professor and stolen the skull, so she was on the lookout for a behemoth bald guy.

"What's that?" Garin asked.

"Well, there's the cross pattée on the gold sutures. A symbol we know the Templars used, so obviously that makes the skull the actual skull, yes?"

"Yes and no. The gold could have been put on later."

"Exactly. And this could be any old skull. Because I don't buy that the skull and crossbones symbol began with the Templars."

"Why not?"

"When I researched the Skull of Sidon it stated the child's skull was found atop the Maraclean woman's crossed thigh bones, which instigated the skull and crossbones imagery. It just spread from there."

"That's what I told you, as well."

"But why, if the knights took vows of chastity and were all about doing good, would they then adopt a symbol that celebrates necrophilia? It makes little sense. Hey, guys, one of our own did something nasty with a dead chick. Let's take that imagery and use it on our flags and tabards and let the whole world know we approve."

"They weren't as wholesome as history tells, Annja."

"I know that. I've read about freemasonry. The devil worshipping."

"Head worshipping, actually."

"What's that about?"

"It was said the Knights Templar worshipped a severed head. Theories place it as the severed head of John the Baptist, which leads to theories on the Holy Grail actually being the tray upon which his head was carried to Salome."

"Interesting. And yet another grail legend attached to the Templars. There can be only one. And I don't think any of them are correct. But for argument's sake, and if we go with the head worshipping, it could have been our skull? That's a head. Partially."

"Who knows? Though some theories do place the Maraclean woman as a symbol of a virgin birth, while the lord of Sidon was a pirate, which ties the grail and the skull and crossbones together nicely."

"Nicely? I don't know about that. Eerily, more like." Annja tapped the window glass with a knuckle as she tracked the passing sidewalks for signs of Serge. "You ever have any dealings with the Templars?"

"Before my time."

"But there've been many recreations of the organization."

"Organization?" He smirked. "You have an interesting way of putting things, Creed. Do you see anything that side of the building?"

She shook her head. "He's not on the property anymore. Let's take the streets and see if we can spot him. I'm sure he's long gone by now. If the guy is smart, he's halfway to Jersey. So you never joined the freemasons or the Shriners?"

"Shriners? Please."

"I understand they do good work for children."

"I've never been a follower, Annja."

"What about Roux? You followed him."

"He was my master. The kindest thing he ever called me was apprentice. I did what I was told, and wisely kept my distance from his backhand."

"But he taught you things. You owe him a debt."

He stepped on the brake. "What dream are you living in, woman? I owe nothing to that man. We are bound together through a bizarre destiny, but that doesn't mean we are brothers or family."

"Sorry." She looked out the window. "'Spose I won't get a Christmas card from you and Roux, then? No family picture?"

She sensed Garin's smile but he looked out the driver's side window.

"Speaking of pictures," he muttered. "You look great nude."

Annja gaped. He'd seen the online pics? Had the whole world?

Garin chuckled. "Don't worry, Annja. I know it's not you."

Affronted, she lifted her shoulders. "How?"

"You forget I know your bra size. And the assets in that picture were a few cup sizes larger. Silicone, I'm sure. You, I can only imagine, are all natural."

About to agree, but feeling too unnerved, Annja left that one to hang. Something must be done about removing that picture. But how?

Silver flashed in her peripheral view. Squinting, Annja made out a very familiar box tucked under the arm of a tall, thin man walking swiftly down the sidewalk. It wasn't Serge. But that was the original box she'd found the skull in. "That's him!"

"You're sure?"

"Nope. It's not the bone conjurer, but that is the skull, I'm sure of it. You drive, I'm going on foot." Annja opened the door. "Can you keep close?"

"No problem. Go get him, sword-wielding warrior woman."

She sprinted down the sidewalk. A good two hundred feet ahead of her, the man turned. The small case the skull had been enclosed in swung out in his grip. He saw her and took off in a run. He dodged right, disappearing from view.

Pumping her arms, Annja forced her pace to long strides. She considered calling the sword to hand, but dismissed that idea. She didn't need it right now, and it would only slow her down.

Taking the turn led into a long narrow alley, which opened on to some kind of building yard enclosed by chain-link fencing. That didn't stop the man. He expertly mounted the fence, and swung himself over.

"Thugs," Annja muttered. "They never cease to surprise me."

Annja hit the fence at a run and landed high, her fingers

piercing the chain links. The curved metal was cold and her toe slipped its hold, dropping her body to hang by her fingers. Working the tips of her boots into the convoluted links, she levered herself up to latch a forearm over the top of the fence. Lifting her upper body, she pushed, and when her chest had risen above the chain link, she dipped forward, releasing the fence and arching her back.

She landed in a crouch. The man ran toward a warehouse.

Garin's Escalade pulled up with a squeal behind the fence as Annja entered the warehouse. It was late. Moonlight cast across the floor at the far wall, but where Annja stood, the atmosphere was hazy at best.

Scattered lumber and plastic-covered pallets stood everywhere. The dusty smell of Sheetrock clued her to a stack of whiteboard to her right.

Before her on the hardwood floor, smeared shoe tracks advertised the murderer's intentions. He'd gone right.

Garin entered with pistol held before him and a keen eye to the surroundings. Annja nodded, acknowledging the trail by pointing it out. He nodded left and gestured she go right.

She dashed between two stacks of lumber piled three feet higher than her head. The building must be a lumber warehouse. Racing to the end, she slapped a palm on a stack of wood. An electric air nailer wobbled.

"Oh, yeah?" Annja grabbed the yellow nailer and gave the trigger a squeeze. No nails were expelled because the safety was on. But it was charged, and ready to use. "Nice."

The clatter of boards alerted her that the man was close. Nailer wielded like a gun, she slunk along a wall of lumber, her shoulders tracing the clean edges, and crept to the end of the stack.

Raising the nailer before her, she decided it would prove a

fitting weapon. With a sword she'd have to put herself close to the danger. With the nailer she could buy herself some room.

Stepping forward to the next aisle of stacked lumber, she dodged a look down the aisle. Empty.

Heavy breathing signaled her quarry was nearby. Putting her back to the next stack of lumber, she guessed he was down the aisle. Footsteps moved closer.

Annja spun her hips and turned her body to stand in the aisle.

The man ran toward her, but seeing she was armed, he abruptly stopped.

Flicking her forefinger over the safety guard, she took aim and fired. His skull snapped backward with impact. Three inches of steel finishing nail pierced flesh, bone and brain. He stumbled a couple paces, slapping his palms against the plastic-covered lumber.

Prepared to fire again, Annja waited for the man to drop. Remarkably, he maintained balance. A gruff shake of head and a growl preceded his wicked grin.

She gaped at the man.

He gripped the two-inch portion of nail jutting from his skull, and yanked it out. A bubble of blood pooled at the nail hole, but didn't drip down his forehead.

He winked.

"You are so kidding me." Annja tossed the nailer aside. "I hate it when I feel like the heroine cast in the movie opposite the villain who just won't die."

The man's feet shuffled. He fled down the aisle away from her. Annja pursued.

In the narrow aisle she couldn't call the sword to her, but as soon as she exited the first row and spotted the man's coattails, she summoned the sword.

Reaching out, her fingers tingled as the sword found its

way from the otherwhere and into her grip. She liked the
solid feel as it made itself whole. It claimed her as much as
she claimed it. They were one.

Annja raced forward. The footsteps in the dust stopped,
but only because she skidded up to a swept section of
cement flooring.

Garin's voice echoed close by. The men must have run
into each other.

The crunch of a fist connecting with bone sounded before
Annja saw either of them. Charging to an abrupt stop at the
edge of stacked Sheetrock, she lowered the sword and caught
her breath.

The warehouse resounded with male grunts. Clothing
whipped with sharp kicks and precise punches. The
murderer possessed some knowledge of karate or judo
and delivered a few direct kicks to Garin's chest. The for-
midable immortal took the violence with little more than
a wince.

Fist to skull crushed the nail hole in the man's temple.
He didn't go down. Of course not; he was the villain who
would not die.

Drops of blood tracked across Annja's forearm. That was
from Garin.

She scanned the floor. Garin's gun lay against a stack of
lumber, thirty feet from where the men fought.

The men matched each other in height and bulk. Yet Annja
wondered what strength the thug could wield against Garin's
very human strength. Just because he was immortal didn't
mean he had superpowers. She'd seen him injured by bullet
and blade.

Something slid away from the clash of testosterone. The
case containing the skull. Annja tracked it as it cut a fine path

through the Sheetrock dust, and came to a wobbling stop against a two-by-four.

"You just going to watch?" Garin said on a huff. He managed a bloody grin at Annja, before lunging to deliver a pulverizing punch to the man's gut.

The man landed three feet from where Annja stood. She tapped him on the skull with the sword's tip. "My turn, big boy. You up for taking me on?"

She allowed him to roll over and jump to his feet. The hole where the nail had pierced was bloody but it hadn't magically healed. He was just a man. She had no reason to fear him.

The man eyed the sword curiously. He spat blood to the side. "I don't normally fight chicks," he said. "But I'll give it a go." He spread out his arms, not a position of preparation but of surrender. "Would you fight an unarmed man?"

She tipped the sword up under his chin. Don't get too cocky, she chided inwardly. You may feel as though you have control here, but if you've learned anything, it's that you never do.

"I hardly believe you would walk about unarmed. Don't have another guitar string handy?" she asked.

He lifted his hands slowly to place palms out near his shoulders. Annja kept the sword tip under his chin. A twist of her wrist pressed it into his neck above the Adam's apple. Flesh opened and blood beaded, a shallow cut.

"Don't know what you're talking about, girlie," he offered. "Watch the blade. Where'd a sexy thing like you get a badass weapon like that? Someone's going to get hurt with that thing."

"You must be that someone. Who are you? You work for Serge?"

"Serge? Lady, I was just taking a casual stroll, then you come along and go all Witchblade on me."

"Wrong mythology, idiot. And I'm not buying your lies. You took the skull from Professor Danzinger after you killed him."

"Never heard of no professor. As you can tell, I never went to no college."

All of a sudden he can't speak properly? Maybe he was an idiot.

"Keep him there, Annja."

The hairs on the back of Annja's neck prickled at Garin's voice. She hadn't been paying attention to him. Now he stood behind her, where the skull case had landed.

The sound of bone slapping against flesh signaled Garin had the skull, and tossed it once in his hand. "This is mine."

Intuition had been horrifically on the mark.

She spun, sweeping the sword around. "You're not going anywhere, Garin."

Her head snapped up as a heavy weight squeezed her throat. The murderer garroted an arm about her neck. Even swinging the sword backward, she couldn't connect with the bastard. To attempt a slice at his leg would first cut her own.

"I'll break her neck!" he threatened.

Garin held the skull before him to look it over. His long fingers stroked the cranium and traced along the gold. "Hmm, let me think about that one. The girl for the Skull of Sidon?"

"That's your choice, buddy." The man tightened his hold, compressing her carotid artery. "She's a fine piece of work."

Annja's vision blurred. Her fingers loosened around the sword grip and it slipped away. Whether or not the murderer noticed, he didn't give clue. She clasped her fingers, trying to fit them around a solid hilt.

Strangulation occurred within ten to fifteen seconds. Garin wouldn't actually…

"You're not very smart, are you?" Garin tossed the skull and it landed in his palm with a smack. "If you'd had a better grip on your sniper, you'd have had this prize days ago."

"What sniper?" The man lifted Annja's body a few inches but loosened his grip somewhat. "Don't know what you're talking about, man."

But Annja did. The sniper who had killed Marcus Cooke. How did Garin know about him?

"I got to him just as he pulled the trigger," Garin said. "He was going to take out my girl after the first guy."

Annja's eyelids fluttered. Garin had been *with* the sniper? Had it been because of him the bullet hadn't gone through her skull? What a swell guy. Seriously. He'd saved her life.

"If she's your girl, then you'll be wanting her breathing. Hand it over!"

If her guess was correct, Garin wouldn't play into this bastard's hands.

His girl? Yeah—no. Not going there.

"You should have offered to trade for her sword," Garin said. He turned the skull so the eye sockets faced Annja and her attacker. "That would have got you this thing in an instant."

"The sword? Where'd it go?"

"Exactly." Garin held the skull from his outstretched arm. "Too bad. You lose."

A forceful wave of *something* plunged through Annja's system. It was as if she'd been hit by a sound wave, yet it physically coursed through her body and pushed her shoulders into the thug's hard frame.

He released his hold on her neck. She gasped, breathing in deeply.

A gust of wind blew her from her feet. And she didn't stop moving.

The man behind her cried out hoarsely. The next thing Annja felt was the brunt force of her body slamming into his, as he collided with the stack of lumber behind them.

The hollow clatter of boards pummeled their heads. Annja recalled Garin's story of the skull killing his enemies. Did he consider her the enemy?

Annja blacked out.

23

Garin raced across the snowy tarmac to the Escalade. The tires spun on thin ice as he drove away. One hand on the wheel, and navigating the tight street, he held the skull in the other.

"Ha!" He tossed it up and down on his palm. "Maybe the second time will be the charm."

As soon as he'd turned the skull face toward Annja, he'd felt the bone vibrate upon his palm, and then—*whack!* Two bodies hit the lumber.

He'd heard groans as he'd run out the warehouse door. Still alive, then. This time the skull hadn't murdered. It had been a risk to hold it before Annja, knowing it could bring her death, but Garin had felt deep down it wouldn't harm her.

She was not his enemy, no matter how she felt about that.

Did he regret leaving Annja behind to fend on her own?

"She's got the sword. She'll be fine."

And if not? That wasn't his problem, was it?

SERGE GOT OUT of the cab at the curb in front of Schermerhorn Hall. He wouldn't attempt to stride up the sidewalk.

Half a dozen squad cars flashed blue and red lights across the darkening winter sky.

The cab pulled away, leaving oily fumes in its wake.

Clenching his fist, Serge swore. He felt a lingering sense of power close by. Not active, but remnants, as if a great force had been utilized. Not on this campus, though.

The sensation made him scan north. Perhaps less than a mile from here?

The intuitive feeling meant someone had beaten him to the skull. And they'd used it already.

Across the street he spied a familiar figure standing outside a dark-windowed BMW. His attention was on the commotion, as well.

Serge sped across the street.

He grabbed Harris by the collar and slammed him against the car. "Where is it?"

"I know you. And I know I don't work for you, you freaky thing, so let go of me."

He didn't need this obstinacy. Swinging the man around, Serge slapped his palm to the back of his scalp and slammed him down. Harris's face dented the top of the car. He sputtered blood and, to his credit, didn't yell or draw attention to them.

"You're insane," Harris whined. Hands gripping the edge of the car, he strained as Serge attempted to force his face again into the metal. He was strong. "If you're looking for the skull, I don't have it!"

"Where is it?"

"In the hands of the NYPD now. Look! The cops are everywhere. My guy is still inside. Getting cuffed, I'm sure. Ouch!"

A dribble of blood pooled on the dented hood.

Serge sensed Harris was telling the truth. If he had the

skull why would he remain on the scene when the cops were swarming?

"You going after him?" Serge asked.

"Are you nuts? Oh, right, you are. Ravenscroft says you talk to spirits. What a freakin' nut case."

Another slam shut up the man. Serge cautioned his anger. If he knocked Harris unconscious he wouldn't be able to tell him anything else.

"You intend to bail him out?"

"That's not my call," Harris said and spat blood.

"Ravenscroft?"

"Yeah, but I'm sure he'll play it cool. Why are you after this thing? Ravenscroft won't like hearing I had this unpleasant conversation with you."

"Tell him what you want." Serge reached inside his coat and palmed the bone biopsy tool. "The skull is mine."

"Not according to Ravenscroft—ah!"

The tool passed neatly through flesh and the scaphoid bone at the base of Harris's right thumb.

The man's shout was loud enough to draw attention. Serge tugged him down against the car door and withdrew the tool as he did so. He dropped Harris near the rear tire. He had passed out.

Inside his pocket he carried a small plastic bag. He placed the tool inside and pocketed it.

He decided to track the skull's latent spirit trail. If it was possible, he might be able to trace it to whoever held it. But he had to work quickly. Already the chill air dulled his sensory awareness of the skull.

PUSHING A BOARD OFF her shoulder, Annja winced. Pain seared through her hip. A good number of two-by-fours had landed her shoulders, but she hadn't felt the impact completely because the murderer's body had blocked the initial blows, and then she'd blacked out.

Now, various parts on her hurt like a mother.

Dragging herself from the Jenga scatter of lumber, she pushed with her toe against something with give. Then she remembered she wasn't alone.

Clearing the boards, she gripped her hip and stood at a forward-leaning angle to counteract the pain.

Professor Danzinger's murderer lay beneath the boards. Dead? She could hope. But as she scanned the length of his body, she saw one of his fingers twitch.

Time to call in the cavalry.

Bart answered on the first ring this time. "Annja, I'm at Schermerhorn Hall."

"You found the professor's body?"

"Yes, and we're dusting for fingerprints now. Please tell me yours will not turn up in the mix."

She winced. "I hope not. I did use his computer."

"Annja—"

"Bart, before you go off on me, I'm standing over the professor's murderer right now. I followed him from the scene of the crime."

"I wish you called me earlier, Annja."

Yeah, so did she. So maybe this was one of those times when she needed to step up and say, *I need help.*

The boards behind her toppled and the man sat upright.

Annja summoned the sword to hand and tipped him under the chin with the point. "Stay," she ordered.

"What?"

"Not you, Bart. I'm in a warehouse about six blocks north of the university. It looks like new construction, maybe a lumber warehouse. I've got your man. We found the skull on him, stolen from the professor."

"We?"

"Me and a—" Most definitely *not* a friend. She'd mentioned Garin to Bart before. But she had never explained their complicated relationship, or that he was immortal. "Will you just come over here, Bart?"

"Is the suspect conscious?"

"Not for long."

IT WAS AS IF THE THING had power.

Annja had felt its force move through her. But when she expected something like that to have burned through her flesh and bone to incinerate, it had been not so much painful as encompassing. She'd held the power within her for one moment, and then it had passed through and she felt the angry force overtake the man who'd held her in a choke hold.

It was difficult to remain a skeptic with visceral proof. Now what she worried about was that incredible power being wielded by a man like Garin Braden.

The ease with which he'd used the skull against her proved one thing—he was in it for himself. And it obviously gave him little concern if Annja was a casualty.

Always thankful for Bart's discretion, Annja heaved a sigh of relief when his voice called through the warehouse. He'd come alone. But not for long, he warned, as he wanted to call this in immediately. The NYPD was up the street at the college; it wouldn't look right if he waited to tell them about this discovery.

"I understand," she said.

Annja led him to the guy sprawled on the floor. Bart didn't know about the sword; she'd knocked out the murderer so she didn't have to reveal how, exactly, she'd kept him at bay until the cavalry did arrive.

"My prints are on the air nailer," she said, nodding at the abandoned weapon on the floor. "That hole in his head is from a nail."

Bart bent over the thug's body, cuffs in hand. "You could have taken out an eye, Annja."

"Seriously? I mean, you're worried I could have damaged a man who murdered my friend?"

"Not at all, do all the damage you like. It'd just be kind of gross to see a guy with a nail through his eyeball."

She smirked and he laughed. The release of tension was needed, and Bart seemed to sense it necessary. He cuffed the unconscious man.

With the thug secure, Bart holstered his gun under his arm, and led Annja to the open warehouse door. He spoke into his radio, explaining he'd followed a perp to the warehouse. Already a police siren gained on them.

Annja felt his breath on her neck before she realized he stood so close. "Need another one of those hugs?"

Did she. But now was no time to go all mushy and start wondering what Bart's hugs implied.

"I can't stick around," she said.

"Don't expect you to. Not sure if I want you to." He grabbed her arm before she could take a step outside. "But I'm still a cop, and I have to follow some procedure. Where's the skull?"

Annja sighed heavily.

"You don't have it?" Drawing her close, he spoke in low tones, his head bowed over hers. "What is going on, Annja?"

"I'm not sure, Bart. There's something about this skull that makes men kill for it. First the thief at the bridge, and now the professor. He was such a nice guy. I can't believe I was responsible for his death."

"How could you be responsible? You couldn't have known someone would go after the skull."

"I could have! I shouldn't have left it with Danzinger after Serge tracked me to my loft."

"Serge? Tracked you to your loft?"

She dropped her raised hands and turned from Bart's eyes. Now he closed her in against the door frame, one of his hands to the wall over her shoulder. "Annja?"

"Yesterday, I returned home from the university to find a stranger waiting for me. My place was trashed. He was looking for the skull."

Bart swiped a hand over his jaw and fixed her with a stare she wouldn't wish on the hardest of criminals. He had a way of looking at her without saying a word that made her feel as if he could read her thoughts as they fired in her brain synapses.

He was a detective. Of course he should have that skill. But she wasn't up on emotion. And she was still feeling out of sorts after finding Danzinger on the floor.

"I didn't want to upset you," she offered. He didn't drop the castigating scowl. "Serge is a necromancer."

"A what?"

"Guy who talks to spirits with bones."

He had nothing to say to that. Annja wondered about pushing up his chin to close his mouth, but she wasn't rude. And she didn't want to rile him any more than he already was.

"Do I need to go in for questioning?"

"You should. But I don't know if I want my coworkers to hear the tale you have to tell. Necromancers and gold skulls? This is not an episode of Indiana Jones."

"It's not a tale."

"I believe you, Annja. But let's keep the creepy skull stuff for the television show, okay? I'll arrest this guy and match his prints at the scene of the crime. It'll be simple murder and artifact theft, only we haven't got an artifact to prove it."

"I'm working on that."

"You know where it is?"

"I have an idea."

"But you're not going to tell me? Maybe I do need to bring you in for questioning. If only because it'll keep you safe."

"I know the guy who took it," she offered. "Remember I mentioned Garin Braden to you a while back?"

"I remember the name. He helped you out of one of those adventurous, bullet-dodging situations you tend to find yourself in so often. Such as now. You've dodged bullets, and the adventure level is pretty high. He's helping you again?"

"Yes." Not really. "I don't know. Listen, Bart, give me a day to go after him and see what's up."

"Let me come along."

"Too risky."

"Then I'm not letting you go."

Bart tugged handcuffs from his belt. Annja shrugged a shoulder against the warehouse door. "Bart, if you arrest me, you'll have to name me as a suspect."

"It's just protective custody, Annja. I wiped the prints from the nailer."

"You did?" That was risky. He could lose his job if anyone discovered his duplicity.

"Let me do this, Bart. You know I can take care of myself."

"Actually, I don't know that. You've given me the call more times than I can count. And each time I sit wondering, teeth clenched and feeling so ineffectual that I can't help you. This has to stop. I know you've got the self-defense moves, but you're not a superhero, Annja."

"Never said I was."

"So don't do this one on your own. Let me help you."

"I'm not in any danger. Garin wouldn't harm me." Too much. "He's a friend." Not really. But she'd never escape the handcuffs unless she convinced Bart seeking Garin was less perilous than it really was.

Still standing in close proximity, Bart leaned over her. She could smell his aftershave. Rebound girl? What the heck was wrong with that?

"Annja, why do you have to do this? Why is this personal?"

It wasn't personal. She had just been sucked into the adventure.

You get off on the adrenaline rush from it now. You don't hate the responsibility of the sword. You crave it. It's so freakin' personal you can no longer survive without the rush, she thought.

So that was it? She'd become some kind of adrenaline junkie? A nutty archaeologist who sought danger and got off on it?

"I know Professor Danzinger," she offered. "Let me go after Garin. I just want to talk to him before it's too late and he's done something with the skull."

"Where does he live?"

"Here in Manhattan. The cops are almost here. Please, Bart, I'll stay in touch."

He leaned back and tucked the handcuffs in his pocket. "I've had partners I've worried less about."

"I'll check in tomorrow morning. Promise."

"If you don't, I'll be sitting on your doorstep waiting for you."

"Deal."

She kissed his cheek. It wasn't an intimate kiss, but it felt pretty deep. Like some kind of promise she was afraid to keep.

"Talk soon," she said as she ran off.

24

"It's been a long time," Garin said to the skull as he set it on the glass coffee table.

He reclined on the couch. He'd placed the skull with the eye sockets facing away from him. It didn't take a genius to understand that's how the thing worked.

Tilting his head, he smirked to recall Annja's surprise at seeing him wield the skull. Had she thought him so cold-blooded? After his story about fleeing Granada with the thing, she must suspect nothing less.

It would serve to keep the woman on her toes around him. She got far too cocky at times. No reason to reveal his true intentions when her suspicions would keep her respectful.

Garin tapped through the contact numbers in his cell phone. His client expected discretion, and would receive it. He'd not gained a reputation for being trustworthy in the company he kept for no reason.

It was 2:00 a.m. in the country he wanted to call. Garin thought better than waking the client. The news could wait another six hours.

He put up his feet on the coffee table near the skull and closed his eyes. Maybe he'd keep this apartment. It had initially been a place to park while he'd brokered the deal. But he did like this city. It had potential. And Annja lived close by.

"I've so much to learn about you, Annja Creed."

And she had a lot to learn about him.

WHERE WAS SERGE? Annja had thought for sure it would be him to go after the professor for the skull. So if he hadn't tracked the skull to Columbia, then who had?

Serge had been unaware of the sniper, or it hadn't seemed he'd been associated with him. So there was another party involved in this mess Annja knew nothing about.

"Benjamin Ravenscroft," she muttered. "Serge mentioned him, as did Garin. Who is that guy? Is he the guy I'm after? Or was he the thug Bart arrested?"

She would have liked to sit in on the questioning at the police station. But she would do well to stay away from any buildings with bars and cells. Bart was worried about her. She could handle herself fine. She gave Bart a lot of credit for not taking her into custody.

Sighing, she tromped up the stairs from the subway station after taking the train back to Brooklyn.

The first place Serge would probably look for her was her loft. She could go to Garin's apartment and wrestle the skull from him. But right now? The best idea was to regroup and think through her options.

At least she was close to home, on familiar ground. And just far enough from Bart that he would not try to follow her.

Walking the sidewalks before a stretch of family cafés and shops, Annja dug out her cell phone. Tugging her hood over her head kept the wet snow from soaking through, but she would be completely wet in ten minutes or less.

Her first instinct was to call Roux, but she nixed that and instead called Bart. He answered immediately.

"You going to take the guy in for questioning?"

"Yes, but any conversation I have with him will be kept in strictest confidence."

So he wasn't going to bring her in on this one? Was it a means to punish her for not allowing him to help her?

Hell, it was his job; he didn't have to bring her in on anything, she reminded herself.

"I'll give you all the information I have, which isn't much," she said.

"Talk."

"The day I brought the skull to Professor Danzinger I returned home to find a guy waiting for me in my loft."

"Yes, you told me."

"His name is Serge."

"Serge who?"

"Don't have a last name. I think he's Russian, if that helps."

"You know it doesn't. What kind of trouble are you in, Annja? Is this Serge guy after you?"

She looked over her shoulder. "Not this second."

Bart's exhale crept through the phone lines and snapped like a finger thumping her skull. "Annja…"

"I don't mean to make you worry. But it's good to know someone does. Will you call me if you get more info on the perp?"

"Don't use cop words like that, Annja."

"Sorry. The suspect. Also I have another name— Benjamin Ravenscroft."

"Sounds familiar."

"It does?"

"Yeah, but I'm not sure why."

"Is it the guy from the warehouse?"

"We'll know soon enough."

"Talk to you soon, Bart. Thanks."

She turned and walked right into a young African-American guy with loose baggy clothes and enough gold on his fingers to start a bank. "Sorry," she said.

"Chill, pretty lady. Little late for you to be out for a stroll in this weather. Hey, you look familiar. Dude, come here." He gestured to a friend equally clad in gold and enough baggy fabric to outfit a whole gang. And no winter coats or gloves. Kids, Annja thought.

"Who's this chick?" the young man said.

Annja stood oblivious as they puzzled her out. She scanned across the street for a place to sit and have a cup of coffee. Suddenly she needed food and warmth, a place to puzzle out her thoughts.

"It's the chick from that TV show about the monsters."

"Oh, yeah, Kristie something."

"Annja," she corrected. "Kristie is the one with the, well…"

"Right." Both guys beamed with knowing smiles and glanced at her breasts. "We like her, too. But you're the smart one."

Gee, thanks. The smart one all the boys walk a wide path around. The only guy she wished would walk around her was a certain Russian necromancer.

She wondered briefly if they'd seen her nudie picture, but then chastised herself for even thinking of it in that manner. *Her* nudie picture? Mercy.

"Dude, can you sign my shirt?"

He produced a marker from a plastic shopping bag and handed it to her. Tugging out the hem of his Knicks jersey, he held a section tight for her.

Annja sucked in the corner of her lip, pen poised for action. "You're sure you want me to mark up this shirt? This is the Knicks. I so don't rate next to them."

"Hell, yeah, girl!"

She scribbled her signature across the white fabric. Many a time she'd been stopped for an autograph, but this was her first shirt. She was one step away from a rock star. Professor Danzinger would approve.

Would have approved, she corrected herself sadly.

"Thanks, guys. Hey, is the restaurant across the street a good place to eat?"

"You want fast food or a nice sit-down meal?"

"Somewhere in between."

"Then go up a block and check out Granny's. They're open twenty-four hours and the waitresses are always cranky, but their coffee rocks. Thanks, Annja."

She shook their hands and walked on. Behind her the guys slapped palms and shared a triumphant hoot. That made her smile. So what if Kristie had posters? She didn't need no stinkin' poster, just give her a dirty T-shirt and a marker.

Inside the restaurant Annja navigated to a corner booth with the shades drawn over the windows. Depositing her backpack on the opposite seat she climbed into the booth and put her spine to the wall, knees drawn to her chest.

She ordered coffee. A framed black-and-white photograph of Carlo Gambino, the Mafia don, hung on the wall behind her. The glass was cracked, but the autograph looked real.

"Friends in strange places," she muttered, thinking briefly of Garin and his on-again, off-again pseudo friendship with her. He'd hug her, then stab her in the back and sink her in the river wearing cement shoes just like a mobster if given the motivation.

There were half a dozen patrons in the restaurant and the heat blasted like a Sahara wind. It felt great. And the waitress wasn't crabby, as the guys had intimated.

So she sat. Alone. Without the skull.

At least Serge didn't have it. Or Benjamin Ravenscroft. Whoever he is.

But Garin did.

What would he do with such a thing? After his tale of the power it possessed, and watching innocents die in the fifteenth century, she thought for sure he wouldn't want it to again wield such wicked power. And yet he'd brazenly used it against her.

She could have been killed! And Garin could not have known otherwise.

Annja rubbed her hip. Nothing was broken, but she'd find a bruise there later. Probably bruises on her elbows and ribs, too. As well, her wrist still ached, and she was feeling in sorry shape.

But the most vexing question was, why had it worked when held in Garin's hands, and yet the whole time she'd had it…nada?

A sip of coffee confirmed it did indeed rock. Annja crossed her arms over her chest and hunched down farther until the back of her head rested on the torn vinyl booth.

She'd never felt so alone. And she felt it in every ache and cut on her body.

Bart's question tormented her. Why *was* she doing this? Who said she had to save the world? Or, for that matter, one tiny skull. Let the bad guys go at it.

She wanted to go home and crawl between the sheets.

It would be great if someone was at home waiting with arms open to give her a much-needed "you tried your best, kiddo" hug. She'd never had one of those before, but had often imagined what it would be like.

Shaking her head at her thoughts, she sipped coffee. "Not going to happen in this lifetime, Creed. Deal with it."

25

CNN played on the plasma television mounted on the meeting room wall. Well after midnight, Ben wasn't close to leaving the office for the day. It wasn't his turn to tuck in Rachel, so he wasn't bothered by the late hour.

A burgeoning migraine gave no regard to the time, either. He should take his medication. Already he was beginning to see spots before him, gray holes in his vision. Though the TV was on, the sound was off. He couldn't see the newscaster's face unless he blinked. That granted momentary relief from the visual spots.

The crawl across the bottom of the CNN broadcast flashed a breaking news story. Ben squinted to read it. A professor at Columbia University had been found dead. He had taught in the Sociology and Anthropology department and was the rock star of the campus. He had been garroted with a guitar string.

Ben pressed two fingers to his temple and rubbed at the sting pulsing in his head. Was there no end to the ineptitude of those he had chosen to work for him?

"I should have taken care of this myself from the start," he muttered.

But he'd always believed leaving the dirty work to others best. Benjamin Ravenscroft was a known public entity. He couldn't afford a slipup, or to be connected to anything immoral or just plain dirty. Not that he didn't positively drool to get his hands on the inept and smash their faces into a brick wall.

He slammed a fist on the conference table. The force toppled the empty paper cups left behind from his afternoon meeting. Anger bled through his veins, pulsing with each squeezing grip at his temple.

Shoving aside the pile of mail he'd been going through, Ben picked up the letter opener.

The headache gripped more fiercely. He squeezed the thin staff of steel. If he was home, Linda would touch him, ease away the pain.

No longer. Once Linda had nursed his headaches, leading him into the dark bedroom and pressing a cool cloth over his pulsing brow. Gentle touches reassured, made him know that, even though he could not speak for the pain, she was there.

But Linda hadn't touched him since Rachel's diagnosis.

Why couldn't she speak to him in anything less than a scream? She blamed him for all their troubles. For Rachel's sickness. For his headaches. For the maid quitting after the dog bit her. She would blame him for the housing crisis if she could.

He was just trying to take care of his family in the only manner he knew—by hard work, and by investigating all means to curing his daughter.

Ben had to prove to Linda he was not the man she thought he was. He would win back her love, her welcoming smile and gentle touch.

A twinge of red pain struck his temple. Ben cringed, leaning over the table. Gripping the letter opener as if to break it, he was about to stab the stack of officious charity requests when a knock at the door stopped him.

Like a guilty child trying to hide the evidence Ben swung the letter opener behind his back.

He'd never escape the guilt of his own ineptitude. His inability to make the world right for those he loved the most. He could sell *air,* for Christ's sake. But save his own flesh and blood?

"What is it?" he snapped.

Harris stepped inside, pushing the door with a careful hand. "Sorry to bother you so late, boss. There's no one here, so I let myself in. You okay, boss?"

No, he wanted to tear out his brain and slam it against the wall. "Just a headache," Ben said. "Your man finish the job?"

"Er…"

"Apparently he did. I saw the news. So where is it?"

Harris rubbed a palm over his knuckles. A bruise near his left temple looked fresh. "There was a snafu," he said.

"Snafu?"

Ben didn't want to hear this. Yet if the operation was going to fall apart around him, he needed to stop it before it bled out. Had to contain the damage. Like his pulsing migraine, it threatened to explode.

His knuckles tightened about the letter opener.

"The police were called," Harris said. "Jones was arrested."

"You kept my name out of the deal, I expect?"

"Of course, Mr. Ravenscroft. I never use names with my men. But the skull…"

"Let me guess. No skull," Ben snapped sarcastically. "But why should I expect success from you?"

"Jones *had* the skull," Harris began, as always tracking the floor with his gaze. "He called me for pickup, said he was being chased."

"By the police?"

"No, by some woman. Then he was cut off. I didn't get there until the police had arrived. I stayed out of sight while they made the arrest."

Ben stabbed the table with the letter opener. The high-gloss mahogany cracked. Damn his frustrations. "A woman?"

One guess who that might be.

Clinging to the shaft of steel, Ben pressed his free palm to the table's slick surface.

"Would that be Annja Creed?" He could not look at Harris. The gray spots had multiplied. "That same slender bit of a woman who managed to fall from a bridge and *not* die, as you would have me believe. Wonder how she managed to rise from the dead? And then to chase a big fellow like Jones? *And* slip away with the skull?"

"She must be working for Marcus."

"The thief? I don't think so. I tracked their e-mails online. She had no clue who he was or what artifact he had before they met. Despite his duality to me, Cooke was careful not to reveal his identity."

"Maybe Serge…"

"Serge?" Ben swung upright, the letter opener tearing slivers of wood.

"H-he gave me this." Harris tapped his jaw. "He was on the scene, trying to find Creed."

Ben hadn't considered the connection, but it was possible. It would surprise him, though, if Serge had made a friend, and one so gorgeous and famous as Annja Creed.

On the other hand Serge was positively clandestine. All the time. The man could have a harem for all Ben knew.

"So Creed took off with the skull?"

Harris exhaled. "No, some man got it."

"Some man? Not Serge? Not Creed? But some person you don't even have a name for?" He hissed madly. "How many people know about this skull?"

"Sorry, Mr. Ravenscroft." Harris tugged at his tie. "Jones texted me from the warehouse just before the police nabbed him. Said a strange man took off with the skull. He said the skull did something to him."

Tapping the tip of the letter opener against his chin, Ben slid a leg along the table. Tightening his jaw, he closed his eyes. "Did something?"

"It was like a hurricane, but inside the warehouse. The other man held it up, and it blew Jones and the Creed woman from their feet."

This was incredible to learn. So the Skull of Sidon did possess powers. But to give all good things? What good was blowing two people away? And not killing them? Unless it was a good thing to the man who now possessed the skull.

Ben wasn't sure how the skull worked. Perhaps the individual bearer determined exactly what goodness could be reaped from the skull.

"Were they together, do you think? Creed and the other man? Did you get his name?"

"No name, but yes, they were initially together. But I think he left her behind."

"You think?" He looked up at Harris, but his vision was littered by blurry gray spots. Nauseous, Ben winced at the command the migraine had over him.

"I wasn't going to get too close to the warehouse. Cops, remember?"

"And you…lost her?"

"Are you sure you're okay, boss?"

"Yes!" Struggling for breath, Ben spoke rapidly. "You didn't follow the woman?"

"There were cops all over like ants to peanut butter."

"Perhaps she left with the police? Did they take her into custody?"

"Couldn't tell. I was busy getting the hell out of there. Whoa—hey now, boss." Harris flinched as Ben tossed the letter opener in the air, and caught it, wielding it like a blade before him.

The migraine threatened to fell Ben to his knees. Going fetal was always a last resort. And not the image he wished to convey to his man.

"Harris…you're fired."

"But, sir—"

He could not see the man's face at all now. But he didn't need to. Controlled by pain, Ben flinched his tightened muscles.

Thrusting, the letter opener slid neatly into Harris's skull through his nasal cavity. Ben barely had to push.

In his fury, he intended to scramble gray matter. Hadn't the ancient Egyptians done something similar before mummifying their dead?

He slapped a hand over Harris's mouth to silence the scream. Shoving the stuttering man against the wall, Ben pushed hard. Pushing away his own pain. Murdering it.

The letter opener stopped, obviously hitting bone. He twisted and was able to cut the blade through the interior. His entire body pressed along Harris's body; Ben felt the man's muscles contract.

Harris dropped, dragging jelly fingers down the front of Ben's shirt. There was very little blood from the hemorrhaging brain.

Dropping the letter opener on the stack of discarded envelopes, Ben stepped away from the damage. His hip jolted against the meeting table. He let out the breath he'd squeezed back since the weapon had entered the man's nose.

His neck flushed with warmth. He lifted his hands to study them. He saw clearly. No blood, yet his fingers shook. Heartbeats pounded with unrelenting vehemence. He hadn't noticed his heartbeat at all while committing the violence. Now he could not hear beyond it.

What had he done? The headache…it had taken control. He did not—

"I…didn't…"

But he had. He'd killed a man.

It had been so easy. Natural. The pain had transferred from his skull, through his fingers and away from his body.

He tugged his foot from under Harris's leg. Thick fluid oozed out the nose and over the man's parted mouth. The head, tilted forward onto his chest, would keep the blood from dripping onto the floor.

"What the hell?" Ben scrubbed fingers through his hair and tugged hard. It alleviated some muscle tightness. The headache had moved to the back of his scalp, just a dull pulse now. "I…have to get rid of this."

Yes. Think clearly. Beyond the migraine. Now was no time to panic. It was too late for regret.

He must know someone who could take this away. Move the body without anyone noticing. What did they call people like that?

"Cleaners," Ben muttered, shocking himself with the knowledge. He stumbled, tripping over Harris's hand. He caught himself against the boardroom table and pressed his face to it.

Ben exhaled and slumped onto the chair. He collapsed forward, arms folding in and head bowing. A glance over his shoulder checked Harris's face. Still no excess blood. When had his blurred vision dissipated?

There was a man he knew who would know the right people. And it was not Serge.

Ten minutes later Ben had been promised a cleaner would arrive within the hour. Stepping over Harris's body, he dragged the door closed behind him. He had to tug. The body had slumped and blocked the door. Harris's ear bent awkwardly. The door dragged flesh, but finally it closed.

He phoned his secretary at home. "I was thinking," he spoke carefully, molding his words before letting them out, "we'd head for the Jumeirah. I want to relax tonight on some luxurious sheets with room service. How does that sound to you?"

"You spoil me, Ben. Shall I give the hotel a call?"

"Yes. I'll meet you in the lobby in an hour. I've got some tidying up to do here and a last-minute phone call with a client on Tokyo time."

"Shall I order champagne?" Rebecca asked.

Champagne to celebrate his first murder?

"Why the hell not?"

26

Garin strode to the front door and, gripping the handle, for a moment wondered if it would be Annja on the other side. It should be.

Unless she hadn't gotten away from the murderer in the warehouse.

Did the possibility of her injury, or even death, bother him? He allowed regret no more than a flash. Regret was best reserved for opportunities not taken and love. Both things he avoided like the black plague.

"Garin!"

Hand still clutching the doorknob, Garin grimaced at the male voice on the other side. Not Annja, but a man he hadn't seen for months. And he never regretted his absence.

He opened the door and Roux charged through. Looking like a silver-screen star with white hair that clashed with his tan skin and sunglasses perched on his head, Roux marched into the living room where Garin had left the skull on the coffee table.

A rush of anger, trepidation and misplaced admiration

battled within Garin. He hated that he could never sort out his feelings about the man. Usually anger won.

Nothing wrong with that.

Roux snatched the skull with a swift hand. He turned on Garin furiously.

"So this is what you're after now?" the Frenchman said. "I thought I'd seen the last of this thing five centuries ago."

"I'll take that, old man." Garin slapped the bottom of Roux's hand, popping the skull into the air. He snatched the small cranium like a basketball and tucked it against his chest. "What brings you to New York? The European women growing stale for you?"

"I could ask the same of you. You never went in for American women."

"I've always enjoyed women. Any nationality will suit."

"So that's why you've bought this place?" The old man's eyes scanned the room. His expression indicated he was not impressed. "New hunting grounds to stalk?"

"It's a rental. But you didn't come here to inspect the decor or marvel over the great deal I got for it."

"I don't care what you spend your money on. Unless it swipes a sweet deal out from under me. How *did* you manage to win that auction in Brussels? I had two buyers to ensure the Fabergé egg would be mine."

"That was you at the Brussels auction?" Garin chuckled. "I had no idea I was bidding against you. But thanks for telling me. Makes the win all the sweeter."

Roux bristled and cast a glance out the window, down toward the park. He was not here for a pleasant chat. His entire frame was stiff, strung tightly. "Where's Annja?"

In an involuntary attempt not to mirror the man, Garin's shoulders relaxed. He swung out an arm.

"You expect to find her here, in my home? I know you distrust me, Roux, but to suspect that Annja and I—"

"You used her to find that damned necromancer's nightmare, then ditched her, didn't you?"

Garin gave the skull a spinning toss. The slap of it against his palm satisfied. When he'd wielded the skull toward his opponents, it had given him good things—the defeat of the opposition and an ability to escape cleanly.

"It is a sweet little thing." He kissed the skull's overlarge cranium.

"You forget your lessons so easily, Garin."

"And you think everything that happens to a man is a lesson. Some things happen for no other reason than that's what was supposed to be. No lesson. No greater meaning. That's it, Roux. I've got the prize and you don't. So I'll be seeing you."

The old man raised a brow. Over the years they'd developed a balance of power between them neither could ever be satisfied with, but which both tolerated.

Roux sat opposite where Garin stood. He would not be shooed from the premises so easily.

There was no love lost between the two of them. Roux had taken Garin on as an apprentice when he was a teenager. More like slave. Though he'd not been beaten, overmuch. Roux had certainly held the teenage Garin in fear for his life should he disobey a command. His master had been rumored to be a wizard, and that frightened Garin into compliance for a good many years.

Garin had taken escape from Roux at first opportunity.

Fortunately for him, he'd gained immortality *before* that escape.

"Did you take a look at the sword while you were with Annja?" Roux asked.

"I did as it was sweeping threateningly before my eyes.

The woman owns the thing, you know? It's like an extension of her now. It is a wonder to witness."

She was a wonder. Garin had not in his endless lifetime met a woman who intrigued him so thoroughly. She may not be the strongest or even close to devious, but she did embrace every situation the sword led her into with a marvelous gusto.

"And when you could not get her to hand it over to you, you took the skull instead," Roux deduced. "Didn't you learn a lesson the first time we wielded that monstrous thing?"

"That was your mistake, old man."

"There is no wise means to handling that abomination. Unless it's now got an instruction manual?"

"Get over it. I won this fair and square. There was a three-way battle, and I emerged the successor."

"Three?" Roux leaned forward. "Don't tell me the bone conjurer was in the mix."

Garin glanced out the window. He didn't want Roux in on this one. The man would be better to walk away and leave the dangerous bit of cranium to him.

"Well?"

"You asked me not to tell you. Make up your mind, old man."

"You are as old as I, so do not toss about the unremarkable moniker. What did Serge do to Annja?"

"It was not the conjurer but a thug who worked for an unknown entity. Annja didn't have a clue who he was."

But Garin did. He'd yet to meet Benjamin Ravenscroft, but he might before he left New York. Opportunity was rattling at his door, and he was just too curious not to crack it open for a peek. As for his original client, well, a little bidding war always sweetened any deal.

Garin sat and leaned forward. "You make me wonder about your attachment to the woman, Roux. Just when I've begun to think you've a sort of father-daughter thing going on, you surprise me with intense concern for Annja's well-being. Do you love her?"

"You are an idiot, Garin." Roux lunged.

Garin saw the punch coming. He kicked high. His foot connected with Roux's gut. The old man grunted. It was a mere tap.

The skull toppled to the floor as Garin swung a fist. Roux blocked the punch with a forearm to his wrist. It was like an iron bar, his arm. For some reason their immortality kept them strong. It was as if each year hardened them—their muscle, their mien, their minds.

They could go at it like this all day and neither would emerge the successor. Hell, why not? Garin had decades—nay, centuries—of anger to get off his chest against this man.

Barreling his head into Roux's chest, Garin and his nemesis crashed upon the coffee table. The glass cracked, dropping them to the floor in a spray of safety glass.

Garin felt the hard metal shape of a gun against Roux's chest. He dug in and palmed the pistol. Trigger finger curling, he knelt over the man, aiming at his head.

"Go ahead," Roux challenged. "The blood will spatter your white carpeting."

"I care nothing about the decor."

The old man glanced aside. The skull sat out of reach, on its side, just behind a leather chair. The eye sockets faced them. Garin winced. It had to be held to work. He hoped.

"The good things that skull gives," Roux said, "are born of evil."

"Listen to you." Garin stood, his aim still on the man's head. "Aren't you the one who recently obtained the Devil's Jade? That thing is evil incarnate."

"I don't use it, I just admire it," Roux said frankly.

"Yeah? Well I've got some admiring to do with the skull."

"You think it'll get you the sword."

Jaw pulsing, Garin didn't answer. It wasn't right the old man knew so much about him. Of course, you know someone for five_hundred years, eventually you're going to learn all there is to know about them.

But this time he was wrong.

"You think I need a magical skull to get the sword? You know nothing. If I wanted it, I could take it from her."

"No, you can't. The sword belongs to Annja. If she doesn't want you to have it, it's gone. Like that!"

"I have my means."

"Seduction will only get you so far with Annja. She's not your average female. If you don't want the sword, then what?"

"That's my business, old man."

"Don't hurt her," Roux warned. "Not for your benefit."

Garin tilted his head. The accusation he would harm Annja cut to his bones.

Roux kicked his ankle, swiping Garin's balance away and toppling him. Garin's back hit the couch arm. The gun fired.

Blood spattered Garin's face.

27

Serge entered Ben's office. An immediate wash of agony chilled over his flesh. He felt as if worms were crawling across his skin. He'd felt this way once before. The man who had given him the feeling was now in jail, serving life for murder.

"Serge."

He craned his neck left and right to snap away the awful sensation, but it would not leave. Ben sat on the leather chair behind the desk, feet propped up and fingers crossed before his narrow dark eyes.

"You summoned me?"

"Yes, but not for the usual business."

He'd been called in at nine in the morning for this? "I am not indebted to you beyond summoning for your business, Mr. Ravenscroft."

"Yes, yes. Come closer. I simply want to chat with you, my protégé. See how the world is treating you. It's been, what? More than a year since you've come to America. You like the apartment?"

"We had this conversation."

Gritting his teeth against the foul aura spilling off the man, Serge cautioned himself against looking about the room. Always he wanted to remain calm and centered when in Benjamin Ravenscroft's presence.

"True. But we didn't finish it. How is your family getting along?"

The word *family* stabbed Serge in the heart. It was harder to hide that hit. And Benjamin wielded it as expertly as a prizefighter's fist.

"I spoke to my father two weeks ago. He is healthy, as are the rest of my family members. My father sends his thanks to my patron."

"Ah. Well, then, do return my best wishes to them next time you speak. I'm all for keeping the family ties strong. A man isn't whole without family, yes?"

Serge nodded. Since leaving his family he had indeed felt broken. Not whole. But he was making a life of his own. Slowly. Tediously. His father was proud of him. Living in the big city, working for a prestigious client. Serge sent money every other week. It put food on his family's table and clothes on their backs, and allowed his father a little extra to save for the new tractor required to till the land.

He would never allow his family to know the sacrilege he made against the ancient craft he'd been born into. Necromancy was an esteemed art, innate in the practitioner. Once his mother decided Serge's tendency to talk to "the others" was a manifestation of that art, she had him tutored alongside the best necromancer in Odessa.

"And you?" Serge blurted. "How is your family?"

Ben's eyelid twitched. Serge knew family was the man's Achilles' heel. So they shared the same weakness. He needed to show he could deliver the blow as well as Ben. This match would not be won with a knockout, but rather with finesse.

"My family isn't your concern, Serge."

"Just trying to be polite, Mr. Ravenscroft. You don't require my services today, then? Just a friendly chat?"

"Let's shove the bull out the window, shall we?"

Ravenscroft stood. His dark shirt was unbuttoned at the wrists and the cuffs were rolled back. He flipped his medium-length hair from one eye and pressed forward onto his fingers over the desk. "I have become aware of what you want, Serge. And I believe you know what I want, too."

A loaded statement. Serge would be foolish to convince himself Ben was unaware he'd been tracking the skull. Hell, he'd accosted his man last evening. The news probably made it to Ravenscroft before Harris returned to the nest.

He'd been less than careful. Frustrated.

The cards had been laid out. There was still a risk in revealing himself, but he didn't have the skull in hand, and was losing options quickly.

"Why did you arrange to have it brought here?" Serge asked his most desperate questions. "How did you learn of it?"

"That's better. Finally, we're talking."

Ben strolled around and perched on the edge of the desk, crossing his arms over his chest. He lifted the end of a letter opener on the desk, twirled it back and forth, then set it down carefully. "I met the man who owns the artifact a few weeks ago. He showed it to me and explained its legend. Fascinating."

"And you believed in the legend?" Serge asked.

"How could I not? I believe in a man who can commune with the dead, bring great riches to my accounts and annihilate my competition with a mere suggestion. A magical skull? An easy leap. What I want to know is how *you* knew I was having it brought here?"

That he kept tabs on Ben through the spirits was not information he wished to divulge.

Ben nodded. "I suspect you have your ways, yes? It's not prudent to wield control over the man who puts coin in your pocket, Serge. In essence, you've been spying on me."

"Not spying. I am simply…alert to entities that accompany my profession."

"Entities. That's an interesting way of putting it. Spirits spying for you? Have they been following me about? Don't answer. I don't even want to know. It's weird enough when you conjure in the next room. I feel so unclean after you leave."

"Really? More so than now? The skull can mean little to you," Serge offered, containing his tight desperation. "It is not a tool to be used by inexperienced hands. It can bring great calamity as opposed to the goodness it promises. What does it mean to you?"

"Do you know what power that thing possesses, Serge?"

"I do."

Ben leaned forward, giving Serge a look he wagered the man volleyed across the boardroom at his competition. "Then you tell me what you think it can do for me. Let's see if we're on the same page."

No, he wasn't going to give up the goods so easily.

"I'd prefer hearing your rendition of its legendary powers," Serge said carefully. "If you don't mind."

Ben smirked. Leaning backward over the desk, he pulled out the top drawer. Sliding aside the contents, which Serge was unable to see, he then pulled out a single photograph. He waved it before him. "Nice-looking family, Serge."

That damned picture. Taken on the eve Serge had said

goodbye to his mother, father and two sisters. Written on the back were their address, the location of his sisters' schools and the hours his father worked. No doubt, Ben kept copies on encrypted computer files, as well.

That night, in a limo, he'd left with Ben Ravenscroft's valet, who had escorted him to the airport and paid for his flight to the States. To begin a new life. To start a journey that would see him financially sound, and able to support his parents and siblings.

He had been naive and open to Ben's wide-eyed visions for Serge's future. New York was a city that welcomed one and all. Serge would love it. He would have his own apartment, a car, fine things, whatever he desired. Ben would make it happen.

And in return, Serge would pledge his summoning skills completely to Ben. He would help Ben do good things, finance charities, build his business and create jobs for many.

Or so he had been promised.

The smell of wrongful death gushing from Ben's body renewed Serge's determination. He would have that skull, and his liberty from this bastard. His family must be free from Ravenscroft's vicious threats once and for all.

There was a taunting flick of the photo with a finger. "Serge?"

"It is said to be the giver of all good things," he said.

Ben replaced the photo in the desk drawer and closed it with a twist of his wrist.

"*All* good things," Ben recited. "That covers quite a lot, wouldn't you say? A man could do remarkable things with such an object."

"Aren't your charitable contributions satisfying enough?"

Ben stabbed him with a look. "You are in no position to question my motives. Remember your place, boy. I made you. I can break you."

And he could, thanks to the team of watchers Ben had placed close to his family's home. He'd taken an afternoon not long after his arrival in the States to show Serge the satellite photos, some positioned but half a mile from his family's home, others posted in town where his mother shopped and his sisters went to school.

"So we both want the thing. You," Ben said, "I can only imagine for some kind of ritual that would serve your usual conjuring."

Serge nodded. It was a guess he could live with.

"Or not." A tilt of Ben's head focused his devious gaze on Serge. "What does a man who conjures ghosts and demons, a man who can manipulate the wills of normal humans through the concentration of the otherworld, want with the Skull of Sidon?"

"I've no desire for riches."

"Nor do I." At Serge's lift of brow, Ben elaborated, "I have riches already. But you—is it power you desire?"

"No more than I already possess." And yet he never felt more lacking in power than when in Ben's presence.

"Then I am baffled as to your desire for the thing. Yet I know you will not tell me. That is acceptable. But must we battle against each other to finally hold the prize? Why not join forces and share the rewards?"

"The rewards the Skull of Sidon offer would be twisted and vile in your hands, Mr. Ravenscroft. I will not be part of that."

"You don't know me at all, Serge. It saddens me. After all I have done for you and your family." One hand thrust out in a slashing dismissal, Ben sighed. "Just so. To opposite ends of the lists, then, we two. You do realize your victory will see your family destroyed?"

Lifting his head to look upon the wicked piece of human flesh, Serge merely nodded. Then he turned and walked out.

He expected to receive a call from Ravenscroft very soon to occupy him, perhaps keep him from pursuing the skull. But he did not.

If he had the money, he'd fly to the Ukraine to protect his family. As it was, Ben kept a very tight rein on his bank account. He could no more afford to buy a new suit. So he'd find the skull, which meant finding that Creed woman.

And he'd beat Benjamin Ravenscroft to the prize.

28

Something clunked dully like pottery hitting stone. Annja woke from a sound sleep. Was someone digging nearby? She couldn't recall getting to the dig—

Her body slid down the vinyl booth. She slapped her palms on the Formica diner table and dragged herself upright.

No dig. Just a weird dream.

Head woozy with sleep, she yawned and winced at the pull in her back.

"Rise and shine, sweetie."

The waitress who'd served her coffee earlier loitered by the table, hand to one very generous hip. Her pink polyester uniform advertised a dribble of ketchup on the skirt, a splotch of grease at the hip and possibly gravy on the hem.

"I fell asleep? Sorry." Not really. She'd intended to catch a few winks. Heck, what was a twenty-four-hour diner good for, if not that? Rest and…gravy.

"No problem, sweetie."

"What time is it?"

"Four forty-five. My shift ends in fifteen minutes, so I wanted to give you a heads-up. The next gal on duty isn't so kind to let her tables be used as bedrooms."

Annja dug in her pocket, mining for a generous tip.

"One more coffee to wake you up," the waitress suggested in a kindly, mothering tone.

Or what Annja suspected was a mothering tone. She'd never had one of those—a mother. But if given opportunity to design her own, this woman's voice would qualify.

"Maybe I can get some breakfast while you're at it," Annja said. "I promise I won't go back to sleep."

"Eggs over easy and a side of bacon?"

"And pancakes."

"With a dollop of whip cream on top for you, sweetie. Sit tight. I'll be back with coffee."

Dragging a folded wad of bills from her pocket, Annja sorted through the cash. She had enough for breakfast and a great tip. If she intended to play it on the down low she needed more cash. She wasn't sure how safe home would be now that Serge had a death wish for her.

Did he know someone else was after the skull? That some stranger had killed the professor to get his hands on it? He couldn't possibly know Garin had it. So that made her the bone conjurer's only target.

She wondered if he still had pieces of her bone. The notion sent a shiver up her spine.

Rubbing a palm over her forehead to ease out the lingering sleep, she shook her head over her moping. "Way to go, Creed. Feel sorry for yourself much?"

She'd literally curled up in this booth like a scared little girl. Alone? No one to care for her?

"Man, I must have been tired. Time to think through this rationally before the necromancer sends ghosts or demons or whatever it is he conjures after me. What is going on with the Skull of Sidon?"

Dragging a foot across the opposite booth seat, she snagged her backpack and dug out the laptop. She scanned for a wireless network, and waited while it searched the area. It nabbed a connection in twenty seconds.

The waitress dropped off a pot of coffee and promised her breakfast would be out in "two licks."

Annja sipped the hot brew and made the guttural sound men do when they've just been java-slapped awake. Now that was some black coffee.

She glanced around the dining room. One patron leaned over the counter at the front. He didn't seem concerned by her sudden vocalization.

After spiking the black brew with four creams from the melamine dish sitting by the condiments rack, Annja started making notes.

Serge wanted the skull. For some sort of bone-conjuring hullabaloo she probably didn't want too many details on. It would be nasty. Nasty didn't require details. But said nasty would have to wait, because he currently did not have the skull.

On the other hand, Serge's last words to her promised he'd track her down.

That meant big-time nasty.

"Bet I could fend him off with this coffee." She stared into the brew, lightened to a rusty shade by the cream. "This stuff could blind a man after a few cups."

After another sip, she typed Garin Braden's name on the facsimile of a yellow sticky note displayed on the monitor.

Garin has the skull. That's the second time in his five hundred years he's held it. He knows it's bad news. *And* it did some kind of mojo on me and the bad guy while he held it, she thought.

So was that the proof? The skull really was the legendary Skull of Sidon? Capable of providing the holder with all good things?

What exactly did *all good things* imply?

Heck, winning the lottery sounded good to most people. Annja glanced out the window. It was snowing again. A nice warm bed and no bruises sounded like a good thing to her right now.

It would be a very good thing, from Garin's perspective, to have me out of the picture so he could walk away with the skull.

That was what had happened last night.

"But then what would he use it for?"

To take the sword from her? He said he didn't want it. This time. That meant he either wanted something greater only the skull could give him or…he intended to sell it.

From what she knew of Garin the latter was the likeliest. The man did like to make a buck. And not from selling office products or Boy Scout Christmas wreaths. He dealt in arms, art and other things she didn't want to know about. When opportunity knocked, Garin Braden answered—with pistol in hand and a devious grin.

But seriously? The five-hundred-year-old immortal guy just wanted the skull to make a buck?

"I'm missing something. Some integral piece to this baffling puzzle."

She tapped the tracking pad with a forefinger. She eyed the coffee. A few more sips were needed to clear her fuzzy brain.

Where had the skull come from? The thief, Marcus Cooke, had gotten it somewhere. And when she'd scanned the Internet she hadn't found reference to the skull being found on a recent dig.

The last place Garin admitted to seeing it had been in a fifteenth-century alchemist's lab in Granada, Spain. And then it was supposedly dropped down a well in a small village on the outskirts of Granada.

It could have been unearthed centuries ago, or been found in an old chest. Heck, it could have been sitting on some librarian's dusty old shelf for a century, the owner completely unaware of what they held.

It could have turned up at a rummage sale as a decorative item. It sounded absurd, but Annja knew that kind of thing happened all the time. It sent her colleagues over the moon to find out a priceless artifact had been purchased for a dollar fifty at a junk sale on the soccer coach's front lawn.

It had no provenance.

That's not true, she told herself.

Annja typed in the few details she had. She knew it was all conjecture, but it was all she had to go on. *Sidon.* And after that *Maraclea.* And also *necrophilia.*

"Some days, I just don't know. I mean, really? Sex with a dead chick? And the Holy Grail?"

There were so many means to twist the origins of an artifact and its history to resemble the grail legend. Garin's story had been one of many Annja had heard.

It was very easy for an ancient rumor to get attached to an artifact that seemed to fit the bill. If she was going to get behind a grail legend, she preferred the one that indicated the platter bearing John the Baptist's head to Salome. It had a macabre romantic twist she enjoyed.

Annja was more prone to believe that theory than to take the leap into the supernatural.

Not that you haven't had brushes with the supernatural, right? she thought.

She smirked and tapped the tracking pad.

But seriously. A skull born in such a manner?

This would make a great episode of *Chasing History's*

Monsters. Too bad Doug is busy thinking of more humiliating assignments for me, like chasing fairies in Ireland. Or posting computer-enhanced pictures of me online. Nope, I think I'll keep this one to myself.

Not that she had anything to herself at the moment. The skull was blatantly missing from her grasp.

Who was the mysterious party who had hired the thief to get the skull? Could it be Benjamin Ravenscroft? Cooke must have feared him enough to want to hand it over to Annja. Not that he'd intended to *give* it to her. He'd merely wanted her to check it out, see if she could identify it. Likely, if she'd decided it was valuable, he may have turned around and raised his price on the buyer.

Might that buyer have been Garin Braden?

It was all conjecture, but it worked for her.

Could it have been Serge who'd hired Cooke? He was the likeliest buyer. But it didn't explain the sniper, whom Serge had no information about.

A sniper Garin had killed to protect her.

"Looking out for me even as he's pulling the rug out from under me. Such a swell guy," she muttered.

That meant Garin knew about the skull well before she'd laid eyes on it. Had he been tracking Cooke or her?

That so many people knew her whereabouts at any given time disturbed her.

"Time to start looking for new digs. Either that or put a welcome mat with a detonating device at the front door."

She eyed the waitress, who headed toward her table with a plate.

If the sniper was working for the same man who hired Cooke, then why shoot the man who held the skull? Resulting in him possibly losing the skull somewhere in the Gowanus Canal?

It didn't make sense. The missing piece…it had slipped under the rug somewhere.

Annja typed *thief* and *employer,* and highlighted both words.

"Thanksgiving breakfast," the waitress announced as she set down the plate. "You spending the day with family, sweetie?"

"Thanks, yes," Annja said, only to avoid the pitiful head shake she'd get if she'd answered truthfully.

Thanksgiving Day? She'd planned to have turkey TV dinners with Professor Danzinger.

"Anything else I can get you?"

Pulled from a momentary sadness over the professor, Annja shook her head. "No, thank you."

The steam rising from the eggs tempted like no gold-decorated skull could. Annja forked up bacon and eggs. The waitress looked over her shoulder at her vigorous enjoyment, and winked.

While munching toast, Annja decided to check her e-mail. A few more from the archaeology list sent ideas to what the skull was. Only one suggested a Templar artifact, but did not link it to the Skull of Sidon as had the previous e-mail.

"PinkRibbonGirl," Annja said. "The kid had been right. Who'd' a thought?"

She knew Sidon was somewhere in Jerusalem. A quick Google search brought up a map.

"Forty kilometers south of Beirut, the third largest city in Lebanon. Its name means *fishery.* The city suffered a succession of conquerors," she read aloud.

It listed many, including Alexander the Great. After the Romans, the city was sacked by the Saracens, the Mongols and the Turks, successively. The French and the Brits took a stab at it, as well.

"Hmm, the biblical Jezebel was a Sidonian princess. Interesting."

But none of it helped her quest.

"Same as Garin told me. This still means little."

A final e-mail made her pause over her toast.

That picture is so sexy, Annja. But I know it's not you. I mean, come on, I've seen the show. And I've seen you in a sweaty T-shirt on that dig in Africa. Not the same size. Heh.

What was better? Having a man drool or say it's not you because your breasts aren't the right size?

"Mercy, why won't this go away?"

Because someone would have to remove the picture for that to happen. And despite her ability to navigate the Internet and put up Web pages and her own JPEGs, Annja had no idea how to remove something another person had placed online.

Would Doug really have done this? she wondered again.

No.

Maybe. Her producer did have a juvenile sense of humor. And he was known to use deviant means to promote the show.

No.

Annja fired off an e-mail to Doug.

Cannot work under these conditions. Please make the naughty picture go away.

He'd likely laugh, then wonder if it really was her body, but knowing she would never pose nude. Either way, he'd take his time considering the picture, Annja knew that much.

"I may have to suck it up and live with it. I refuse to. I will get it removed. Somehow."

The last e-mail in the queue was from Maxfield Wisdom. The e-mail had come from Europe.

"I don't know you, Mr. Wisdom, but let's see what you have to say."

The man introduced himself by stating he lived in Venice and had inherited many artifacts of great archaeological value from his great-grandfather who was a questing adventurer much like he imagined Annja to be.

Annja smirked. " 'Questing adventurer.' Okay, I like that title. Sounds a lot better than 'that other chick who hosts the show.'" She heard that all too often when in the presence of Kristie's beaming smile and fake assets.

She read on.

You posted pictures of my skull! It has been in the family for generations. It was stolen from my home five days ago. I'm sure it is the one, for the pictures of the gold sutures and the cross detail, and those interior carvings. Are they not unique? I have not seen them clearly but have spent hours tracing my finger along the inside. Fascinating. Do you think they mean anything?

She hadn't opportunity to check the interior map Professor Danzinger had managed to get before his death. Annja dug in her pocket. The flash drive was safe.

She'd finish reading the e-mail before uploading the map.

The skull has been sitting in a dusty box for decades. On occasion, I take it out and detail its crazy legend to visitors. How it is believed to be giver of all good things. I don't believe it myself, Miss Creed. It's never done anything but sit and stare blindly at me. Perhaps it is that I believe I have all good things already?

As did she, really. So if the holder did not want for anything—felt they had good in their life—then the skull remained quiescent? Interesting idea.

Anyway, the last time I had it out was to show it to a visiting friend, Benjamin Ravenscroft.

Annja leaned forward; her toast went untouched.

He was fascinated with the legend. I felt a little odd watching him turn the skull over, tracing his fingers along the gold sutures. He's quite the prominent businessman over in your country, or so he told me.

But you have the skull now, Miss Creed, and I would be grateful for its return. Of course, I'd graciously allow you to keep it for study as long as you wish. I believe, after noting your vigilant efforts to track its owner online, I can trust you with it.

Please instruct me what your plans are for the skull, and we can make arrangements.

"Huh." Annja settled in the booth, the last pancake on her plate drowning in a pool of syrup. "Mystery solved. It belongs to some dude in Venice."

She clicked open the photos he had attached. Three of them, featuring anterior, lateral and inferior view. "That's the same skull, all right."

A skull Mr. Wisdom did not name the Skull of Sidon, yet had detailed the same magical powers the legend spoke of. But if it belonged to his family, then she had every intent of returning it to its rightful owner.

"If I had the thing."

Scanning through the e-mail again, her eyes stopped at the friend's name. "Benjamin Ravenscroft. Why does your name keep coming up in association with this skull?"

It was about time she searched his name.

Forbes was the first site to bring up his name. It had just published its famous lists. Benjamin Ravenscroft was number twenty on the Top-Earning CEOs list. His company, RavensTech, auctioned intangibles and had a huge hand in the burgeoning enterprises in Dubai.

"Intangibles?" Annja was completely out of her element with anything white collar, Wall Street or high-tech.

A click on the CNN site brought up an article published a month earlier about RavensTech's surprising rise to profitability. Who was Benjamin Ravenscroft, it posited? Where had he come from, and why was the world just hearing about him now? The man sold nothing. Or rather, things that could not be held, but only made, designed or promised for some future creation.

Like patents, air and domain names. Air? She read further. The guy started out in college selling air space to cell phone companies. Well, I'll be. I bet he's even sold the Brooklyn Bridge a time or two.

And yet each article about Benjamin and RavensTech also expounded on his charitable contributions. He'd established a foundation for children with bone cancer after his own daughter had been diagnosed. The most recent charity event had been held a month earlier, and had raised 3.2 million dollars. Unfortunately, the disease was a nasty one, and doctors forecast many decades before a cure is in sight.

"Sounds like a likable enough guy. Bummer about his kid."

Annja scrolled through the search engine listing. They were all the same, listing Ravenscroft as the CEO to watch and extolling his charity work.

"And yet he's had his hands on the skull once, when in Venice. Could he be the one who hired Marcus Cooke? Because I don't think Serge did. Although Serge has had his eye on the skull ever since it arrived here, I'm sure. Are Serge and Ravenscroft connected?"

To think on it a few seconds tweaked a muscle at the corner of her eye. Really? Could he possibly? Annja reasoned the mystery behind Ravenscroft's rise could be attributed to one certain bone conjurer.

Why not? He can summon the dead. Why not help a man make millions? Roux had said something about manipulating people and seeing the future. What a dream to see the future stock market.

The article had conjectured about his sudden rise over the past year.

She could go there with the theory. Hell, she was starting to believe a necrophilic liaison produced a skull.

Wonder how long Serge's been in town? I'll have to ask next time we chat. Because she knew she hadn't seen the last of the necromancer, by any means.

Neither Serge nor Benjamin Ravenscroft holds the skull right now. And I think I'd like to keep it that way.

But the option of Garin Braden holding the skull wasn't desirable, either. It belonged to Maxfield Wisdom, and Annja would see it returned to him.

Five minutes later her plate was clean, and she'd downed another cup of coffee. Annja had a plan. "Manhattan, here I come."

29

"You just don't care anymore, Ben! You didn't even come home last night, and Rachel is not feeling well."

Ben rubbed his temple and considered laying his cheek against the cool desktop. Instead, he propped an elbow and caught his head in a palm as he listened to Linda rage over the phone.

"How dare you say I don't care about Rachel?"

"You don't know the meaning of caring, Ben. Starting a charity means little. You're just doing it for the media exposure. You don't even know what Rachel's T-cell counts were the last time she was at the doctor, do you? Do you!"

"I'm doing my damnedest, Linda."

"Well, it's not enough. I can't do this anymore, Ben! I'm tired. I—I can't look Rachel in the eye when she asks me when she's going to be better."

"Linda, put the whiskey back in the cabinet. It's too early in the morning for that nonsense."

"Don't tell me what to do, Ben. You don't get to tell me

what to do since you're not even in this family. I can't do it, Ben!"

It had become Linda's script. She'd call him up after she'd had a few drinks, then rail about her inability to cope.

He was an asshole for hating her slip into drinking. An even bigger asshole for not being able to rush home, wrap her in his arms and promise he'd make everything better.

Ben didn't know how to make things better through normal means. He wasn't wired to be compassionate and offer gentle words of reassurance. He only knew how to get a deal done. And he'd be damned if the skull was going to slip through his hands.

He would make things right for Rachel. No matter who he had to kill.

"You're a bastard, Ben."

The slammed phone surprised him. Nowadays most people couldn't slam the phone anymore. But Linda insisted on using the landline because she thought cell phones caused cancer. She also thought processed food, plastic and anything artificial could do the same—invade your healthy cells and kill you.

Rachel's cancer had seeded Linda's paranoia.

Now Ben did press his face against the cool desk and stretch his arms out above his head. "I'm trying, Rachel," he whispered.

ANNJA SWIPED HER MetroCard and got on the train. The subway car was fairly empty except for a young guy, probably early twenties, with blond dreadlocks who bobbed his head to tunes. He did not look up to acknowledge her; his attention was on a textbook. Annja couldn't see the spine, but it made her smile to see a young man with his head in a book.

Across from him sat an elderly woman, head bowed, snoozing. Annja thought perhaps she was homeless, for the layers of sweaters that bulged out beneath her tattered jacket.

It was early morning, the weekend, so there were no commuters to jockey for position or seats.

Before the doors closed, two men rushed on. Each wore a long dark coat and dark sunglasses. Annja shook her head. The *Matrix* look was so over.

She had a fifteen-minute ride, she estimated.

The car's gentle rumble lured her to close her eyes, but she didn't. She kept one eye glued on the men in black.

She hadn't had much sleep in the diner. What she really wanted to do was to go home and crawl between the sheets. Calling Bart to stop by her loft and give it a once-over would not be a bad idea, but she didn't want to upset him.

Hell, he already knew about the body in the river. And the body in the university.

She smiled. Bart had no idea she was the bearer of Joan of Arc's sword. Telling him something like that might put him over the edge. But he had to wonder about her for the many times she'd called him to help her out of a bind, or to avoid the scene of a crime that may have her fingerprints, or yes, to let him know how the victim had been murdered because she'd witnessed it firsthand.

Good old Bart. He was the best friend a chick could have. It had been a while since they'd paired up for bar trivia. When they teamed no one in the Brooklyn area bars could compete.

But what if they paired for more than that? Like dating? Or sex?

Never work, she told herself. I'd hate to lose a good friend over something like sexual incompatibility. And I can't tell him the truth about the sword. That would really kill him.

"Miss Creed?"

A chill zinged up Annja's spine. The fiberglass seat next to her creaked as one man in black sat next to her. The other loomed over her, clinging to the vertical steel pole extending from floor to ceiling.

She closed her eyes and took a deep breath. This didn't feel right. And she'd learned to trust her intuition. It was rarely wrong.

There was the kid at the end of the car. A sleeping woman. And a few stops between here and Manhattan that might introduce more riders.

"You know me," she said, tilting her head to look directly at the one next to her. "Must have seen me on TV, huh?" Keep it light, Annja. Protect the innocents. "I haven't a pen for autographs…"

The man standing before her slid aside his coat to reveal a knife tucked in a shoulder strap under his arm. She couldn't see the blade. Had to be a big one to secure it that way. "We're not here for an autograph."

"I guessed as much." She planted her feet. The man to her right likely also wielded a knife or pistol. "Can I ask who is so interested in me?"

"He'll tell you when you meet him. He's asked us to escort you to his office."

Did Serge have an office? He'd come after her himself, she felt sure. So that left Benjamin Ravenscroft. Much as she'd like to meet him, the current circumstances offered no appeal.

She had no intention of going anywhere with these thugs. Much as she wanted to know who was behind this, she'd gone one too many times with thugs before, and it never turned out in her favor.

"Think I'll pass," she said.

She stood. The man who'd been sitting also stood. Cornered, she looked at the young man down the way. He was oblivious to anything but his tunes. The woman still slept.

She was right-handed, but in times like this, ambidextrous was the way to go. Annja thrust out her left hand, opening her fingers to receive the sword. She slid it through the air, cutting across the man in front of her. He yelped and grasped a shoulder.

Feeling the icy cut of blade across her right forearm, Annja hissed. She stepped toward the center of the car. The second man approached. His knife glinted with her blood. If he was smart, he should see the futility of his blade versus her three-foot-long battle sword, she thought.

Tossing the sword to her right hand, Annja swung toward the approaching man. He dodged. He was more agile than she expected from such a hefty man. Points for him.

She backed her spine against a pole. Dropping the sword freed both hands. Gripping the pole near her hip, she lifted her legs and kicked. Her hard rubber soles landed against the man's face. He stumbled, and went sprawling backward against the doors.

Red tunnel lights flashed swiftly. The prerecorded conductor's voice announced the next stop.

The other thug had recovered and wasn't about to play stupid. Annja dodged a flying blade. It soared over her head. She followed its trajectory, wincing as it flew just six inches before the reading guy's face. That got his attention. He tugged out his earbuds, and flashed her wide eyes.

"Get to the end of the car!" she shouted at him.

He nodded, and scooped up his book. He left the woman. So long as she stayed asleep she might not become a hazard.

The train stopped, whistles blowing and the doors opened. *Just get out!* she should have yelled. No new passengers entered the train. The doors closed and they jerked into motion again.

Grabbed by the shoulder, Annja swung her free arm, but

her position was wrong. Elbow connecting with steel, she became twisted about the pole. Back to the thug, and the pole before her, she couldn't swing across her body and turn.

Fingers gripped her hair. A vicious shove banged her forehead against the pole. Bright colors flashed behind her left eye.

Mental note: give up pole dancing.

And keep the bad guys away from the innocents.

Annja gripped the pole with both hands and kicked up and back. Someone grabbed her ankle and twisted. Her grip slipped. She landed on the floor of the rumbling car on her back and shoulders. A colorful gum jungle was stuck beneath the plastic seats.

A kick to her hip made her cry out in pain.

With a stretch of her neck she could see the book guy had jumped to stand on his seat. His fists were up, but he was acting out of fear. She hoped he'd stay put and not try to be a hero.

A kick to her side forced her stomach against the steel pole. Another stop was announced and she prayed no new passengers joined the melee.

This was not going the way she planned for it to go. It was time to start swinging blindly and hope for an advantage.

Slapping her palm on the floor, she summoned the sword. It emerged from the otherwhere, the blade stretching along the floor with a glint. She gripped it and swung backward, using the moving train's momentum to strike through fabric, flesh and bone as another kick was aimed for her elbow.

The thug yelped and stumbled backward. The blood spraying the floor told Annja she must have hit an artery. Served him justly for kicking a girl when she was down.

Jumping and landing four feet away from the thugs, Annja put her back to the book guy. The old woman was still sleeping, her head against the window and her lower jaw sagging.

"Stay there," she called to the young man. "I've got things under control."

"That's cool with me, girlfriend." He was too afraid to make a move—to get off the train or to summon help.

Thug number two charged her, knife in hand. Annja leaped to a bright orange seat and, two hands gripping the sword, sliced it across his forearm. Blood flowed, but she hadn't cut too deep. She didn't want to sever any body parts, especially not in front of college boy. Gross anatomy, this was not.

The thug growled at her and tossed the blade to his unwounded hand.

She kicked. He slashed and managed to cut up under her calf. The sudden pain startled her and Annja toppled forward, losing her stand on the seat. She clutched an arm about the pole and swung out wide, coming to a landing in a crouch.

All right, so maybe pole dancing had it advantages.

The thug charged. She swung wide, cutting again through his shoulder and sending him veering left. The arc of her swing was powerful. Annja followed it through, spinning at the waist, and drawing the sword low. She halted its course. The tip stopped just below the college kid's neck. A heavy dreadlock bobbed on the blade.

He squeaked and swallowed.

"Sorry." Annja thrust back her arm, releasing the sword into the otherwhere as she did so.

The train came to a stop. The guy's eyes fluttered. He was ready to faint.

She gripped him by the jacket and helped him to stand. "Let's get you out of here. People are plain unfriendly today, don't you think?"

She steered him over the fallen thug, and shoved him hard to quicken his steps and keep him from looking too closely at the one who bled profusely.

A glance to the sleeping woman startled her. She wasn't sleeping—she was dead. No. Maybe passed out?

Annja knelt on the hard plastic seat next to her. Alcohol fumes wavered off her body and, sure enough, there was a pulse.

"Drunk. But good for you, you missed the show."

"They wanted to kill you," the guy said. "I'll testify. You don't have to worry about a thing."

"Thanks." She patted him on the shoulder. "But I'll be okay."

"What happened to your sword?"

"Sword?" If the kid ever figured out who she was, and remembered the sword, things would not go well for her.

She lifted the book he clung to. "Anthropology? Great career choice. I love an old pile of bones, myself."

"Yeah, I want to be like the chick on TV who works with the FBI. Er, not that I want to be a chick. I mean, I'm a guy."

Annja rubbed a hand across the back of his shoulder. He was scared and shaky. "Why don't you get out of here?" The train rumbled to a stop and the doors opened. "I'll take care of calling the cops. Thanks for being so brave."

He nodded, and smiled, but the smile faded too quickly. "You're not going to stay? With those guys?"

"Leave. Now!" She gave him a shove.

He shuffled off, making a fast line to the stairs, turning once to wave back. But the warning signal pealed, and the doors closed.

With a sigh, Annja tugged out her cell phone.

"Bart is going to flip over this one."

30

Before Annja could knock, Garin's dark mahogany front door swung open. A seething half-naked warrior stood glowering at her.

"Now what," he growled. When he realized she wasn't who he expected, his tense jaw softened. He smoothed a hand down his sculpted abs and hooked his arm along the door. "Annja."

Dragging her eyes down his fine form, Annja had to force her gaze to meet his. "Didn't expect me?"

"Actually, I did. But sooner. Does it always take you an entire day to retaliate?"

"I've been plotting my revenge. That kind of thing takes time."

"I see. Wouldn't want to charge in gangbusters? And yet, I've seen you go gangbuster before."

"I like to mix things up. You going to invite me in or give me the third degree?"

"Come in."

He left her at the door and strode off into the living room.

With a peek down the hallway to where his bedroom was located, Annja listened, waiting—wondering when she'd hear the giggle.

"I'm alone," he called back. "Close the door behind you."

"Right. So, why don't you go put on some clothes and I'll wait in here."

She strolled into the living room, her eyes straying to the window to avoid the real tourist attraction who stood posing before the couch. Bright sunshine had melted most of the snow they'd gotten over the past two days, and it actually felt balmy outside. If you could call twenty degrees balmy.

Garin slowly reclined on the couch, stretching his arms behind his head and propping his feet on the coffee table. Annja expected a cheesy come-on line, but he didn't rise to the prospect.

"Take me or leave me," he growled.

"I could take you much better if you weren't half-naked."

"You're a big girl, Annja. Get over it."

Many scars marked his ribs and abs. A particularly thick one dashed right over his heart. She recalled him mentioning he'd once almost been staked as a vampire. What disturbed her was that there were still people in this world who believed in bloodsuckers enough to go so far as to attempt to stake someone.

"I assume you've come to snatch the skull from me and trundle it off to some dusty old museum?" Garin asked.

"I see you know the script. You could save me the trouble and simply hand it over," she said.

"Can't do that."

"Didn't think so." She gripped her fingers about the semblance of the sword's hilt, but didn't summon it to reality.

"Don't even bother." Garin noticed her grip. If anyone was able to guess what she was thinking, it would be the one man in the world who wanted said sword. "On the other hand, if you want to show me your pretty weapon, I'd like to take a look."

"Not sure there's room on you for another scar."

"You wouldn't get that close, sweetie. Trust me."

"I can throw the thing and stab you."

"Really? Then would it disappear if I tried to pry it from my heart?"

"I think so. But, hey, if you want me to give it a go, we can both learn the answer to that one."

He flashed a mirthless grin at her. "I don't have the skull, Annja. See this?"

He tapped the edge of his jaw. Annja noticed the bruise now. A modena decorated his deeply tanned skin. Funny she hadn't seen that right away. The six-pack abs shouldn't have been that much of a distraction.

Her hopes falling, Annja sighed. "So does that mean Serge has it now? Or did you sell it to the highest bidder?"

"Nada on the Ukrainian. Thought the guy had eaten you for breakfast."

"No, but the man in the warehouse was eager to take a bite. You are the sweetest man, have I ever told you that? Tricking me into helping you track the skull, then abandoning me to the dogs when push comes to shove."

"I couldn't trick you if I tried. You're smarter than that, Super Action Chick."

"Please, no comic-book monikers."

"No? Look at you. Annja Creed, the comic-book heroine. Average unassuming archaeologist by day, supersexy crime fighter by night."

"I have been known to pull out the sword in full daylight."

"All you need is a cape and a tight leather bustier with gold wings or some such emblazoned on it."

"So long as I don't have to do the tights. I don't like tights."

He chuckled and the sound of his relaxed mirth nudged a smile onto Annja's mouth. For two seconds. No more Miss Nice Super Action Chick. This goose chase of musical skulls was getting tedious.

"You could have killed me. You have no idea about the power of the skull. And you had just finished telling me how it had killed dozens of people the first time you held it. Bastard."

"I knew it wouldn't kill you."

"Impossible."

"Intuition."

"Liar."

"Annja, I don't want you dead."

"Yeah? So what, then? Only slightly maimed?"

He looked aside, brushing his jaw with a palm. "You want an apology?"

"No, it could never be genuine." She spoke over his protesting gape, "So who's got the skull?"

"Roux."

That was the last name she'd expected to hear. "What? How the—? He's in town?"

"You didn't know? Here I thought he'd hooked up with you. So the man *is* working by himself. Clever. Should have expected as much from him." He leaned forward, sliding his elbows along his thighs to rest on his bare knees. "I am sorry. But you don't look the worse for wear."

"Seriously? Dozens of two-by-fours fell on my head and body. I bet I've got bruises bigger than yours. My wrist still hurts. And some goons tried to fillet me on the subway as I was coming here."

"Classic Annja Creed. You want me to fix you up? Hey, you're bleeding."

She looked down at her forearm where the knife blade had

skimmed her. Her blue shirt was stained with her blood, but it was dried.

She felt her neck. "That's the second time in two days someone has tried to take me out and missed. It's just a skim. I'm fine."

"Come with me." He gestured for her to follow, but Annja remained where she was.

His back view was spectacular. Scars in plenty, but also wide shoulders capable of balancing a desperate heroine across each side. Not that she was desperate. She didn't need any man to rescue her. Not even from a grave.

"I was almost out," she muttered under her breath. "Didn't need his help."

Garin gestured down the hallway. "No tricks. Promise. At least let me dab on some alcohol and bandage it. You wouldn't want it to get infected. Come, Annja, comic-book heroines need medical attention every once in a while, too."

She resisted with forced stoicism. "Do we have to?"

"Judging from the blood staining your sleeve…" He rubbed a palm thoughtfully over his tight abs. "I think we do."

The bathroom off Garin's bedroom was the size of Annja's entire loft. Marble floors, walls and a huge walk-in glass-tiled shower gleamed. The tub and toilet were black. Very macho. Doorknobs, drawer handles and faucets glittered, and she wasn't sure, but they could be real gold. It was an embarrassment of wealth. But it fit Garin Braden to a T.

"You going to take off your shirt?" he asked with a grin.

She sneered as he sorted through the closet for supplies. "Not in your lifetime."

Sitting the edge of the black claw-foot bathtub, Annja rolled up her sleeve.

"That's a hell of a long time." Garin dabbed the knife wound with a moist cloth.

"As far as you know," she said. "Do you have any proof your immortality wasn't stolen when the sword was put back together? You could be dead tomorrow."

"Come now, Annja, would you wish that on me?"

She wasn't sure. After yesterday he deserved it. No, probably not. Maybe. "No. Ouch!"

"It's more than a skim. You should have stitches."

"No emergency room. I'm a big girl."

"Yeah? But do you possess the comic-book powers of instant healing?"

"Do you?"

"Not instant by a long shot. But faster than the average man. I've got some medical tape in the cabinet. Don't move."

She hung her head and stared at her dirty boots. It seemed sacrilege sitting in this pristine room in her dirty clothes. It was also wrong to be sitting in the enemy's lair. Garin was the enemy. He'd proved that time and again.

And yet, she couldn't resist the offer of kindness, no matter how forced she suspected it must be. What girl could? It annoyed her she wasn't able to just up and leave.

Because when he wasn't backstabbing her, he was romancing her in a weird kind of friendly come-on that intrigued her immensely.

"So what did you find on me when you were snooping yesterday?"

To deny it would just be wrong. "Nothing of interest. I was looking for clues to why you'd want the skull."

"Why not just ask?"

"I did. You gave me the runaround."

Garin bent before her. "Think we'll ever come to accord?"

His heavy male sigh sifted over her hands. Something about a man and his innate scent and just...*being* always made Annja marvel. Men were so...male. No matter their shape, height or penchant toward fisticuffs or bookish avoidance, she did like them.

She needed to consider making time for dating once in a while. Just so she didn't forget the easy comfort of a man's presence. And sex. Nothing wrong with sex.

But not with this man.

Garin's muscled body blocked the light, and Annja did not look up because that would put her eye level to his bare pecs.

"Do you want that?" she asked. "Peace between us?"

"Not sure. It's amusing, the clash of wills and the quest for things we don't have and perhaps never will have, don't you think?"

"Depends on who's getting hurt in the process."

Now she did allow a look over his stomach. Her gaze landed on his hip. "That one's huge," she said.

"Why, thank you."

She chuffed. "You know I'm not looking that low. That scar. How'd you get it?"

He tilted his torso, which tugged at the white flesh as thick as a night crawler that crossed from his side and to the center of his chest. "Almost lost my spleen that time. Not that I knew what a spleen was back then. It was one of many adventures Roux and I barely escaped by the skin of our teeth. Good times."

Resisting the urge to touch the scar, Annja nodded. The man might like to extol the many ways he despised Roux, but when he spoke of their adventures reverence and respect tainted his voice. They were alike. In fact, the only two of their kind in this world. They needed each other more than they would ever admit.

"You must have been laid out a while from the wound," she said.

"A couple of days. You can't imagine my wonder, in those early days after Joan's death, over my own ability to survive what should have been fatal wounds. Roux and I hadn't yet figured out we were immortal. That would take surviving the entire fifteenth century before we finally wrapped our brains around that reality."

"I suppose when one gains immortality—unless they're specifically told, and given the instruction manual—it is a wacky surprise."

"Exactly. Wacky. But good, you know?"

"I don't know. Don't think I would ever take immortality if it was offered."

"Oh, you would, Annja."

No, she was sure she wouldn't. But she'd allow Garin the fantasy of being right this time. Skeptic that she was, she still found it hard to wrap her head around the living five hundred years thing. It would be a gift. It would be a nightmare. She was perfectly happy with eight or nine decades, thank you very much.

"You really don't want it for yourself?" she tried. "The skull."

"Nope."

"Then you intend to sell it."

"Assumption."

"But correct."

"Annja, would you believe I think the thing needs to be dropped down another well, and this time covered over with thirty feet of cement?"

"Not sure. Gotta think that one over."

"You do that."

His fingers tugged at the wound as he placed the tape over it. The smell of antiseptic cut through her brain and in its wake Garin's aftershave wavered. The spicy scent curled her toes.

"You can touch," he commented.

"Wh-what?"

"You've been eyeing my abs since you walked in, sweetheart. Go ahead, touch. I won't break."

"That's it." Annja paced over to the vanity, hand to her hip.

The nerve of him to suggest she wanted—whatever. So she was getting a little soft and melty around the guy. Time to get back to business.

"You said Roux has it? Where's he staying?"

"Haven't a clue." Garin dropped a wad of bloodied gauze into the sink. "Would you like to join me for lunch? Griggs is preparing haddock and asparagus."

Food sounded divine. And Annja knew Griggs was an amazing chef from previous meals. But she'd had breakfast. And she'd had enough of Mr. Poser here.

"No, I'm finished with you."

She marched from the room, making damn sure she didn't call out any apologies for her abrupt departure, or thank him for the medical attention.

Women could be like that sometimes. Worried about offending someone or acting aggressively. She wasn't like most women. Garin knew that. He probably enjoyed their little tête-à-têtes.

Just as much as she did.

31

"You say the skull isn't in hand? How can I trust you even know where it is?" Ben tapped the corner of his phone on his thigh. How the caller had gotten his number disturbed him, but he wasn't about to admit that.

"My associate has it," the gruff male voice said. He'd said his name was Braden. That's all. Ben didn't know if that was a first or last name. "She's a professional when it comes to handling artifacts."

She, huh? Annja Creed's image popped into his mind. Could he be so lucky to be pulled back into the search for the skull with a simple phone call?

But he wasn't willing to shell out the amount of money Braden was asking for. Five hundred thousand wasn't chump change. And Ben felt sure he could get the thing for nothing now he knew that Annja Creed held it.

"I'm interested," he said.

"Great. I've got another bidder who wishes opportunity to match bids."

"I'll go as high as is necessary," Ben offered. It wasn't true, but Braden didn't have to know that.

"I'll be in contact soon, Mr. Ravenscroft." The phone clicked off.

Ben hit a speed-dial number.

SERGE RETURNED to the warehouse where Annja Creed and the man he did not know had been with the Skull of Sidon. The police had arrested the man. He'd been working for Harris, which meant he was one of Ravenscroft's employees. He had to track the skull before Ben got to it.

He hadn't been able to track Creed from the warehouse, and she hadn't returned to her loft. He'd headed home to obtain his supplies. This setback was not acceptable.

To be safe, he'd left his cell phone in the car. The frequency of Ben's calls of late did not bode well for Serge's concentration. The man suspected something but Ben could not possibly know why Serge sought the skull.

Yet he hadn't anticipated Annja Creed. An archaeologist? What stakes did she have in obtaining the skull? Unless she also sold artifacts to finance—*what,* Serge did not know. Her loft had been nice enough, but far from richly furnished. The woman must make money from her television appearances. Why would she need to sell artifacts?

Unless she had a drug habit or an expensive vice Serge could not know about. The woman appeared in control of her faculties.

"No, not drugs," he muttered as he walked inside the warehouse.

The extreme scent of cut wood overwhelmed the latent tendrils of arsenic likely used to preserve the wood. There were many footprints in the lumber dust on the floor. Difficult to determine a specific track, or if one might be a woman's footprint.

Serge wandered about until he found an upset tangle of two-by-fours, and what looked like signs of struggle. Attuned to the world and the energies left behind by its inhabitants, he sensed the lingering whisper of…

Power.

The skull had been in this warehouse. He knew it.

He knelt and emptied his pockets onto one of the boards. He didn't have the proper substance to mark a circle, but in a pinch, anything would do. Shuffling up a pile of sawdust, he then leaned over the small dune and blew it out evenly over the concrete floor. With his forefinger, he drew a circle large enough to sit inside.

He tapped the vial of bone powder remaining from the sample he'd taken from Annja Creed out onto the board, spreading it into a fine circle with a fingertip.

Picking up a lighter from the contents of his pocket he waved the flame over the crushed bone fragments until the bits began to smolder. They would not light to flame—bone required high heat to burn—but would instead simmer to a hard black coal.

Leaning over the smoking bone, Serge drew in the scent. Humming deep in his throat he began the low droning that would center him and push away the world. He must focus to connect. The souls he could contact would read the bone and tell him all he required to track Creed.

An icy trickle scurried down his forearm. Touched by the otherworld. A presence had arrived.

Communicating was achieved through a high keening he altered in tones. He was about to ask after the Creed woman when he choked on the smoke—and rocked onto the heels of his hands. His mind fuzzed over with the scent of burned bone and the clatter of cars rushing by outside.

This wasn't right. What had brought him out from the trance?

He winced as another twinge attacked his temple. Was it the souls? Had he asked too much?

"Damn it." He fought to lean over the smoking bone, to concentrate on drawing in the essence, but the summons would only increase until it became unbearable.

The spirits no longer wished to communicate about Annja Creed. Interesting. It was as if they held back information about her. Or did not deem him worthy of knowing.

Serge returned to his car and slid inside, but didn't start the engine. The phone rang.

He picked it up, and didn't say a word.

"We need to talk," Ben said.

32

Serge stood in the center of Ben's office.

Ravenscroft strode before him. He'd removed the pinstriped suit coat and rolled up his crisp white shirtsleeves to reveal tanned forearms. The diamond Rolex must have put him out tens of thousands of dollars. Likely thanks to Serge's conjuring.

"It's not working, Serge. We're both going after something the other wants, and neither is having much luck in nabbing it. We really do need to join forces."

"Why do you want the skull when you can have all that you wish through my summonings?"

Ben smirked. "Serge, you surprise me. You've refused me the only desire that means anything to me."

"I've told you I do not have the power to give or take life!"

"She's already alive," Ben hissed. Curling his fingers into fists, he said, "You simply need to ensure that remains the case."

If he could, Serge would move worlds to save the little

girl's life. Ben had told him about his daughter's disease months earlier. She was dying from the bone cancer that had invaded her skull. Ben wanted Serge to make her new again, not sick, but free from the disease.

Serge had gone home that day and attempted to channel the spirits to ask for the girl's life. It wasn't so simple as that. The disease had come from the chemicals man put into this world. The spirit world could no more stop her death than medical science could.

And though he could speak to the dead, summon them to his bidding and learn about the future from them, the dead did not bring others to their realm, nor did they refuse those destined there.

If some had suffered due to the summonings Serge had performed for Ben it was because Ben had tainted the information Serge provided and caused it to happen. Serge's hands were clean.

Yet he could not erase the blackness association with Ben had seared upon his soul.

He would do nothing for this man he was not forced to do.

"Ask me for anything but life and death," Serge said quietly. "I am yours to command, as you have seen to exact the bonds about me."

"So dramatic, Serge. Dance about your fancy words but avoid my daughter's dying soul? When she's dead will you then offer to summon her for me? What am I do to with my dead daughter's soul? You bastard!"

Ben lunged and punched him in the chest. Serge allowed the man to beat upon him. His punches were ineffectual, and hurt his pride more than his flesh and bone. He could not move away. He would not. The dark demons inside Benjamin Ravenscroft needed an outlet. They needed to push fists into another man's flesh and pound at his bones. A small justice for his dying daughter.

A wicked backhand across his jaw snapped Serge's head smartly.

"Fight, you idiot!" Ben stalked off, rubbing his bruised fists. "Have you no mettle?" He leaned over the desk, snatching the burning cigarette and taking a drag from it. The scent of cloves infused the air.

"I merely wish my freedom, Mr. Ravenscroft."

"Freedom?" He gasped on his inhale like an addict fighting to hold in the smoke. "Is that what you believe the skull will give you? You don't like working for me, Serge?"

"I do not like the results of our association. Your heart is black."

"My heart?" He rapped his chest with a fist. "My heart? You! You are the necromancer. You dally with dead souls every day."

"It is not a black magic unless the conjurer makes it so."

"Ah? So it is me who has twisted you?" Ben sucked in another long drag, his back to Serge. A flick of the thin brown cigarette sent ash particles to the marble floor. "Always someone else's fault. It's my fault Rachel's sick, you know." He glanced over a shoulder at Serge. "My wife blames me. Me? How is that possible? I only lost sight of her a few minutes that day in the park. Getting lost does not induce cancer. It's not fair. It's just…not fair."

Serge sensed exhaustion purl from the man in waves.

Lauded by his peers, Ben had achieved much in the past year of their alliance. Serge had read the headlines at the newsstands. Benjamin Ravenscroft was a futurist and a philanthropist of the highest order, they claimed.

But in the time of their association, Ben's family had suffered from his misdirected greed. While Serge knew the girl's disease was not caused by her father's neglect, he was aware of Ben's affair with the secretary. No man should treat his wife so cruelly.

Karma had a way of slapping the most deserving.

Serge had compassion for the Ravenscroft family. But not so much for Ben.

"Very well." Ben approached, his hands at his hips. "I've got a bargain for you."

Serge let out a breath. A devil's bargain, surely. He did not wager in evil. At least, he tried to avoid it.

"Your freedom for my daughter's life."

All he wanted was freedom. But the man did not understand!

Serge shook his head. "That is impossible, I have already explained…"

"Listen, necromancer," Ben said sharply. The sweet spice waved before Serge as the man slashed the cigarette through the air. "The skull is yours after I've had my go at it. I get my daughter's life, then you can have your freedom. You just need to put the skull into my hands."

The man's logic was fractured. If Serge got to the point where he could put the skull into Ben's hands, there was no way in hell it would happen. He'd be long gone from New York City before then.

"You double-cross me," Ben added with a dagger glare, "your family dies."

Serge had no doubt a phone call is all it would take for them to die. Cruelly. Likely gunned down in front of one another.

Damned, he was bound to serve this man!

But could he trust when the skull was obtained, and handed over to Ben, his wicked employer would then hand it over to him?

Erratic heartbeats pleaded with him to rationalize, not jump, into any traps. Once he'd trusted this man, and look where that had got him.

"I must have more than your word," Serge said.

"But you do. You, Serge, have my truths." Ben looked up at him through a fringe of dark bangs. "If I try to swindle the prize from you, then you can go to the media and tell them all about Ben Ravenscroft's dealings with the spirit world to get to where he is today."

How stupid did the man think him? He may have come from an impoverished country, but he wasn't naive. Go to the media? That would go over like a lead balloon. Serge could see himself being wrangled into a straitjacket and carted off while Ben stood atop his marble empire laughing all the way to hell.

And with the skull in hand, who was to say Ben wouldn't be able to kill Serge with it? No one knew the skull's true power. It gave all good things. That covered quite a lot of ground. And he felt sure the Skull of Sidon—unlike him—had the power to give and take life.

"You're thinking too much, Serge," Ben said slyly. "Take the deal. I only want that one thing. You've already put me on the top. Where else have I to go?" Spreading his arms like a deity, Ben mastered his empire. "I'm here. The hottest young CEO in New York City on a meteoric rise to the top. No one can touch me. I've got the world at my fingertips."

"At the sacrifice of your family."

Ben slapped a hand on Serge's shoulder. "Worry about your own family, man."

Serge tried to move away. He could not. It stunned him. Ben's grip, not so tight, but more a heavy weight warning of his future, did not relent.

If he had known a year earlier that Benjamin Ravenscroft

had more in mind than taking a simple man to America and helping him start a new life, Serge never would have followed. But the carrot Ben had offered—money to support his family—had been impossible to resist.

Just a few conjurings, Ben had promised. He'd wanted to improve his life, perhaps start a few charity foundations. All good, he'd said encouragingly.

He'd asked Serge to summon the best means to funnel research dollars to hospitals and medical organizations. The spirit world had eagerly complied. While Serge did not understand the stock market, he received stock tips that had tripled Ben's charitable investments.

Soon after, Ben had started calling Serge in weekly to look at the stock market. To enhance his business. One couldn't front a huge philanthropic movement without the business success to back it up. The spirits had complied, and Ben's knowledge for what intangibles were going to bring in the biggest returns grew.

Within months Serge began taking the subway to Ravens-Tech daily. Ben kept him busy. The spirits gleefully obeyed. And Serge realized instead of garnering a good life and business contacts, he was journeying farther away from his pursuits and into evil.

"We work together, then." Serge finally surrendered.

"Good! So where's the woman? Annja Creed. She's our target. You have a fix on her?"

"I know where she lives."

"Excellent. We'll search her place—"

"I've already done so. She doesn't have the skull. There's another man who has obtained it. I don't know who he is."

"But he knows Creed?"

"I believe so, yes."

"Then that's where we start. Take me to her."

"Very well, Mr. Ravenscroft."

"Just so you know—" Ben eyed Serge's fist "—I've got a contact who checks in with me on the hour. If I do not respond your family is dead."

ANNJA WALKED THROUGH her open front door. This time she was not surprised it was open. Summoning the sword to hand, she called out.

A dark-haired man popped his head out from the kitchen. He set the open box of cereal on the table behind him and offered her a smile.

"Your housekeeping skills leave much to be desired, Miss Creed," he commented. Stepping carefully over a toppled pile of research books, he waved dismissively at the sword. "You won't need that. I come in peace."

"I've heard that line before."

A fashionable five-o'clock shadow stubbled his jaw. His dark complexion was probably a tan. Gold and diamonds flickered at his cuffs and fingers. He wasn't ugly or villainous. Rather attractive, moreso than his pictures online. She could sense he wielded charm as a means to get what he wanted.

"Why has my home become the revolving meeting place for Thugs of America?" she asked.

"Oh, that's rich. You been having trouble with security? There are protection systems you can get for that. And really, I must protest. I'm not a thug. Serge showed me here."

"The guy is giving tours of my home? I gotta get a new profession."

"I'm Benjamin Ravenscroft."

"I know," she said.

Serge had lured the most elusive member of her gang of skull chasers right to her. Ravenscroft didn't appear too threatening. The business suit he wore must have set him back a few Gs. And she'd bet that was a manicure. He smelled…expensive, and looked as though he'd just stepped off the cover of a business magazine.

But Annja wouldn't let down her guard.

"We need to talk," Ben said.

"Let me guess. You and Serge are working together?"

"In essence."

"Didn't sound like he was on your side when I last spoke to him."

"We work together on various levels. We've recently joined forces on a pressing matter. Do sit down. And please set the sword aside. Nice. Don't often see women wielding swords in New York unless it's in the theater district. Hey, I caught your show the other night. It was the Transylvania one. I sure as hell hope they pay you for those nonsense forays."

"I don't like the feeling I'm getting about you."

"Huh. I like you," he offered with a shrug. "You fascinate me, Miss Creed."

"Can we cut the small talk? What do you want?"

"You know what I want."

What everyone else wanted.

"Haven't got it," she said.

"But you know who has it. I spoke to him earlier. A friend named Braden has been in touch with me."

That information didn't surprise Annja as much as she thought it should. It was further proof Garin was in this one for the money. And obviously tracking the highest bidder. So he had the skull, after all.

Ridding the world of it? Yeah, right.

"Whatever he says he has," Annja said, "he doesn't."

"For some reason I believe you. This disappoints, then. I

had thought the man was at least telling the truth about his associate having the skull. That associate, I assumed, being you."

She was Garin's associate now? Man, did she need to put that guy's head straight.

"Why do you want the skull?" Annja asked.

Ben spread his arms and stated plainly, "It has the power of God, yes?"

"I haven't heard it termed in quite that manner, but I suppose one could go there. I've come to learn most villains won't waste their time for anything less than godlike power."

"Villain? Annja, you hardly know me, and yet you label me so viciously."

"Yeah, well, if the shoe fits." She glanced to his leather loafers. She couldn't even make a guess how much they'd cost.

"Such power could come in handy," Ben casually tossed out. "Haven't you ever wondered what you would want if granted all good things?"

"Nope. Not going there, either. Seems like your life is going well enough to judge from the magazine articles touting your riches and philanthropy. As well, you employ a necromancer to see you get anything you desire. So I don't get it. Why do you want more power?"

"You have family, Annja?"

Sighing heavily, Annja maintained her grip on the sword, but fought against rolling her eyes. And why was that? Why did the family question prick at her like that? She had a great family—of friends.

"No," she said.

"Some don't." Ben shrugged. "It's the way of the world. But it also leads me to believe you'd never understand my motives. I'm not going to get into the greater meaning behind my quest with you. It's not worth the effort, especially when I'm not particularly pleased staring at your weapon."

"Girl's gotta protect herself."

"I'll grant you that. Perhaps I need to stick around while you wait to meet with Maxfield Wisdom?"

The man knew far too much. And Annja was tired of having her private property trespassed on. She swung the sword. Drawing the blade tip along the buttons punctuating Ben's suit coat, she tapped him roughly under the chin with the flat side of the steel.

"Get out of my home, Ravenscroft."

"You're not going to kill me."

"No, but I am in the mood to poke someone. Do you have any idea how many times my home has been broken into lately?"

"I am only aware of myself and Serge visiting."

"Visiting? Leave, or I'm calling the cops. I've a direct line to a detective who can be here in minutes. Are you willing to have me introduce the two of you?"

"No need to involve the police." He stepped backward toward the door, arms raised and hands splayed. His attitude changed from arrogant nonchalance to guarded. "I don't need to be here to keep tabs on you. And I'm guessing my resources for obtaining the prize are greater than yours." He nodded. "Good day, Miss Creed. Despite the rude treatment, it was a genuine pleasure to meet a celebrity of your stature."

He left swiftly. Annja clasped the sword with both hands and whisked it through the air.

"You might have the resources, Ravenscroft, but you don't have the skull."

For that matter, who did have it?

33

A few more swishes of blade served to slice the steam from her tension. It had been weeks since Annja had practiced the swordplay exercises Roux had taught her. Confidence arrived when the hilt fit into her grip. She knew how to lunge, thrust, riposte, dodge and down-and-dirty go-for-the-arteries with it. Practice kept her muscles toned, as well, her mind strong.

Deciding an impromptu practice session was just the thing, Annja lunged at the curtains and almost severed them when the doorbell rang.

"Bad guy back so soon?" It had been ten minutes since he'd left. "Must have forgotten the departing wicked laughter and evil rubbing of his fists."

Sword in hand, she answered the door to someone she wasn't sure she was happy to see. "Haven't seen you in a while, stranger."

"And you greet me in such a manner?"

Roux waited for her to step back before entering. He smiled at her ready position, which was so strange Annja finally realized she stood, elbow up and blade angled in preparation to behead the man.

She thrust out her right arm, opening her fingers with dramatic flare. The sword vanished.

"That never ceases to amaze me," Roux said.

Same with her. That's why she did it.

"Garin said the two of you had a grand reunion."

"Always a pleasure to spend time with the man."

"Liar."

"Yes, well." He turned his head to reveal a dash of red through his brilliant white hair.

"Is that blood?" Forgetting her need to remain distant, Annja touched the wound just above his ear.

"From a bullet."

"Garin tried to kill you?"

"You say that with such surprise, when you know it's not the first time. No, he just wanted to piss me off. He succeeded."

"Let me take care of it."

"It's an abrasion. I've already cleaned it."

"I thought you liked it when women fussed over you?"

"Certainly, it is a pleasure one mustn't refuse. But I suggest we hold this conversation elsewhere."

She followed his gesture. A small camera LED blinked in the corner, above the curtain rod. Not something she had put there.

"There's one in the hallway, too. To judge from your surprise, I assume that's not your security system?"

"What security system?" Ravenscroft must have planted it. He had said something about not needing to be near her to track her. And that Roux had noticed it immediately and she had not annoyed her. "I need to have a conversation with my landlord. He'll obviously let anyone into the building."

Annja summoned up the sword and used it to pop the

camera out from the wall. She let it drop to the floor, which didn't break the hard black plastic shell. A stomp of her foot put the LED to rest.

"Come on." She propped the blade against a shoulder, picked up her backpack and wearily gestured toward the door. "I'll sweep the hallway and stairwell on the way down."

They shuffled down the stairs and headed to the sidewalk. Annja gestured they walk north. She surveyed the building soffet but didn't spot other cameras.

Technology sucked when it was used against her. What did Ben think to gain by spying on her? He'd thought to have the upper hand in locating the skull, so why bother with her anymore?

He'd also mentioned Maxfield Wisdom. Not good. She should contact him, and soon, but there was little she could offer him without the skull in hand.

"So to what do I owe the pleasure? If you came from Garin's place, then you must know he has the skull."

"He did."

"Did?" Roux's pale blue eyes glinted marvelously. "So he wasn't lying! You've got it now?"

"Indeed, I do."

"So what now?" she asked as Roux matched her brisk pace. "You have plans to rule the world?"

"Not interested in that job. Could you imagine? It would tax a man something terrible. The pay would be horrendous. No days off, either, I'd wager."

Good old Roux. And yet, if he held the skull she wasn't going to fall for any sweet-talking diversions.

Like she had for Garin's flirtations?

"It's yours," he said as they waited at a street corner for a green light. Snow fell like pillow down, melting on the black leather shoulders of Roux's coat.

"I know in your hands, Annja, the abominable thing will find a proper resting place. Believe it or not, there are some valued treasures in this world I'd rather not obtain. But if I hand it over to you, I must be guaranteed it will be disposed of properly. Do you have any idea what you'll do with it?"

"I've located the skull's owner. It will be returned to him."

"I'd prefer the bottom of the ocean, but I suppose I've no choice in this matter, right?"

"You do until you hand it over. But you know, Garin said the same thing about wanting to get rid of it. I didn't much believe him, either."

"He was lying."

"And you're not?"

"Cross my heart. Garin wants to sell it."

"I know that now. I believe his buyer was the one who planted the camera in my loft."

"And here I thought you were suddenly into kink."

Annja dropped her jaw and gave him a soft punch. "Watch it, old man. I have a sword and I know how to use it."

"Sorry, couldn't resist the humor."

"No offense taken. I know between the two of us, if there's any pornographic footage out there it's not going to feature me."

And yet that awful doctored picture of her was currently flashed for all to see online.

Don't throw stones, Annja. Because someone will toss one back, she reminded herself.

"Where is it?"

"In my car. Which is parked the opposite direction we are walking."

Annja stopped in the middle of the intersection. People brushed past them, swearing and muttering about how rude they were. "Why didn't you say something?"

"I thought you were the one with the plan." He spread out his arms and smiled, which reached his blue eyes with a glint. "Lunch?"

The light changed and cars honked. Annja strode back the way they had come. Roux followed cooperatively.

"I'm not hungry. Yes, I am. I don't know. I'm getting very tired of this 'who's got the skull' game. It's like a round of hot potato, and I never did like that game. I mean, why a potato? And why were we supposed to imagine it hot? And if you don't have it in hand, then I don't trust that means you'll keep it in hand. Let's make sure the thing is where you say it is, then we'll talk food."

Roux flipped open his cell phone and punched one number. He spoke to his driver and then to Annja. "Wait here. It'll be a minute."

When the limo pulled up, Roux said, "It's in the trunk."

"Let's take a look."

"We're blocking traffic."

"I don't care. Driver, pop the trunk."

Amidst a stream of honking, swerving cars, Annja went around and peeked inside the trunk. Wrapped within a blue silk shirt she suspected cost more than her monthly rent, she found the skull.

Parting the silk and drawing it out, she examined it. For all the exchange of hands it had made the past few days, it was still in good shape. The gold sutures were tight and it didn't appear as if the bone had been chipped.

She tapped the forehead. Giver of all good things?

"Wonder why it doesn't do anything biblical for me, like part that damned canal the other night after I'd fallen into it? Isn't it supposed to do good things for the holder?"

"So I've been told." Roux peered over her shoulder.

His presence blocked the feeble November sunlight. Was

it so wrong to think of him as a father figure? A very frustrating, backstabbing, opportunistic father—but still.

"You didn't give it a try? See if it works?" she wondered.

"No interest. At least, not in this century."

"Garin told me about Granada."

"Surprising. The man doesn't often tell tales of our past. I was foolish then. I'm much more careful about the occult artifacts I seek nowadays. I suspect it doesn't work if the holder is already a bearer of good things," he added. "You do live a good life, Annja."

"Not so good as yours."

"Wealth and prestige may look good on the outside…" He didn't finish the thought. Instead, Roux opened the limo's back door. "Hop inside. The weather is turning nasty."

Tucking the skull to her, Annja slammed the trunk and slid inside the warmth of the limo. Roux offered wine, but she refused. She was still riding the buzz from this morning's coffee. That stuff had been high octane.

"You think we could go to the drive-through? I'd kill for a burger."

Roux scoffed.

"What is it with you immortals? It's not like a little artery-hardening grease is going to knock you off. Up three blocks, driver, and turn left."

The driver complied, and Annja cast Roux a winning smirk.

Only when she was situated with her bacon double cheeseburger did she strike up a conversation with her annoyed cohort.

"So, you flew here from France? Must have been worried about me, huh? And yet, you first went to Garin. Not feeling the love much here, Roux."

"I initially stopped by your loft. You weren't in residence. Garin's place was my next guess. I did get the skull back for you. And I've yet to hear a thank-you."

"Thank you. Innocence worldwide thanks you. I think. I'm still not overly convinced of its power. Could have been a fluke at the warehouse."

"What fluke? You saw the skull working?"

"Garin wielded it against the thug and me. It released a tremendous wind that pushed us back and, well, took us out. He escaped while we were barraged by lumber."

"The fool. Despite his protest to the contrary, he hasn't learned a thing from when we first held that damned skull."

"Oh, he has. Things like how to make a buck and trick your friends while trying."

"Friends? You and Garin are getting close, I see."

"Best buds." She crossed her fingers, then shook her head. "Please."

Annja was aware Garin used their flirtations as bait against Roux on occasion. She didn't like it. And it surprised her that it did get a rise out of Roux.

Her burger box was gone. When had she sucked it down? She should have ordered a large vanilla shake, too.

"Tell me about this bone conjurer," she said, crumpling the bag and tossing it to land the front passenger seat.

Roux gave her an admonishing shake of head.

"Sue me." She stretched out a leg across the center divider on the floor and nestled into her corner of the seat, arms crossed. "You and Garin were pretty freaked to hear about Serge. So what am I dealing with?"

"The necromancer is very powerful. He summons the dead to control the living."

"Ghosts?"

Roux shrugged. "I've never attempted the practice myself, but I assume that's what you'd call something dead but now risen."

"I think they're called revenants." If she recalled one of her producer's pleading phone calls correctly. Doug always had a bead on the latest hauntings, monsters and paranormal activity.

"Revenants, sure, but then we're getting into zombie territory," Roux said. "I prefer to stick with ghosts."

"And these ghosts give Serge all the answers and do dirty, evil deeds for him?"

"I assume so."

"That's nonsensical." She leaned forward. "I mean, ghosts? Why would they have answers? Or for that matter, power? They aren't even corporeal. Why would a ghost have any more knowledge than the human body had while alive? I mean, you die an idiot, you're pretty much still an idiot. Am I right?"

"Are you saying all ghosts are idiots?"

"No, I'm saying I don't think any of them would have the kind of knowledge the necromancer is looking for. I believe Ben has been using him to tap into stock market futures. How can anyone know that? Most especially a dead someone?"

"Move beyond your skepticism, Annja. We are all one. All part of the greater consciousness. When the body dies it is buried. But the soul—the mind and spirit—become part of the collective."

"You just went New Agey on me, Roux."

"I did, didn't I?" He gave an unexpected shudder. "Must have been Roxanne. She read my cards last week. Told me I was going to have a long and prosperous life." He chuckled. "Tell me something new?"

The old coot.

"This sounds too Nostradamus scam to me."

"The man was a soothsayer, Annja. The true seers are in such a minority the majority will never believe them. Which is both good and bad. You cannot judge time from point A to point B," he explained. "All time is happening at all times. That's the only way you can ever conceive of a person's or an entity's ability to know the future."

"Not going to touch that one. I buy the immortality bit," Annja said. "I don't have a choice. And I can even buy the monsters and supernatural voodoo, because I've seen it."

"Show you the truth and you're a believer."

"Exactly."

"I promise if you are on the receiving end of a necromancer's voodoo, as you call it, you will believe."

"I'm still not buying it. This skull…" She picked up the beheaded entity from the seat next to her thigh.

Setting it on her lap, she let the silk spill away, turning it so the eyes did not look directly at her. She remembered it had been so in the warehouse. As soon as Garin turned the eyes on to her and the thug, something freaky had happened. They hadn't glowed. But she had felt its power.

"It is rather plain," Roux commented. "I see some idiot decided to add gold. I thought it was originally silver or even a simple base metal."

She held up the skull. "Why did you take this skull from the alchemist?"

Roux gripped the forehead and turned it so the eye sockets were facing down into her palm.

"I'm waiting."

He sighed. "It was about two years before Joan's death. It was one of the first items on my list."

"Your list?"

"That's none of your business. A man has a right to gather certain items that intrigue him, if he wishes. But I will tell you I witnessed its power. Garin and I were being attacked in an almond grove outside of Granada, and it set back the attackers. But it didn't discern evil from good. Many were slaughtered later that day. Quite a few innocents."

"Garin told me. You must have been awed."

"Not really. More frightened."

"Garin said he was the one to throw it in the well. You wanted to keep it?"

"Did he say that? Never. I was distraught, Annja. I had just been responsible for the destruction of innocents. I was not in my right mind. I'm grateful Garin was able to think straight and dispose of the thing. I was thankful to lose it. I'd thought Garin was, too. But obviously not."

"So do you know about its origins?"

"The necrophilic liaison?" Roux chuckled.

"You don't buy the Templars were involved?"

"Didn't say that. I don't need to buy anything, Annja. I just *know* it works, no matter if it was birthed because of a macabre copulation, or if it came from aisle nine in Wal-Mart."

"I'm going out on a limb to guess you've never graced the aisles of Wal-Mart."

"Am I that transparent?"

"No, just too rich to bother. So, anyway, the legend is supposed to be the origin of the skull and crossbones."

"Pirates were not the first to use the symbol, nor, I suspect, were the Templars. It's a bit before my time, you'll recall. But does it matter?"

"It does to place it on a time line, and verify it is actually this skull we all believe it to be."

"Annja, you tire me with your skepticism. You've seen it work."

"Yes." She sat back again. "Sorry, I can be a little stubborn on the uptake sometimes. Where are we headed?"

"To my hotel. Are you all right with that?"

"I could use a nap."

"I've got a suite, and I promise to be quiet."

"Then let's go!"

THE GUEST BEDROOM was standard luxury hotel fare. King-size bed, 900-thread-count sheets and rich jewel colors. Nabbing the mints placed on a silver tray on the pillow, Annja quickly downed all three.

She set the skull on the bed between her feet. Eye sockets facing away from her, she leaned forward, tapping the skull gently.

"You've been handled rather poorly in the past few days," she said to the ancient artifact. "Sorry about that. I intend to get you on your way home."

Leaning to the side, she turned to her laptop and brought up her e-mail program. Maxfield Wisdom had replied to her request for his phone number. She grabbed her phone and dialed.

As it was ringing, she calculated what time it must be in Venice. It was early evening in New York. That would make it around midnight there.

A groggy male voice answered. Annja winced. "Sorry, Mr. Wisdom?"

"Yes. Is this Miss Creed?"

"Yes, I just got your phone number. I apologize for waking you."

"S'all right. Needed to answer the phone."

At least he could find the joke in it, she thought. Then it occurred to her, if Ben Ravenscroft knew she had communicated with Wisdom, could he have seen this same e-mail?

"First let me ask, has Benjamin Ravenscroft been in touch with you?"

"No. What would be the reason?"

"The skull. He's hot on the trail for it."

"I suspected he was more interested in it than should be."

"Don't worry," Annja rushed to say when his tone wavered through the phone line. "I've got the skull."

"Excellent. I could catch a flight in the morning and be there before nightfall tomorrow."

"That would be great. In the meantime, I hope you don't mind if I take lots of pictures and document the skull as completely as I can?"

"Be my guest."

"I'd like to have it properly dated, but haven't been able to find a contact who can do it."

"It's still in one piece, I hope?"

"Yes. Been joggled a bit, but it's a survivor."

"Much like you, I wager. I did some online research on you, Annja, after you contacted me. You've got quite the impressive résumé."

"I travel a lot for the TV show." Fingers crossed he hadn't stumbled across the nudie pic.

"I like a woman who's comfortable anywhere in the world, with the dirt as her bed and the sky her ceiling."

Did he now? Annja hadn't done the same research on Wisdom, but had assumed he was an old coot after reading his claim to have held the skull for generations. But she realized that didn't necessarily make him old. His voice did sound young.

"Perhaps we can spend an evening discussing the skull when you get here? I know a great restaurant in Manhattan I've been eager to try."

"That's the best offer I've had in months," Wisdom said. "I'd be delighted."

"I'll make sure a car is waiting for you at the airport when you arrive," she said. She could finagle something with Doug if she made him believe this was research for a show on… Venetian…mermaids. Yeah, that would work. "E-mail me with your flight information when you have it."

"I will. I look forward to tomorrow night."

Now all she had to do was make sure no necromancer or business mogul got to Wisdom before she did.

34

It was easy to track Maxfield Wisdom's moves online. Ben had spent his teenage years building his own computers and hacking into local banks, the DMV, and he'd even made it through the CIA firewall for about four seconds before they'd sicced their security on him. He knew his way around online security and there wasn't a firewall that could keep him back. He could find anything he wanted on any person.

Wisdom had booked a flight to New York early this morning. He should arrive at LaGuardia Airport in less than six hours.

Interesting. He distinctly remembered Maxfield telling him that his vast collection of ephemera had been acquired mostly through gifts and inheritances because he rarely traveled.

Something in New York must be worth the trouble, Ben mused, but little humor found its way into his expression.

MAXFIELD WISDOM LANDED at LaGuardia with a nasty case of nausea. He numbly navigated his way through customs and barely arrived in the men's lavatory before losing the contents of his stomach. Thankfully, he was the only one in the bathroom at the time.

As he washed his hands and patted them over his face, another man entered, nodded and headed for the urinals.

Wisdom rarely traveled for this very reason. He had a loose stomach and an even looser brain. Didn't take much to joggle it around and make him ill. Equilibrium was a precious thing he battled to maintain.

He couldn't take a date on a romantic gondola ride. The waves made him dizzy. Same with nightclubs. The raucous music mixed with flashing lights and pounding beats worked a number on his system.

He hoped Annja Creed preferred more subtle forms of entertainment. He did look forward to meeting her. She was gorgeous, and had led such an interesting life. She had visited most every country, and was never afraid to get her hands dirty, and learn all she could about the culture, people and its history.

Very well, so they would never travel the globe together, but Maxfield could dazzle her with his esoteric knowledge of the skull. Knights Templar. Necrophilia. Supernatural powers. What wasn't to love about that hodgepodge of legend?

A night spent conversing with an intelligent woman was something he looked forward to.

Tugging out a brown paper towel from the machine, he pressed it to his face. Perhaps he'd extend his stay in New York from an in-and-out two-day trip. He needed time to recover his bearings and prepare for the return flight. Maybe he could manage some sightseeing. The Statue of Liberty was not to be missed—and, oh, why not, a Broadway show could be the thing to lift his spirits.

He'd traveled with only his carry-on bag, and followed the signs to the ground-transportation desk where he was directed outside to the area where Miss Creed had promised a driver would be waiting.

He liked Annja Creed. She was a good person to want to see the skull swiftly returned to him. She hadn't asked to keep it, only to be allowed pictures for further research. She said a professor at Columbia University had been able to map out the carvings on the interior.

Maxfield looked forward to seeing that map. He'd oft pondered over the meaning of the carvings, never able to discern their completeness for the limited view through the foramen magnum. Perhaps they were Celtic or Templar related. It would be exciting to learn more about the artifact his family had owned for well over a century and a half.

But magical? Hardly. He'd never once sensed the power the skull was rumored to possess. Giver of all good things? Maxfield had a good life; he saw the world as a blessing and his every breath a gift. He didn't need more good things, so if the skull was to up and offer him the prize, he'd politely refuse.

Gripping the cuff of his sleeve he wandered toward the bright sunlight that beamed through the windows along the pickup bay. The light made him woozy. He needed a nap in a dark hotel room before calling Miss Creed.

Spotting a female figure walking toward him, he wondered if it was Annja. The sunlight shone from behind her, shadowing her face and body. Tall, slender and nicely curved. She wore a dress and high heels, which didn't seem to fit the adventurer he had familiarized himself with, but then he had no clue how she liked to dress when not on digs.

"Mr. Wisdom?"

"Yes. Annja? I wasn't aware you were going to meet me."

The woman stepped under the overhead awning and beamed a bright smile at him. Her hair was redder than the brown he'd seen in the pictures online at the *Chasing History's Monsters* site.

"Is there something wrong? Did you have a good flight?" she asked.

"Yes, no, er, you're really Annja Creed?"

"You don't look so well, Mr. Wisdom."

"It was a trying flight."

"The car is waiting." She pointed over her shoulder. "There's ice water inside."

The driver offered to take his bag and Maxfield reluctantly relented. It had served a comfort to hold it to his chest.

Annja smiled at him as she stepped for the back door. "What is it?"

"It's just…you're different than I had expected."

"Prettier?" she asked.

Hmm, not really. And what an odd question from someone he'd presumed rather at ease with her looks and femininity, so much so she didn't do the hair and makeup thing.

Ah, well, he was no judge of character. But if she was going to dress so fancy tonight, he'd have to send out for a suit coat before dinner.

"Would you be bothered if I asked to sit in the front seat? My stomach is a bit unsettled from the flight."

"What's the holdup?"

Maxfield bent to see who had spoken from within the car. A man sat on the opposite side of the backseat. He couldn't see his face for the shadows. The diamond ring on one finger glinted as he offered his hand to shake.

"Maxfield Wisdom, I am Benjamin Ravenscroft. We meet again. You prefer to sit in the front? Do get in."

THE JARRING BUZZ from his cell phone popped him out of
focus on the back of Mr. Wisdom's head. "Rachel, sweetie,
what's up?"

"Daddy, I don't feel well." The warble in her voice put his
heart in his gut.

"Where's Mommy?"

"She's sleeping."

Ben checked his watch. It wasn't even eight in the
evening. "Bring the phone to her, will you, Rachel?"

"Can't. Her door is locked. Daddy, can you come home?"

Linda had locked the bedroom door?

"I'll be right there, sweetie. Driver, head home. I need to
check on something before we go farther. Just a small detour,
Mr. Wisdom, hope you don't mind."

HE WAS ONLY A LITTLE worried Ravenscroft had made him
on Annja. It was expected the client would try to dupe him.
He had means to keep the man under his thumb. And he did
want to know where all the players in this skull chase were.

Garin speed dialed Roux and, as he did so, wondered why
he *had* the man on speed dial. There were so many other
people he would place above the old man for his precious
one-number dials.

Roux answered with a bored, "Now what? I'm in the air
and halfway across the ocean."

"Don't tell me you're leaving so soon?"

"Nothing to keep me there. What's up? Annja hasn't lost
the thing again, has she?"

"Again? She has it now?" Hell, he hoped not. He could take
the thing from her again, but going against a necromancer
didn't sit in his gut at all well. "Of course she does, because
you gave it to her. As long as she has the skull you know she's
not safe. I'm stunned you would leave her in the lurch like this."

"It's not like you to worry over our girl, Garin," Roux said.

Our girl? Yes, he supposed she was theirs. In a manner of speaking. They were, the three of them, connected because of the sword. And whether or not he ever again laid hand to the sword, was able to break it or merely claim it, Garin could admit he did have a soft spot for Annja Creed.

Could be because he hadn't bedded her yet. A challenge, that woman. To his sense of honor, to his will to protect, and yes, to his libido. And yet, once bedded, would the blush slip away? Would he lose all interest?

Never.

"I think someone should keep an eye on her until we've either secured that damned skull or seen it returned to the owner," Garin said.

"The owner is on his way to New York right now," Roux offered. "I wager he's arrived and is already shaking hands with Annja."

"Maxfield Wisdom."

"Er, yes. You're not still determined to take the thing from her, are you? It won't ever get you the sword, you know that."

Garin sighed and rubbed a thumb along the vein in his temple Roux's admonishing tone always managed to twang. Even after five hundred years.

"Why did you buy an apartment in the same town as Annja?"

"It's a rental, and it has nothing to do with being close to her. Christ, Roux, you are one suspicious bastard. Fine. If you don't care a whit about her, then I guess it's up to me to ensure she comes out of this one unscathed."

"Or, at the very least, bruised, but still standing."

"Exactly."

"Garin?"

"What now?"

"Do save our Annja. And while you're at it? Try not to take over the world."

Garin clicked the phone off and shoved it in his pocket. "Imperious old man."

35

Maxfield Wisdom stood outside in the sleet, back to the black limo. He stared at the estate his host had insisted they stop at. The driver stood right beside Maxfield to keep him in place.

He'd never liked Benjamin Ravenscroft. Now, he wasn't quite sure what the man wanted from him. He didn't have the Skull of Sidon. Did he hope to use Maxfield to get it from Annja Creed?

He felt nauseous again.

He shivered, but didn't want to get inside the limo. The cold air cleared his senses. And if he could figure out a way to distract the driver so he could start running, he was all for that. But who was he fooling? He'd get about two houses down the sidewalk before the driver caught him, huffing and slipping about on his dress shoes.

He felt quite sure the besuited chauffeur was also packing a weapon, for his coat strained across one shoulder where Maxfield assumed a leather holster must run.

Is this the kind of adventure Annja Creed experienced? He'd initially thought following her an intriguing notion, but now…

LINDA LAY SPRAWLED on their king-size bed in the pink silk nightgown Ben remembered giving her for their fifth wedding anniversary. A bottle of Vicodin sat on the night-stand, half-empty. He had no way of knowing how many pills she had consumed, but when he slapped her face gently, she didn't rouse. Her skin was clammy. He found her pulse along her neck. Slow.

"Daddy?"

"Rebecca, take Rachel to her bedroom."

The secretary complied. She was nervous, but not frantic. He gave her points for that. A strong woman, who took orders well.

"Daddy?" Rachel cried as Rebecca tried to shoo her from the doorway.

"Rebecca's a new babysitter," he tried, hating the lie, but blurting out the first thing that came to mind. "I think Mommy isn't feeling well. I'm going to take her to the doctor."

"Like me?" Rachel's voice cracked and tears started. She pulled at Rebecca's gentle insistence.

"Go with Rebecca, please, Rachel. Mommy is going to be fine. Not like you." Stupid. Why had he said that? "Just listen to what Rebecca says, and I'll call you as soon as Mommy wakes up.

"Fuck," he said as he touched the side of Linda's neck. Heartbeats should be faster. "What the hell are you trying to do? Kill yourself? Leave our precious daughter alone? Stupid woman."

He glanced to the phone. He should call for an ambulance. Could the limo get her to the emergency room faster?

Wisdom waited outside in the car. He knew Ben was not allied with Annja and had nervously tried to open the door as they'd driven from the airport. Rebecca had shown surprising sanguinity when she'd offered to hold the gun on Wisdom. It made Ben feel a little like Bonnie and Clyde.

Hell, he shouldn't be thinking like that! Not now. Not here in his family's home.

This night was not right. He had things to take care of. A means to save his daughter was out there. So close. All the elements to obtaining it had come together.

And now this…this distraction.

He tugged down the skirt of Linda's nightgown and stood to pace at the end of the bed.

"Ben?" Rebecca popped her head in the doorway. "I gave her some milk and cookies. She won't go to sleep."

"That's fine. Will you stay with her while I take Linda to the hospital?"

Rebecca nodded. "What about the guy out in the car? You want the gun?"

"No." Ben exhaled. He could do letter openers, but guns?

On the other hand, he had vowed to do whatever was necessary to save his daughter. Linda was slowing him down. He didn't need this complication.

"New plan. I'll call an ambulance. You meet them and explain you're the babysitter who arrived to find Linda like this, okay?"

"You're going to leave me with the kid?"

"She's my daughter, Rebecca." He allowed her to embrace him from behind. It felt great. Strange, though, standing in another woman's arms while his wife slowly died just five feet away on the bed. "You love me? You love my daughter."

"I'll do it, Ben. But I worry about you and Mr. Wisdom."

"Give me the gun, then."

She slipped the Ruger LCP from the pocket of her skirt. The small pistol was perfect for concealing. "You know how to use it?" she asked.

"Doesn't matter." He checked the safety. It was on. "I just need to make it look good." He kissed Rebecca's mouth, full and warm and always ready for him. "I'll call as soon as I'm able."

He slid the pistol into a front trouser pocket, and strode toward the stairs. Then, realizing he'd have to pass Rachel's room, he detoured toward the back door, stepping softly so she wouldn't hear.

ANNJA ADJUSTED THE GREEN screen hanging in a corner of her living room. Standing back, she studied the lower left corner. That was the only place torn during Serge's rampage. She'd fixed it with duct tape to the back and a coating of clear nail polish on the front. Not a perfect fix, but she couldn't see the tear, and it shouldn't show on film. And until she had the extra cash to invest in a new one—or could convince Doug Morrell to foot the bill—this would serve.

Chasing History's Monsters may be winning some decent ratings, but it was still a strictly low-budget venture. She sometimes recorded spots for her segments in her living room or out in the field, and hoped Doug didn't insert something like fangs on a local librarian or wings on the backs of a trio of schoolchildren walking away from the camera.

The man had no morals when it came to ratings. Wasn't Kristie Chatham proof enough of that?

But would he go so far as to doctor a photograph of her? Annja couldn't decide on that one. And she hadn't heard from him after e-mailing him about it. Did that mean he was hiding in shame? Or laughing because he'd gotten away with it?

Her loft had been returned to a semblance of normality. She'd spent a few hours going over it, tossing two bags full of damaged food from the kitchen. A terrible waste. She'd even managed to dust the curtains. Hey, a few flicks of the material out the window worked better than a feather duster any day.

There were two books Serge's rampage had damaged beyond repair. The spine had been ripped clean away from the signature pages on *The Three Musketeers*, published in 1894 with illustrations by Maurice Leloir. It was still readable, but her heart sank to her stomach at the destruction. This was one of her favorite volumes.

Now she sat on the couch and sipped a can of Diet Coke. She should hear from Maxfield Wisdom soon. His flight had landed half an hour earlier.

The skull sat on the coffee table, now bare of her collection of manuscripts. She'd tucked those in a neat pile on a bookshelf. A little cleaning never hurt anyone.

"You've caused a lot of trouble, you," she said to the cranium. "I wish I could decipher the markings inside."

Following that spark of curiosity, Annja went to her desk and spread the printouts Professor Danzinger had worked on beside the laptop. The design had a very Celtic look to it. There were interweaving ribbons and it was all very symmetrical. The Celts had invaded France a long time before this skull had been born.

"Fourth century," she muttered. "The Templars weren't established until the twelfth century."

So while the design could be Celtic, she decided it probably wasn't. It wasn't her field of interest, though she had read a few papers about them in college. With the professor gone, she had no idea who to contact who might be able to help her.

But did it matter? Returning the skull to its owner was imminent. End of story. She'd go on to the next adventure. What would knowing what the markings were meant to say prove?

"Maybe they invoke some dark spirits?" She chuckled. "Annja, you've been chasing too many monsters."

But she had found some real monsters during those chases. It meant there were many things on this earth that must be believed, if only one could open their mind wide enough.

"Maybe I should consider this as a segment for the show?" She pondered the carvings until her eyes unfocused and the dark squiggly lines blurred. "Necrophilia might be too extreme even for Doug. Ha."

The phone rang and she nearly toppled from the chair. Dashing to the coffee table, she grabbed her phone. "Hello?"

"Miss Creed. I've got something you want." The voice was familiar.

"Really?" Couldn't be Wisdom. She had something he wanted. "Who is this?"

"Benjamin Ravenscroft."

Right. She should have detected the sense of entitlement in his tone.

"Can we arrange to meet?" he asked.

"That depends. What is it you've got you believe would interest me?"

"Maxfield Wisdom."

Annja exhaled. "You picked him up from the airport?"

"Yes, I told him you sent me. He was very agreeable until he decided I wasn't going to take him to you. We've had to restrain him, poor fellow. The sooner you can get here with the Skull of Sidon the quicker the man can be undone and set to wander free. What do you say?"

"Why is the skull so important to you?"

"Does it matter when a man's life is at stake?"

"You'd kill Maxfield?"

"I'm losing patience, Annja. I need that skull!"

"Why? Someone die?"

"You bitch!"

"Whoa." She'd touched a nerve.

"Let's meet in an hour. Why not somewhere in your neighborhood? Sunset Park. It's private and out of the way, but that's for the best, don't you think?"

"Where's Serge?"

"You haven't stumbled across him? The fellow does have a manner of chasing in circles. Don't worry, he won't bother us."

That meant Ravenscroft must have no idea where the necromancer was. Annja wasn't sure she needed a bald bone conjurer thrown into the mix right now.

"An hour?" she said.

"At the Bush Terminal Piers," he said. "Shall I send a driver to pick you up?"

"No, I'll find you. Don't hurt Maxfield, because if you do, I'll hurt you."

"You make me tremble, Annja. I must admit it is a thrill to feel threatened by a woman. I like your spark."

"Yeah? Remember that when I'm forced to beat you bloody." She hung up and put her head to her knees. "I can be so rash sometimes. I have no idea who this Ben guy really is or what I'm dealing with. And he's holding an innocent man hostage."

With Serge out searching for her, and Ravenscroft gunning for her, this night could prove interesting.

She reached to switch off the laptop but startled. The image of the interior skull map showed…

"Words? In…Latin."

She tapped the screen and read, *"Non nobis Domine, no nobis, sed nomini to da glorium."*

"'Not unto us, O Lord,'" she interpreted. "'Not unto us, but unto Thee give the glory.'"

"I know that quote. It's…Templar."

36

Annja wondered what she'd be up against. She'd have her sword, but that meant she had to get close to anyone who wished to harm her. And those anyones would likely have guns that didn't require *they* get close.

She was certain Ben would have muscle, with weapons, waiting for her arrival. She had no backup. She should have backup. But Roux was gone, and she was determined not to go running to Garin with a pitiful plea for protection.

She could do this. Exchange the skull for Maxfield, and pray Ben had no reason to kill them. But to be safe…

To his credit, Bart didn't bemoan her call as giving him a heart attack. Instead, he listened carefully as Annja summarized her adventures and the showdown she expected to come.

"What warehouse?" he asked. Annja heard the scribble of his pencil as he took notes. "Along the pier? There's a lot of old warehouses out in Sunset Park. Some are destined for demolition. Others they've recently fixed up."

"I'm not sure. I'm guessing one of the empty ones."

"That seems obvious. Don't go in until I get there, Annja."

"Are you going to be my backup?"

"Do I have a choice?"

She touched the cool skull bone nestled in her open backpack. "In the wrong hands, this skull could do some serious damage, Bart. I can go so far as to say it's evil."

"Then I'm in. But remember, wait for me."

"Thanks. I owe you Cuban—"

"And another one of those hugs next time."

Zipping up her down-filled jacket against the chill, Annja tugged her cap lower and walked onward. A long stretch of warehouses paralleled the Upper New York Bay.

The cranky bark of a car horn forced her onto the sidewalk. Resisting the unnatural urge to turn and give the finger to the driver, Annja checked her emotional gauge. She was angry. That would never serve when entering a dangerous situation.

"Chill," she coached herself. "He's on the *Forbes* list. He won't risk damaging his reputation any more than I will risk Maxfield's life. We're on a level playing field. So Ravenscroft gets the skull for a bit. I'll get it back."

That was her focus. She'd have to hand the skull over to save Maxfield, but then she had to plot a way to get it back. It didn't belong in the hands of anyone who intended to use it nefariously.

If he even could.

Maxfield had said the skull had done nothing for him, or any of his family members. It hadn't shimmered with ineffable vibrations or granted any good while in her possession. Nor had it helped the professor.

Yet why had it worked for Garin?

"Something about whomever is holding it." Garin had

seen the skull once before. Touched it. He'd said it had whispered to him. "The holder must have a connection to the skull. Maybe. A Templar connection?"

Did Ben Ravenscroft have the same connection? As far as Annja could figure, he hadn't ever had it in his hands except for the one time he'd held it at Wisdom's home. Ravenscroft must have been the one who sent the sniper after Marcus, and was ultimately the man who hired Marcus. It made weird sense. Perhaps the sniper had been acting beyond orders. Ben would have never ordered the man killed if he knew he held the one thing he wanted.

So were he and Serge working together? She'd had the thought a necromancer could help a man rise in his career. Made sense, again. Supernatural sense.

But it didn't seem as though Ben and Serge were on the same page now. Both wanted the skull. Yet Serge had seemed bitter about Ben. Could the skull be a means to retaliate against Ben? For what?

Turning down the street, Annja stretched her gaze across the building fronts. Half the area was active business, the other derelict industrialism. Sunset Park had done a great job of prettying up the area, but there was yet a lot of work to do.

At this pace, she'd beat Bart. And did he really think she'd wait for backup?

It bothered her that, of all the people she would expect to produce results upon holding the skull, one of those people was not her. She wielded a magical sword. Why wouldn't a magical skull work in her hands?

Or was it she was only allowed one magical weapon to her arsenal in this crazy world of legend become reality?

Annja had no idea how the sword actually worked for her—coming to her grip when needed, and sometimes not appearing when it wasn't needed, though she called for it. It worked, that was what mattered.

So did the skull only work in one specific set of hands? Why Garin's? It was hard to tie Garin to a necrophilic skull that gave all good things. He wasn't some chosen warrior set to change the world. Heck, warriors weren't even in vogue anymore.

Or maybe he was. She had no right to judge. There were greater forces operating in her life, and in the lives of those orbiting about her. Roux and Garin were two of those orbiting planets.

Annja slowed. Her hair stood up on the back of her neck.

The warehouse was compact, yet six stories high. A bright light beamed out from the multipaned windows tracking the first floor. It was older, probably built in the industrial age, and likely marked for demolition. There were lots of buildings in the city that should have been demolitioned ages ago due to safety hazards.

Feeling as though she was the only one in the yard before the building, but sensing that couldn't possibly be true, Annja instinctively held out her arms, putting up her hands in show of surrender. Her backpack with the skull inside hugged her shoulder.

Behind her, water slapped the decaying pier. She was in no mood for another swim in November waters.

As she approached the door she heard footsteps move up behind her, sloshing through the slush of snow. She stopped. Intuitive prickles tightened across her scalp.

A man called for her to stop. A little late, but she never did rate thugs too highly on the smarts scale.

"Hands behind your neck," he ordered.

She complied, hating the vulnerable position. Wide male hands moved over her arms, patting her down in search of weapons. They groped down her torso and thighs.

A tug at the backpack prompted her to tug in return. "I only hand it over to Benjamin Ravenscroft," she said. "Or the deal's off."

It was a lousy argument. They could shoot her, take the backpack and be done with the entire thing.

"Let her hang on to it. She's clean," someone said.

The door before her was shoved open by a man clad head to combat boots in jungle camouflage. He hugged an AK-47 to his ribs. The dark glasses were utterly inane this late at night.

Given a wide berth, Annja passed through the doors and into a vast empty room. She couldn't determine what kind of factory it may have once been. There was no equipment or large industrial machines. The concrete floor was cracked and littered with building debris and bits of twig from overhead birds' nests.

Ahead, light beamed over a man tied to a chair, his arms wrenched around behind the back of it. Blood dribbled from the corner of his mouth and down his chin.

Annja felt the need to hold the solid hilt of her sword. But she cautioned quick action.

Behind her, four thugs loomed. One stood close enough she could hear his labored breathing.

"Miss Creed, once again it is a pleasure."

A man in black suit and silver tie stepped into the light beside the seated man.

"Your pleasure is my headache, Ben."

"Yes, you can use my first name, if you desire. Most call me Mr. Ravenscroft."

"I'll keep that in mind, *Ben*. Is this Maxfield Wisdom?"

The man on the chair, his mouth gagged, looked to her with pleading eyes and nodded profusely. He couldn't be much over forty. He had a narrow face and was dressed in safari khakis.

"I'm sorry, Maxfield. I hadn't intended for things to go this way," she said to him. Then to Ben she said, "Why don't you extend the olive branch and let him go? I'm here. I have what you want. There's no need to further involve Mr. Wisdom."

"You're an impatient woman, Annja. That surprises me, knowing you spend your days digging fruitlessly about in the dirt in hopes of now and then snagging a bit of bone or pottery."

"When I'm not pothunting—" she used the derogatory term loosely "—I seem to be negotiating with one or another type of bad guy. I've become very good at it."

"Really? I knew something remarkable had attracted me to you. For a woman, you've got balls."

She shook her head. "Can we quit the dance and get to the showdown?"

"Yes. Time is, as they say, of the essence."

With a nod of his head, Ben laid out a silent command. Annja was gripped from behind, her left arm twisted across her back. The backpack strap, hooked over her right shoulder, slipped to her elbow.

"Is it in there?" Ben approached. "Give me the bag."

She struggled, but allowed him to take the backpack. Until Maxfield was free, she couldn't be too quick to fight. Especially not with the thug standing in the shadows with a machine gun aimed on the bound man.

The thugs handed the backpack to Ben. He set it carefully on the ground.

"You have it, now let me take Maxfield and leave."

Ben squatted over the backpack, making great show of slowly drawing down the zipper and reaching inside. "You don't want to see if it works?"

"It doesn't," she said. "I don't know what you think an old skull is going to do for you, but it certainly isn't going to bring riches or raise the dead."

Ben's smile wavered. He stood, the box in both hands. "You know nothing about me, Annja Creed. You think I'm some evil man who wants to kill, maim or destroy to get what he wants?"

"I'm a pretty good judge of character. I call 'em as I see them."

Ben caressed the box and lifted it to study. Now he reminded her of a wicked wizard who held Pandora's box and intended to unleash untold evils upon the world.

Oh, Annja, you've been watching far too many fantasy movies lately, she thought.

"I already have the riches," Ben said. His dark eyes searched hers.

Annja saw the glint of life in his eyes. They glittered. With madness? No, there was something so sad in the dark depths she momentarily wondered if he was truly mentally disturbed.

Hell, he'd hired a necromancer. He believed a skull could give him power. Of course he was disturbed.

"But I do need to ensure one destined for death is granted a reprieve," he said.

"What does that mean? We're all destined to die sooner or later."

Ben tucked the box under an arm and tilted a quizzical look upon her.

"Annja, what if you knew you were going to die. It was fated. Let's say, tomorrow."

"If that's when I'm meant to go…so be it."

"Ah, but what if you knew something was out there to reverse that fate? Would you attempt to utilize it?"

He didn't want to know her philosophy of life and death. He must be talking about someone close to him. Who else would a man try so desperately to save?

"You think the skull can stop death?" she asked.

"That would be a very good thing, don't you agree?"

She could only tilt her head and offer a doubtful shrug. If Maxfield's guess that the skull only worked in the hands of those who had not received enough good already, she figured it would produce a maelstrom for Ben.

"I would give my very heart to have it work." Ben clenched a hand over his shirt. "I would rip it out and hand it over to you, if you could tell me this skull can stop death."

"I…I can't do that. Who do you need to save?"

He was starting to frighten her now. And with her arm twisted uncomfortably behind her, she was in no position to escape.

The man with the machine gun had moved closer to Maxfield. "Let him go," she tried again.

"Ben!"

Annja recognized the voice yelling from the doorway behind her. She flinched as the sound of bullets ricocheted in the room—and struck flesh and blood.

The man guarding Maxfield dropped to the floor. The thugs behind Annja engaged and prepared.

"Hold your fire!" Ben shouted. He held the box, unflinching.

Tears ran down Maxfield's face.

Annja was able to stretch a glance over her shoulder. Two men were down. Serge approached with a pistol in each hand.

"I thought you weren't into taking life, necromancer?" Ben challenged.

Annja struggled against her captor, but he held her wrists behind her back firmly.

Serge didn't answer Ben. Instead, the tall bald man aimed for Annja and pulled the trigger.

37

An SUV slid to a stop at the end of the pier. Bart paused from inspecting the warehouse fronts. Thick snowflakes dusted the black night sky. The world was strangely silent, save for the rumble of the engine. A huge man with hell in his eyes swung out from the car and stalked toward him.

"Who are you?" he growled at Bart. He reached inside his leather jacket, as if going for a weapon.

Not easily riled, Bart flicked his jacket to expose his detective badge. "NYPD."

He had no time for a harried husband with a pregnant wife needing to get to the hospital, or a drunk looking for a fight. Annja would not wait for him. He knew that better than he knew his own mind.

Then the guy surprised him by asking, "Where's Annja Creed?"

"Why don't you tell me who you are, and—I hope that's not a gun under your coat."

"It is." The man propped a hand at his hip, boldly revealing the weapon. "Annja's in danger. And I'm Garin Braden."

That was a name he had heard. A couple of times.

Bart nodded once. "Bart McGilly."

"I've heard of you…"

"Seems we're both in Annja's circle. I don't think we should waste time chatting about her, though, do you?"

"Nope. Benjamin Ravenscroft may have her," Garin said.

"Shit. You know which warehouse?"

"Haven't a clue."

"There's only a few on this block that aren't occupied, but the buildings are huge. Let's split up. But keep your weapon holstered, buddy."

The man didn't reply, only rushed down the sidewalk, leaving Bart damn sure his warning would go unheeded.

THE THUG'S BODY SLAMMED into Annja's back as he took the bullet from Serge's pistol. Pulled down by the man's drag on her wrists, Annja stumbled forward, landing on the ground on her stomach.

"Stay there," Serge commanded her. One of his pistols was aimed at her head. "And you won't be harmed."

It was a good option. For now.

Pressing her palms flat, Annja inched onto her knees to assume a ready-to-move position.

Serge's long strides passed her as he approached Ben. All of Ben's guards were down. Unless he had some hidden out of sight for emergency. Good villains always stashed a few thugs for such an occasion, she thought.

"We are at an impasse," Ben said to Serge.

"Only from your perspective. Hand over the skull."

"And then you shoot me?"

"No. Then I walk away with my freedom," Serge said. "You've been served your part of the bargain. You got the skull. Now it's my turn."

"But I've not had the opportunity to use it," Ben argued. "Hell, I haven't even looked at it. She could have put anything in this box."

"Open it," Serge commanded.

Annja tilted to rest on one hip and Serge pointed the gun at her leg. "Be still."

"Gotcha," she muttered.

The idea of holding the sword hummed loudly in her brain. It was as if the sword wanted to become whole, while she still felt it wasn't the right time. She could sweep up and kill the bad guys and rescue Maxfield.

But she wasn't so sure Serge was a bad guy anymore. He could have shot her. Instead, he'd granted her freedom by shooting her captor. Nothing made sense.

"You must allow me to use the skull," Ben said as he snapped open the locks on the box. "You would not allow an innocent little girl to die, Serge. I know you. You're compassionate."

"I am. But I've told you the skull does not hold the power of life."

"We'll see. If it can cure my wife, it'll cure Rachel."

"Your wife?" Annja said.

"She tried to kill herself earlier. A few hours ago. And my daughter has bone cancer. She's suffered so much. You see why time is so desperate?"

"Did you call the police about your wife?" Annja asked.

"My secretary is with her. Why do you care, Annja? You, who would ignore a little girl's plea for help."

"I'm not following you, Ben."

"My daughter e-mailed you a few days ago about the skull. She told you about it. You didn't bother to reply. Busy TV star too good for the little people?"

"She e-mailed me?" Annja didn't have to think hard to remember. "PinkRibbonGirl?"

"Yes. She was excited to have contacted a woman she looks up to. She watches your show. She wants to be like you someday. And you ignored her."

She had dismissed the girl's suggestion the skull was the Skull of Sidon. Until she'd learned differently. "I would have never purposely ignored her, Ben. I get a lot of e-mail. I can't answer them all."

But that didn't make her feel any better. She should have replied to the e-mail.

"Enough! I will walk out of here with this skull. My daughter's life depends upon it. I can save her!"

Annja caught Serge's droll look. The bone conjurer said, "He's not so magnanimous. He's been using me to steal and extort."

"Yet you helped him," she argued.

Serge's eyes burned into her gaze. "He threatened my family."

"I gave you a home and pay you well," Ben interjected.

Annja glanced to Ben, whose focus was on the skull.

"What if the skull doesn't work for you, Ben?" Annja tried. "It's been in many hands lately, and hasn't done a thing. You're not going to give your daughter hope and then let her down. A caring man would not do something like that."

"What about the man in the warehouse?" Ben asked. "Garin Braden. He's with you. He held the skull on you and my man, and defeated you both."

"He's not working with me. And that was the wind."

"The wind! You're not a good liar, Annja."

"I don't care what you think of me, Ben. Just give Serge the skull and be done with it."

She caught Serge's hopeful glance. Yeah, I'm on your side, she thought with a shrug. For now.

Ben dug in the wool inside the box. "You don't want it anymore?"

"Of course I do. Well, I don't. It doesn't belong to any of us. It belongs to Mr. Wisdom. And it will be returned to him. But suddenly I'm thinking I'd rather stand on Serge's side, if I have to choose sides."

"I want my freedom," Serge said. "To keep my family safe."

The ache in the bone conjurer's voice took Annja by surprise. His freedom? From Ben. The bastard had threatened Serge's family to get him to perform his necromantic arts for him.

And yet, who was she to judge? Ben had as good a reason as Serge for wanting the skull. Twisted as it may be.

"Can it really prevent death? Cure cancer?" she asked. "Serge?"

He shook his head no.

But hope was a powerful weapon. She'd seen it work in her own life, many times. Some people thrived on hope and prayer. She would not dispute the power of positive thinking.

You can't be the one to deny a little girl because your beliefs don't mesh with her father's, she told herself.

Annja turned to Ben. "Very well. You keep the skull. I don't want to be the one who destroyed a father's hope for his little girl." She lifted a hand at Serge's sudden gasp. "Do you believe in karma, Ben?"

He smirked and crossed his arms. "Of course I do. Why the hell do you think I donate millions to charity every year? A man can't employ a necromancer and expect the balance to remain."

"So charity is your way of covering your spiritual ass?" she asked.

The guy didn't get it. Probably never would get it. People

like him needed a metaphysical smack every now and then. Sometimes they got it, sometimes they didn't.

Yet she was prepared to step back and let the universe work its mojo. Said mojo was currently itching at the fingers of her right hand.

"It will work!" Ben took the skull from the box. "I will prove its power."

Ben held the skull up and turned the face toward Annja and Serge.

38

"No!" Sword in hand, Annja lunged. The sword tip connected with an eye socket on the skull.

The skull soared into the air, turning end over end, high, so high.

Using Ben's gaping focus on the skull, Annja released the sword into the otherwhere and lunged for him. She shoved his chest, landing both of them on the floor. Straddling him, she grabbed his tie. Ben gripped her by the hair and yanked.

"A sissy fighter, huh?" She punched him in the jaw. He spat out blood. "I never expect much from you business suits."

The punch to her gut came as a surprise. Ben slipped a leg around hers and twisted her onto her back. Fists to her jaw pounded like iron.

"You think so?" He smirked. A dribble of blood trickled down his chin. "I've recently lost my aversion to violence. Let's see how you like this."

Out of her peripheral vision, Annja saw the skull falling through the air and a hand reach up to grab it.

Ben's fist connected with her ribs. Wheezing out air from her lungs, she choked. The floor was hard and cold against the back of her skull. He pummeled her abdomen, taking far too much glee in the process.

"You're killing an innocent little girl," Ben growled.

She lifted a knee and managed to swing out, kicking the back of his thigh. He toppled off balance, slapping the concrete beyond her head, and putting his chest to her eye level. And his groin to knee level.

Ben took the kick with a wincing gasp.

"If your daughter is dying, perhaps you should have allocated some of those charitable dollars in her direction." She instantly hated herself for saying that.

"I have. There's no cure for bone cancer, you bitch!"

Where he'd kept the knife, she couldn't know, but Ben slashed across his chest and Annja felt the icy bite of steel below her chin. It tracked a vicious line across her throat. No blood oozed down her neck. It couldn't have cut too deep.

"Now you're starting to piss me off." She reached out to grab for the sword, but something caught her attention.

It wasn't Maxfield scraping across the floor on the chair in a desperate attempt to escape this insanity.

It wasn't the wounded thug crawling toward an AK-47 twenty feet away that she knew she'd better dispatch sooner rather than later.

It wasn't the swinging door creaking in the wind and letting in a thunderous rain that seemed to have come from nowhere.

It was the strange orange and blue light that surrounded Serge as he held the skull aloft over his head, staring up into the empty eye sockets.

"Oh, no, not on my watch," she shouted.

Standing, Annja struggled with the hands Ben gripped

about her ankle. Sword coming to hand, she stabbed him in the shoulder. "Stay there like a good boy, or I'll have to do more than wound you." She bent over him. "Got that?"

Gripping his shoulder and cursing her, he managed an acquiescent nod. "My daughter…" he whispered.

"Cannot be saved by an ancient skull," she said, regretting her harsh words, but knowing there was nothing better to say.

With no time to lose, Annja raced toward Serge. Another man entered the doorway, pausing to take everything in. His broad shoulders dripped rain. Garin.

"No, Serge, don't do it!" she yelled.

The necromancer didn't listen. He was making a strange keening noise and the lights spread around him. The floor rumbled, as if there was an earthquake. It literally moved her boots and made traction difficult.

Windows burst. A vicious rain of glass slivers poured over a fallen thug, who screamed as he was repeatedly sliced.

Annja entered the orange light and swung Joan's sword.

The world slowed to a single heartbeat.

Her sword scythed the air, cutting through the supernatural light as if cleaving open the universe. It swung smoothly, an extension of her arm. The first touch of steel to bone found no resistance. The blade moved forward. Annja followed its lead.

Serge did not cry out in protest. Or if he did, she did not hear beyond the thunder of her own abnormally slow heartbeat.

Annja came to a stop, the blade swinging around in front of her. Momentum tugged her muscles, stretching them tight. She let out a grunt of exertion. Sound shattered like the glass. Heartbeats accelerated.

Two skull halves clattered to the floor. A hollow echo amidst the chaos.

A thin red line opened the flesh on Serge's throat. A sad grimace tugged down his mouth. Annja waited, panting. The slice did not open wide and begin to gush. She had not injured him mortally.

"You destroyed all that power," he said sadly.

Staggering, she swung back her sword.

He'd only been seeking freedom. The man had been enslaved to serve a more evil power, at the risk of his family's lives. He should have that freedom now Ravenscroft had been taken down.

"I'm sorry," she gasped.

"You were following the sword," Serge said. "It has power, too. I respect that."

Somewhere across the room, Ben cursed her.

Annja stepped forward into a waiting embrace. But Garin didn't hold her or offer comfort. Before her, the sectioned skull wobbled on the floor.

"You had no choice," he said. His hand squeezed her shoulder. "The sword decided that one."

"The sword is not a thinking thing. I did this." She pulled away from his touch. "I took away that man's hope. Could his daughter have been saved?"

Slashing the blade through the air she'd severed the contact with the immortal. She just needed….

She needed.

To not be responsible for it all. To not feel the weight of the world. To just…walk away from it all. She'd almost done that by granting the skull to Ben. And yet, some greater compulsion had led her to destroy it.

Perhaps Serge was right. The sword held power she merely followed.

Behind her she heard the sound of bone clacking. Garin inspected the damage. He'd been cheated of the prize.

A little girl had been cheated out of the opportunity for a cure. At the very least, hope.

An imprisoned man had been cheated freedom.

Because of her.

No, you did what was right. You know that. Don't question it. Accept it.

"I can accept it," she said to everyone. Because it had been the right thing to do at the time.

Turning, Annja scanned the warehouse. Many had fallen. And those standing were not necessarily friends. How had Garin known to find her here?

Striding purposefully toward him she held up the sword and looked aside the blade at him.

She was not ready to give it up. It was hers. She controlled it, when it was not controlling her. She and the sword had an ineffable connection. And she liked that just fine.

"Skull's broken," she said. "Hope you weren't expecting to make a fortune on it."

"Not at all."

"Liar."

"Truth? My initial hopes were to make a couple of bucks, yes. But I had a change of heart. I've been considering that empty grave as a good spot for its final resting place. I don't think it was something that should have been circulated in the first place. I know Mr. Wisdom has taken excellent care of it, but in the wrong hands…?"

"Why do you think it worked for Serge and not Ben or this guy here?" Garin gestured to Maxfield.

"And you?" she posited. "You've held it twice, Garin. What's your suspicion?"

He shrugged. "I wish I knew. Is it because I'm immortal?"

Annja saw Maxfield's head whip around to inspect Garin, but he remained silent.

"Could be. And the necromancer has a connection to spirits and souls."

"I expected it to work in your hands, Annja."

"So did I." She caught the skull half Garin tossed to her. And she tossed it back to him. "Keep it. Bury it deep, deeper than an open grave."

"It will give me great pleasure to do so."

"On second thought, Bart may need it for evidence."

"Annja!" Maxfield called out. He inched across the floor, still tied to the chair.

"Here." She handed Garin the battle sword. "Hold this a second, will you?"

The mighty man gaped. Almost reluctantly, he opened his fingers to take the sword. It remained solid in his grip. It did not disappear into the otherwhere. Because she did not want it to leave this realm. Not yet.

Annja nodded and dodged to the side to untie Maxfield. "Sorry about the skull," she said as she worked the rough hemp rope free from a knot.

"It was the right thing to do," he offered. "I wouldn't have believed it unless I'd seen it. It has power. It is evil."

"Not evil. Just something that should be lost for good."

"I agree."

Hands and ankles free, Maxfield stood and ran his fingers through his sweat-laced hair. He exhaled and then bent forward, catching his palms on his knees.

"You going to be okay?"

"Yes. Just give me a moment." He clasped her hands and left out a heavy breath. "Thank you. For believing."

"I try to believe in what is shown to me," she said.

Garin had not moved since she'd handed him the sword. He tilted the weapon, studying the blade. It caught the light. Each turn of the blade glinted in his eyes, a silver flash. Greed or lust or something deeper, like fear?

Crossing her arms, Annja waited to see what he would do.

If he turned and attempted to run off with it, could she wish it from his grasp and into the otherwhere? There was no telling now that she'd given it freely to him.

"I have not held it since long before it was shattered. An exquisite sword. Not so fancy. A fine battle weapon." He smiled and, with a wistful smirk, handed it back to Annja. "Next time."

She took the sword, swung out her arm and released it into the otherwhere. "We'll see. But I must say, what you just did was impressive."

He offered a devil's smirk. "I'm just not ready for the adventure to end," he said.

She lifted a brow.

"Like I said—" he smoothed fingers along his goatee "—next time."

"If there is a next time."

"There's always a next time, Annja."

She could definitely get onboard with that.

"You want me to clean up the mess?" He strode across the floor. Garin lifted Ben to his feet and inspected his wounded shoulder.

"I'll have you arrested for murder," Ben said with a nod toward his men.

"Will you shut him up?" Annja said to Garin.

"With pleasure, my lady."

A punch reduced Ben to a heap at Garin's feet. Garin gave her a pleased grin. He inspected the carnage, then started collecting scattered weapons.

Bart charged through the open doorway, taking everything in. Pistol held before him, he didn't call out until he'd surveyed the entire room. "Annja?"

"You took your time getting here, Bart."

"You didn't tell me which warehouse it was. Looks like things are under control. Braden." He nodded to the bigger man.

Annja noted their acknowledgment of each other. When had they met?

"You okay, Annja?"

"It's been an interesting day, Bart," she said.

"Looks that way. You're safe?"

"I'm fine."

He lowered his pistol but still held the grip ready, and approached Annja. "You're cut. On your throat."

"I'll survive. The skull is destroyed. Garin subdued Benjamin Ravenscroft over there. Not sure what you can charge him with. Though an accessory to murder comes to mind."

"Is he the guy you think hired the sniper at the canal? The thug in the warehouse?"

"I'm sure your investigation will prove it," she said.

"Who's he?" Bart nodded toward Serge, who knelt over the skull pieces.

"A necromancer. I'm not sure he's committed a crime beyond communicating with the dead."

She watched Bart struggle to maintain his composure. "I'm calling for backup. I'll need you to stick around for questioning this time."

"I'll go wherever you ask, Bart."

His shoulders relaxed and he nodded. He spoke under his breath. "You need another one of those hugs?"

She didn't respond, and instead embraced him. She noticed Garin's curiosity at their embrace. Indeed, it had been a very interesting day.

39

Dinner, as she'd promised Maxfield Wisdom, was out of the question. He'd gotten a call from home and had to fly back immediately. Without the skull, which made her feel badly, but he reassured her the Wisdom family had many more mysterious artifacts to boast about.

The man could not know what that statement did to Annja's thirst for curiosity. She got his address in Venice and promised to visit as soon as she could swing a trip overseas.

She had spoken briefly to Serge before he'd been handcuffed and taken way for questioning. Deeply saddened at the loss of the skull, he did say he felt he'd done nothing wrong and looked forward to his freedom from Ravenscroft.

Annja hoped it would work out for him. He had a family in the Ukraine that she understood he supported by working here in the United States. It wasn't clear if he would move back home, but any suspicion regarding him wanting to harm anyone had been alleviated.

Even though she had a hole in her wrist from him. He'd

only been trying to track a means to his escape from a maniacal man who wanted to control Serge for his benefit.

She was waiting for Bart. He wanted to escort her to the police station for questioning. That was fine with her. She didn't mind interrogation by a friend and had nothing to hide. Though they'd certainly get an earful when she started talking about the necromancer.

Bart would probably want her to tone that down a bit.

He pulled up in his car in front of her building and Annja slid into the front seat. Heat blasted from the vents. It felt great.

Her phone rang and Bart adjusted the heat so she could hear the caller talk over the noise. "Doug?"

"Annja, got some less than positive news for you."

"When do you ever have positive news, Doug?"

"Ha. It's about your sexy online pics."

"They are not my pics. Someone made them up. And it's not plural—it's just the one. Right?"

"Right, just the one—that I've seen. If we want them removed from the site it's going to take a slew of lawyers. I say you just let it slide."

"Doug, if I let that picture slide, then what do I do about the next one, and the next one?"

"You have more?"

"Doug!"

"Sorry. Kidding. I've got a friend who's an expert at all things Internet. I'm going to give him a call and see what he can do. Maybe spam the site or…I don't know. I'm trying, Annja."

"I know you are, Doug. I appreciate it."

"I thought about putting a disclaimer on the show's Web site. Something like 'Ms. Creed has never posed in the nude and that picture is a fake,' but I figured that would just drive more traffic to the pictures."

"Not plural, Doug, don't forget that. I just want it to go away. Thanks for trying. Talk later."

"Bye, Annja."

"Picture?" Bart stopped for a red light.

Releasing a sigh, Annja shrugged. "There's a nudie pic of me online. It's not me," she rushed out when his eyebrows lifted and his smile grew lascivious. "My head, someone else's body. That was my producer, Doug Morrell. He's trying to have it removed from the site."

"Good luck with that."

"Thanks. I think the best bet is to forget about it. Not call too much attention to it."

"Probably. I'm sorry, Annja. I can't imagine how that makes you feel."

"Just the fact you do wonder how it makes me feel is great, Bart."

"My pleasure. So, a necromancer, huh?"

"That's what he tells me. He can foretell the future by speaking to the dead."

"Right." Bart signaled and turned onto a busy street. "I took the skull into evidence, but I don't think we're going to see it do anything magical. Are we?"

She smirked at his worried tone. "It's dead now. But if you knew about its parents…"

"Do I want to know?"

"Nope."

"Then keep that gem to yourself."

"Did you send someone to Benjamin Ravenscroft's house after his daughter?" she asked.

"Yes. The child protection agency has already reported that her aunt has been contacted. She'll be placed with a family member until it can be determined her mother is fit to care for her."

"Poor kid. To lose both parents in one day. She's got cancer, you know. PinkRibbonGirl."

"What's that?"

"She e-mailed me a few days ago. About the skull."

Bart shot her an alarmed look.

"I don't think she could have had any idea her father was looking for it. Maybe. She was the only one, of all who answered my online query, who knew what the skull was. Isn't that remarkable?"

"You tell me."

"Yeah. It is."

"Too bad her father is a nut case."

"Maybe. Maybe not. Benjamin Ravenscroft wanted to believe in something so desperately he couldn't see the truth. And maybe the truth could have done something for his daughter. We'll never know."

"Things happen for a reason, Annja." He reached over and patted a palm reassuringly on her leg. "Now about this Garin Braden guy."

"What?"

"What does he mean to you?"

Annja tilted a curious stare at Bart. Was he serious? Because he'd just asked, not as a cop, but more as a guy. A guy who might be interested in knowing about any men who had an interest in her. Huh.

"It's a long story, Bart."

"I think I want to hear it."

James Axler
Outlanders®

OBLIVION STONE

A shocking gambit by a lethal foe intensifies the war to claim planet Earth…

In the wilds of Saskatchewan, a genetically engineered Annunaki prince returns after 4,500 years in solitary confinement to seek vengeance against the father who betrayed him. And his personal mission to harness Earth's citizens to build his city and his army appears unstoppable.…

Available August wherever books are sold.

JAMES AXLER

DEATH LANDS®

Baptism of Rage

In the Deathlands, the future looks like hell—and delivers far worse...

Of all the resources Ryan Cawdor and his group struggle to recoup, hope for escaping the grim daily life-and-death struggle has suffered most. But reports of a fountain of youth appear to be true, luring Doc and the others on a promising journey. But the quest proves to be tainted and the survivors soon discover the deadly price of immortality....

Available July 2010 wherever books are sold.